THE EDUCATION OF HÉCTOR VILLA

Other Books by Chilton Williamson, Jr.

NARRATIVE NONFICTION
Saltbound: A Block Island Winter
Roughnecking It: Or, Life in the Overthrust
The Hundredth Meridian: Seasons and Travels in the New Old West

FICTION
Desert Light
The Homestead
Mexico Way

NONFICTION
The Immigration Mystique: America's False Conscience
The Conservative Bookshelf
After Tocqueville: The Promise and Failure of Democracy

THE EDUCATION OF HÉCTOR VILLA

by Chilton Williamson, Jr.

Chronicles Press
Rockford, Illinois
2012

All of the chapters first appeared in *Chronicles: A Magazine of American Culture.*

Cover painting by Stephen Warde Anderson (*stephenwardeanderson.com*)
Cover design by Melanie Anderson (*www.kisstudio.net*)

ISBN 978-0-9843702-7-6

To Brooke Cadwallader

CONTENTS

I

The Villas of New Mexico

"**H**EY, *COMPADRITO*—bring the mail along with you when you come inside!" Héctor Villa shouted through the open window to Jesús Juárez, who was just letting himself into the yard by the front gate where the mailbox, painted red-white-and-blue, stood on a barbershop post.

Héctor "Pancho" Villa was having a pleasant Saturday morning in June, sitting late at the kitchen table over morning coffee while his wife AveMaría weeded the garden patch behind the house and their daughter Contracepción minded Dubya, named for Héctor's greatest hero after the late Francisco Villa, Centaur of the North. (As Héctor and AveMaría had agreed that the little boy should be their last child, Héctor had thought it particularly important that he bear the name of a great man and a patriot.) Master of all he surveyed (if he didn't lift his chin too high toward the Manzano Mountains east of Belen, or glance too far to the rather prim and, to his mind, sterile houses left or right), he felt satisfied and assured, altogether pleased with himself as his sight caressed the artistic assemblage of art objects arranged before him on the front lawn: the miniature drill rig painted orange, yellow, and purple; the windmill nearly as tall as the house itself that drew water upward from a tank buried in the ground beneath it; the wooden birds—bright-painted, eagle-sized, and mounted on poles—endlessly flailing backward on wings rotated by the ceaseless high-desert wind; the tall clay ovens shaped like broad-bottomed, headless giraffes, tastefully placed by AveMaría in surprising places where nobody would normally expect to find an oven and that you could actually fry tortillas and roast corn in; the four-, six-, and eight-foot-tall Trees of Life—ceramic confections, hauled up from Ciudad Chihuahua, in which the serpent, Adam, and Eve were grouped with various saints and animals among spreading arboreal foliage; the Army Jeep that had had its motor pulled and its engine compartment filled with dirt and planted with sunflowers. From inside the house, Héctor could not contemplate directly the huge, two-dimensional, rainbow-colored silhouettes of birds, butterflies, and flowers tacked all round the exterior walls, the side facing the street most heavily. He could, however, imagine them. Past all this splendor, just beyond the turquoise-blue picket fence and the patriotic mailbox, the new-model GMC van, also painted red-white-and-blue and emblazoned with the words PANCHO'S COMPUTER SERVICE, stood parked half on and half off the strip of narrow sidewalk. If only (Héctor mused, leaning on his thick forearms above the coffee cup as he watched Jesús approach the house with a bundle of mail under his arm, dodging statuary as he came) the padre back in Namiquipa years ago, who'd warned him as a boy that he was Hell-bound, could behold him now: fat, dumb, and happy (as they said in America), at his ease in the Promised Land! (He had quit thinking of the USA as "El Norte" years ago.)

"Hey," Jesús (known as "Eddie") greeted him, as he dropped the mail heavily on the table, nearly upsetting Héctor's cup—"so what do you know to-*day*, man?"

Jesús "Eddie" was no Mexican but a Rio Abajo New Mexican, with the rather odd speech typical of his kind that made him, in Héctor's eyes, seem slightly un-American. Rio Abajo folks—like the *rioar-ribenses* up north—disliked Americans (whom they called "Anglos") and Mexicans almost equally. Unlike the northern inhabitants of New Mexico, however, who felt superior on account of their supposed direct descent from the Spanish *conquistadores*, the Rio Abajo people south of Albuquerque thought of themselves as *nuevomexicanos*—more superior still. Though he sometimes resented his air of conde-scension toward immigrant Mexicans, Héctor was fond of Jesús and enjoyed having him around—so long as he kept his hands off Con-tracepción, who had recently turned thirteen and was fast becoming a woman in all the recognizable places. So far as a husband for their daughter went, nothing would do, Héctor and AveMaría were deter-mined, but a patriotic Anglo boy her own age who would consent to tying the knot in one of the evangelical churches. (The Villas them-selves happened to belong to the First Assembly of God, which they'd joined after the local Catholic priest had refused to baptize Contra-cepción under her given name.)

"Not a whole lot, *amigo*. Help yourself to a cup of coffee and a chair." While Jesús "Eddie" drew coffee from the automatic brewer on the countertop, Héctor glanced quickly through his mail, which included a couple of letters from relatives back home in Namiquipa, a notice of some sort from the City of Belen, a mailing from Hijos de Pancho Villa (an organization of Villa's descendants and others who wished they were) in Parral, and the May MasterCard bill. The relatives would be requesting remittances, and Héctor was certain he couldn't face the credit-card bill over coffee. He was about to push the pile away from himself when he noticed that the city-hall letter had DATED MATERIAL: OPEN IMMEDIATELY stamped in red on it. Héctor slit it open with his penknife but left the contents inside the envelope for the time being. He'd paid the water and trash bill only the week before, so he wasn't overly concerned to know why the *alcalde* and his friends should be in such a hurry to get his attention now.

"And you," he asked Jesús "Eddie" as his friend seated himself across the table, "how goes *your* day so far, *hermano*?"

Jesús "Eddie" rolled his eyes toward Heaven. Then he passed his brown hand from his forehead down over his chin. When he had done this, his face wore an entirely different expression.

"It is bad what goes on up in Santa *Fe* these days," he said, darkly. "The goddamn *An*-glos—they want to outlaw cock-*fightin* in Soccorro! All the f--kin movie stars, the environmentalists, f--kin *PETA*— it's cultural *gen*-ocide, man!"

Héctor nodded, trying to look sympathetic. He'd never been much of an enthusiast for the sport himself, even when he lived in Namiquipa. "I know, I know . . . Well, listen, *compadrito*: We need to educate the gringos, you understand what I'm saying to you?—get them to accept our culture. They're halfway there already—Jennifer López, salsa, Taco Bell, everyone wanting to speak Spanish to you at the bank, George Dubya's amnesty plan! Pretty soon they won't *have* any culture, except for ours! You just have to be patient, *amigo*."

Jesús "Eddie" shook his head and struck the table with his fist. "You don't understand! *We* were in New *Mex*-ico hundreds of years before *they* were, man! Why should *we* have to make *them* understand *any*-thin?"

Héctor pushed back his chair, went over to the cupboard, and returned with a bottle of tequila.

"It's Saturday, *compadrito*. Put some of that in your coffee and see if you don't feel better, *inmediatamente*."

Jesús "Eddie" poured a finger of tequila into his cup and stirred the mixture gloomily with the end of the ballpoint pen he carried in his shirt pocket.

"You got a letter there from city *hall*," he observed sourly. "The *Anglos* have taken over the town *coun*-cil. What you suppose they're buggin you about *now*, man? Probably to tell you *you* can't keep fightin cocks in *your* backyard, neither."

"No idea. I don't owe them nothing." Héctor took up the envelope, slid the letter from it carelessly, and unfolded it. The thing had an official look, apparently a summons of some sort. In sudden alarm, he held it out at arm's length and squinted at it. "Let's see, let's see."

"What do the *cabrones* want now?" Jesús "Eddie" demanded suspiciously.

Héctor's roars brought the family running from the yard into the kitchen where the head of the household stood behind the table with his hands on his hips, glaring ahead of himself like Pancho Villa preparing to order the attack on Agua Prieta in October 1915.

"What has happened, Panchito?" AveMaría cried.

While her husband groped for words and attempted to bring his voice under control, Jesús "Eddie" was covertly admiring Contracepción, who stood just behind her mother holding Dubya in her arms. The girl was definitely good-looking, he thought, though far from being as intelligent as his own niece of about the same age. He'd always suspected her name reflected her parents' lack of trust in her to protect herself without some sort of subtle reminder present.

"¿*Panchito?*" AveMaría repeated.

Héctor turned to face her, his moist brown eyes soft and tragic. "The zoning board—my house—an 'eyesore'! A 'public nuisance'!"

AveMaría took a single lurching step backward, put her hands to her face, and took them away again. She threw back her head suddenly and began to wail.

"*¡Ay, madre mía!* They will come for us and take our house, first. Then, they will deport us—all the way back to Namiquipa again!"

It was no more than a technicality and easily overlooked in the event. Héctor and AveMaría had been strongly discouraged by both the menacing Arab immigrants and the coyote who guided them all from presenting their papers and requesting asylum at the border, in the uninhabited desert east of Douglas, Arizona. In twenty years, no one had thought to trouble them about this detail of formal citizenship. The hospitals and schools they had had to deal with had been most understanding—in particular, the state university branch where Héctor had received his degree in computer science.

"They can't deport us, *tonta*," Héctor told his wife dully. "Contracep and Dubya are citizens of the United States—just as much as the President of the United States, George Dubya Bush, himself! Anyway, we've had drivers' licences for years and now these Social Security cards I had made."

"They could change the law," she persisted. "And the cards are obviously fake, even if you did pay too much money for them. What if that *hacendado* Buchanan was to run again for president, next time?"

But Héctor was no longer listening to her. "Ten days to 'comply with standards,'" he muttered. "The best-decorated yard in town and one of the three or four most beautiful homes" (he'd considered offering it for the Parade of Homes tour at Christmastime last year), "and they tell me to comply with 'standards'!" He was angry; more than that, he felt deeply wounded in his heart. Nothing he had ever experienced in El Norte had made him feel so unwelcome, so misunderstood, as this, including the time an admiring leftist student at school had mistaken him for a Sandinista.

"What have I been saying to you all mornin?" Jesús "Eddie" demanded. "The Anglos have *sto*-len New Mexico from us. You should ask yourself, *What would Pancho Villa have done in this situation?* I'll tell you what he would of done, 'mano: He'd of rounded up a couple hundred of his *villistas* and attacked Los Lunas—just like he did Columbus. *¡Viva Villa!*" Jesús "Eddie" shouted, thrusting his fist in the air.

"*¡Viva Villa!*" Héctor echoed him in a dull voice. He'd never known Jesus "Eddie" to express enthusiasm for the Centaur before.

Now Contracepción was looking at Jesús "Eddie." He looked very handsome, she thought, striking a revolutionary position; even the gray at his temples appealed to her as sexy. Still, he was probably too old for her, and Papá would be certain to have a fit.

"What are you going to do, Héctor?" AveMaría asked, speaking in her normal voice this time.

Héctor had no idea what he was going to do. Therefore, he was silent.

"Why don't you just pay the *alcalde* money?" Contracepción asked. From visiting relatives in Namiquipa for several weeks every summer, she understood a thing or two about how the world works.

"Be silent, Contracepción," her father told her. "It isn't the same up here as there. You think George Dubya gets paid to do, or not do, what he *should* do in the White House?"

"I will organize a demon-*stra*-tion, *hombre*," Jesús "Eddie" promised him. "Everyone from the local MALDEF and LULAC chapters in Albuquerque, and others, will show up here, for sure."

Later that morning, when AveMaría had taken her Prozac and Contracepción was away shopping at the mall in Los Lunas with her girlfriend Luz, who had a driver's license, Héctor took a walk round his yard. The shock he'd received that morning had worn off, leaving a deep depression in its place. This thing that had happened to him was incomprehensible, he felt. As his eyes wandered from one object to another in the vast display of carefully selected and painstakingly arranged lawn ornaments, not one appealed to him in any way as an eyesore but rather as an element of the good taste and cultural enrichment the Villa home represented. Though Héctor had allowed Jesús "Eddie" to depart full of plans for a large demonstration outside the municipal center, the last thing he really wanted was a bunch of noisy demonstrators making a public nuisance of themselves on his behalf, in this way calling attention to his shame and public humiliation. As a further consideration, a demonstration might not work: The city fathers might fail to be impressed. How often had he noticed this strange truth about democracy in America: While you might occasionally get the result you wanted at the national level—the reelection of President Bush, for instance—you hardly ever got it at the local one, where everything seemed sewn up tight. The answer to the present crisis, Héctor understood instinctively, did not exist in the political world. He needed to look instead to an alternative arena of hallowed American activity for a solution.

It came to him suddenly, like a fireball in the desert sky overhead, as he stood staring at the old Army Jeep, a relic of World War II, now sprouting sunflowers where the hood used to be. In the toolshed behind the Jeep were his buckets of leftover paint and several squares of fresh plywood. Héctor dragged everything outside and set to work at once with his paintbrushes in the hot sun. Now, perhaps, he could pay off the entire credit-card bill on time and avoid paying interest at eighteen percent.

He worked fast, so that Contracepción, returning with Luz from

the mall, was greeted by three separate signs, facing in different directions up and down the street and decorated brilliantly in all the bright-
est colors of Mexico. The Villas of Belen, as the entire city was about
to learn, were holding a YARD SALE!!!

Reconquista de Villas

HÉCTOR VILLA was discovering the hard way that running afoul of the authorities in America is like riding a horse into quicksand, as Rodolfo Fierro, the Centaur's chief executioner, had had the misfortune to do. You escape from the fatal mire only by miracle (something God had not seen fit to grant poor Fierro).

For months after Héctor had wound up his yard sale, follow-up letters had continued to arrive almost weekly from the Belen municipal building—letters which, while stating very little in nearly incomprehensible English, appeared to threaten bankruptcy, sanctions, prison, and flogging in the public square. In desperation, he'd considered pulling up the red-white-and-blue mailbox by its post and renting an anonymous P.O. box downtown to alleviate the sense of personal violation he suffered in receiving the harassing communications at his own home. He was on the verge of actually doing so when, late one evening in September, his telephone rang—and Héctor found himself facing a crisis compared to which the hovering city fathers of Belen appeared less like ravens than meadowlarks.

For ten or twenty seconds, he heard only a crackling buzz on the line, punctuated by the chink of coins being fed into a coin box. The sound was followed by cuss words in Spanish, before the line went dead. Héctor hung up and was halfway across the room when the phone rang again. Swearing himself, he retraced his steps and snatched the receiver from the wall.

"*¡Diga!*"

"*Oye!* It is your *primo*, Eufemio Villa in Namiquipa, speaking! From a pay phone in Candelario's Cantina! How goes it in El Norte, *compadrito?*"

Eufemio's words were nearly drowned out by the soundtrack of a Spanish-language romance AveMaría and Contracepción were watching in the TV room next door. The flash of resentment Héctor felt at that moment had nothing to do with the uproar, however. He had sent generous remittances by Western Union to his cousin over the past three months, and he was beginning to feel that enough was enough.

Just the fact of residency in the U.S. of A. didn't make you a piggy bank waiting to be sledgehammered by every lazy, unenterprising *campesino*—kin or not—south of the border.

"It goes well enough," Héctor told him shortly. "Look, Eufemio, I sent you $100 by wire last month, and $150 two months before that. I'm not made of money because I have a computer business, understand? Who do you think I am—Bill Gates? I didn't invent the goddamn machines; I just work on them, that's all."

"Wait, *compadrito*, wait—you are not understanding! I do not ask you for money this time—only for a favor, a very small favor; that is all!"

Héctor, still suspicious, said nothing. The last time someone had asked him for a favor, it had been to borrow his driver's license to present to the welfare office in Albuquerque where the document had been temporarily confiscated, with great embarrassment to himself in getting it back after a lengthy and highly unpleasant bureaucratic procedure.

"Me and the family are coming north next month to try the U.S. for ourselves! I've paid the coyote the $3,000 he asked for already; he's going to bring us through near Columbus, where there aren't enough *migra* around these days to catch everybody. . . . Listen, *hombre*: I see by looking at the map Columbus is just a couple hundred kilometers south of Belen! From the photo you sent me of your beautiful home, only two Christmases ago, I know it is a large one, Héctor. There's only eight of us coming north—ten, if we bring two of my niece's sons as well—and so I feel certain, *primo*, you must have plenty room for—"

Héctor experienced something like panic, followed by the same violated feeling the city-hall letters had given him. Somehow, the spirit of *Mi casa es su casa* failed to carry across international boundaries. His house, simple as it was (though also tasteful, of course), was his castle, for which he had worked hard and sacrificed much. Now his good-for-nothing relatives back home in Namiquipa seemed determined to piggyback on his success by moving north—and, what was unimaginably worse, moving in.

"Eufemio, you do not know what you are saying! In the picture, perhaps, my house looked big to you. In reality, it is not so large! Consider, *hombre*, there are four of us, with—!" He'd been about to add, "with a fifth coming along," but held back this lie just in time.

Of course, Juana—Eufemio's wife—would know AveMaría had had her tubes tied immediately after the birth of George Dubya two years before.

"Listen, *compadrito*, you mustn't worry about a thing! We can sleep out on the lawn or on the roof until the weather turns cold, and after that—we'll see, we'll see! Anyway, the company's trying to cut us off, and I'm out of pesos to feed the phone with. . . . I'll call again in three or four weeks, just to let you know we're safely across the border and headed north to Belen! A million kisses to Contracepción—and AveMaría too, of course. *¡Hasta luego, primo!*"

As Héctor had expected, the womenfolk responded badly to the news when he broke it to them. AveMaría protested there was no place in her home for a lazy toad like Juana Villa, while Contracepción wailed that she'd never be able to enjoy a wink's sleep at night under the same roof as Máximo—at sixteen, Eufemio's oldest son—whom she accused of having tried to seduce her while she was visiting Namiquipa the previous summer. Since the remote wasn't working after Dubya dropped it into the toilet bowl the day before, and neither mother nor daughter seemed willing to get up from the sofa to turn down the volume by hand, their uproar, added to the din of the TV movie in which the lovers were being serenaded by a mariachi band outside of the Big Cat House at the Mexico City Zoo, was finally more than Héctor could stand. Clutching at his graying, but still thick, hair, he fled to the kitchen where, gripping the tequila bottle in one hand and the telephone in the other, he settled down behind the kitchen table to seek consolation from Jesús "Eddie" Juárez, upriver a few miles in Los Lunas.

For the next few weeks, Héctor tried to put the Eufemio Villas out of his mind—partly in the hope that, like a bad dream, they would vanish at the first penetrating ray of reality, and partly from guilt, since, when he *did* think of them, he found himself fantasizing that the entire family had been apprehended by the *migra* this side of the border and deported back to Namiquipa in the nick of time. Mostly, he existed in a state of grim dread, like a man expecting a fatal medical diagnosis, as he awaited the next phone call from the south. It would surely come collect, he thought scornfully. Eufemio, excepting only in the few months after Juana received a small legacy from a rich uncle, had never had so much as a peso to his name.

On a bright hot late afternoon in September, Héctor was in his garden, weeding the chrysanthemum bed and wondering, as he worked, whether city hall would tolerate his placing the antique sod-busting plow he'd admired at a local flea market in the southwest corner of the lawn where it wouldn't show too much from the street, when a white school bus with the words SOUTHSIDE PRESBYTERIAN CHURCH, TUCSON painted in blue along the side panel slowed and rolled to a stop beside the mailbox. From his knees, Héctor glanced up briefly at the bus, then returned his attention to the chrysanthemums. His mind noted, vaguely, that for a church bus this one was awfully noisy: people screaming and shouting through the raised windows. "Hey, *compadrito!*" The voice, bellowing out above the general confusion, sounded horribly familiar. "We made it, *hombre!* Here we are, safe and sound, all of us—the Villas, at last, have arrived in El Norte!"

Héctor took a careful count as Eufemio's family piled off the bus. They made thirteen or fourteen, he couldn't be certain which. Everyone wore a daypack on his back and clutched several bulging Wal-Mart bags. His heart sank as his cousin—a large, stout man with drooping mustaches, wearing a dirty white T-shirt and a baseball cap—waddled toward him, followed heavily by Juana who, though at least a foot shorter than her husband, appeared to be twice his girth. The Eufemio Villas, so far as Héctor knew, were still Catholic, and the distasteful thought occurred to him that she could be pregnant yet again. Unnerved, Héctor turned his back on them and shouted toward his house, as though for help.

"AveMaría! Contracepción! The *villist*—that is, the Villas are here!"

The family stood grouped alongside the bus, watching impatiently while the driver—a pale, weak-chested, bespectacled young man—struggled to carry a dozen or more cardboard boxes tied about with string and sealed with duct tape down the steps and dropped them in exhaustion on the sidewalk. They'd actually been apprehended at the border (Eufemio explained to Héctor as they stood together watching the young man at work) after their coyote abandoned them and fled into the desert, loaded like animals into a van with barred windows, and driven to a detention center in Deming, where they were held overnight without tortillas or even TV. The next day they were visited by a gringo attorney who advised them, as descendants of the "social bandit" and revolutionary Pancho Villa, to request political asylum on the grounds of possible persecution by the PAN government in Mexico City. With the attorney's help, Eufemio had filled out the required paperwork. The day after that the church bus arrived, chauffeured by the young man who'd offered to take them north to Belen for no money. When Héctor suggested he might be willing to drive them as far as Chicago, or maybe just Albuquerque, Eufemio said no, that wouldn't be necessary; Belen was a good town, full of opportunity, and, anyway, the *familia Villa* needed to stick together if they hoped to survive in a racist imperialist country.

After the bus drove off, AveMaría announced that, if she was really expected to feed all these people, she would need to do a big shopping at the Albertson's store in Los Lunas. She left in her new Subaru, taking Contracepción along, while Juana went into the bedroom to lie down in the big double bed with its Shape-U-Up mattress and Héctor and Eufemio seated themselves at the kitchen table.

"I was bringing you a bottle of José Cuervo from Namiquipa," Eufemio explained, "but the *migra* stole it from my hands at the border—*¡hijos de la chingada!*"

"It's OK," Héctor said helplessly. "I got plenty tequila in the house already." A hard winter lay ahead of them, he could see. He'd better try to get used to this.

After the first drink, Héctor felt slightly better. After the third or fourth, he was barely aware of the din around him as a dozen young children and adolescents surged back and forth through the house with a confused roaring sound, like a dirty tidal wave. The two men were still drinking when AveMaría and Contracepción returned from the supermarket and carried in the groceries they'd bought—bags and bags of the stuff, causing them to make three or four trips in from the car, and costing, Héctor guessed, three or four hundred dollars. And tomorrow he'd have to go to the liquor store and stock up, big time.

AveMaría, with help from Contracep, prepared an enormous pot of menudo and a platter of hot dogs wrapped in fried tortillas. When the meal was ready, Juana came from the bedroom to join them and the adults—Contracepción and Máximo included—sat down around the table in the kitchen, after AveMaría had served the kids on paper plates and shooed them out into the yard to eat. Partly to be hospitable, and also for survival's sake, Héctor produced a gallon bottle of

Gallo wine and six water glasses. By now he hardly knew what was happening to him, or cared—after all, he reflected stupidly, *mañana* is another day.

Later, when Juana had retired to the bedroom again and AveMaría and Contracep were washing up, Héctor and Eufemio, taking the wine bottle with them, wandered out into the yard to watch the sun set behind Ladrón Peak, which stood like an eruptive volcano against the western sky. Around them on the grass, the Eufemio clan—plus a few others of whose identities Héctor remained ignorant—were spreading their blankets, whacking each other with pillows, and tuning their transistor radios for the night. Off in the southwest corner of the fence, where Héctor had in mind to place the sod-buster plow, Contracepción and Máximo stood embracing in a manner that caused her father to avert his eyes. In just a few hours, his home had assumed the aspect of a *barrio* in Chiapas. What (Héctor agonized) would the neighbors have to say about this small corner of the Third World set down overnight in their pleasant and comfortable neighborhood?

In the bad Old Mexico of Pancho Villa's day, when peons amounted to property, like so many yard ornaments, a convenient solution to his problem might have existed. In the circumstances, there was only prayer to trust to—prayer, and the honorable worthies at the Belen city hall.

Día de los Muertos

FALL HAD ALWAYS BEEN Héctor Villa's least-favorite season. This year, as the days shortened and his cousin's stayover in his home lengthened inexorably, he felt his substance as a householder drain away in exact proportion to the diminishing quantity of the pale indirect light. Four days after the shortest day of the year comes Christmas. Already AveMaría had her credit cards out, and Juana was promising to pay her share of the debt as soon as the local economy picked up enough to allow Eufemio to find a job.

Though born to a family of *campesinos*, Héctor had never before lived in a *colonia*, and he found it difficult to adjust to the experience now. True, by comparison with the Juárez *colonias* visible from Interstate 10 in the neighborhood of the ARCO plant in El Paso, his home in Belen was a palace. Unfortunately, it was also crowded to bursting—unlike the seemingly deserted *barrios* across the brown trickle of the Rio Grande, at whose empty and precipitous dirt streets Héctor gazed wistfully now each time he made the trip to the border, though formerly he had found Ciudad Juárez dirty, distasteful, and depressing. Like it or not, he'd be visiting the place again at the beginning of November for *Día de los Muertos*—the Day of the Dead, Juana Villa's favorite holiday. Héctor expected he would need to rent two vans to transport the families there for a three-night stay at the Holiday Inn Express on the Paseo Triunfo de la Republica, in the vicinity of the condemned Plaza Monumental bull ring. Maybe even a third, to hold all the Christmas presents the girls bought at the *mercados* along the Avenida Juárez. It gave him a sick feeling just thinking about it. On top of everything, he would have to endure the wrath of his Assemblies of God church if Brother Billy Joe learned he'd attended a heathen festival in Mexico. Of course, celebrating *Día de los Muertos* wasn't actually a sin, like going to Mass at the Cathedral of Our Lady of Guadalupe. Still, Héctor suspected, it was sin enough—in the preacher's eyes, anyhow. He consoled himself by reflecting that, after nearly two months, his regular visits to the Taberna Aztlán on the road between Belen and Los Lunas in the company of Jesús "Eddie" Juárez had yet to be revealed to a scandalized world. Though not what is known as a drinking man, Héctor found the *taberna* a refuge from the chaos the Eufemio Villas had made of his once-comfortable home, a relatively quiet place where he could get away for an hour or two after supper to relax while conversing with his friend. Since Jesús "Eddie," as a candidate for a seat on the local school board in the coming fall elections, knew everything that went on at the city hall these days and seemed more than willing to share it, Héctor was content to let him do most of the talking, while he drank beer and listened.

"The goddamn *An*-glos," Jesús "Eddie" was complaining on a chilly evening in mid-October as the two men sat across the table from each other beside the big plate-glass window looking out on Highway 47, considered the most dangerous in New Mexico on account of its narrow shoulders, frequent curves, and entire fleets of drunk drivers. Directly across the road from the *taberna* a large billboard, lighted from below, read VOTE JESÚS "EDDIE" JUÁREZ FOR SCHOOL BOARD DISTRICT NO. 2 in huge red letters. "They are wantin to take over our public school *sys*-tem, *hombre*! All these immigrant white kids from Chic-*a*-go, Minnesota, O-*hi*-o! Hundreds of thousands of them in the last ten *years* alone! Ten more, and our teachers will have to speak *En*-glish in *class*. Then the *An*-glos will have stolen our culture from us for *good*! Listen to me, *compadrito*—it is time Eufemio's kids went to school here, in Belen. We need all the brown ones we can get—even if they are wetbacks from Mexico!"

"Eufemio can't risk enrolling them until he has the necessary documents to show," Héctor explained patiently, for at least the fourth or fifth time in a month. "He's got a *tipo* in Canutillo drawing them up now." Héctor didn't add that he himself was paying for the forgery, to the tune of a couple of thousand dollars or so.

"You need to get the boy, Máximo, out of the house as soon as *poss*-ible, *compadrito*, before he finds mischief to get into." By "mischief," Jesús "Eddie" meant Contracepción, though he didn't dare say so. While grudgingly aware that he himself was too old for the girl (in her father's eyes anyway), he found the thought of the younger man having her intolerable. Seeing the way the kid made out with the girl when he thought her father wasn't looking made him squirm with jealousy and frustration.

"I'm driving everyone to Juárez for *Día de los Muertos* in a couple of weeks," Héctor assured his friend. "We can stop in Canutillo for the papers on the way down there, if they're ready by then."

Jesús "Eddie" froze suddenly, the tequila bottle poised above his glass, to squint resentfully at the billboard where one of the electric lights had just burned out in a sudden small explosion.

"When *I* am a school *board* member," he said darkly, "the *migra* won't dare come snoopin around, askin to see people's papers—you see if they don't, *hombre*."

With November's approach, disagreement emerged among the Villas—the Héctor as well as the Eufemio branch of the family—concerning the proposed trip to Ciudad Juárez at the start of the month. Eufemio, it seemed, detesting *Día de los Muertos* as a superstitious relic of the Catholic religion for which, since his arrival in El Norte, he'd conceived a violent dislike, preferred to attend the stock-car races in Alamogordo instead. Héctor had been relieved by the prospect of having to rent only one van to make the trip, before Contracepción began pleading for permission to accompany Luz at a three-day open-air rock concert at the state fairgrounds in Albuquerque.

"Too much money," he decreed shortly. Besides the cost of the fabulously overpriced ticket, there was also the combined expense of gas, meals, and two or three nights in a big-city hotel to consider. "Here I am, supporting half the village of Namiquipa out of my own pocket, and my daughter expects me to pay for her to attend a *fiesta de percusión*?" Since the alternative was her share of a room at the Holiday Inn Express and meals, money was not the true ground of Héctor's objection. His nephew Máximo was.

"You'd have to pay for me anyway, in Juárez," Contracepción reminded him. "In Albuquerque we can sleep in the car, or in sleeping bags at the fairground. Besides, they give me extra credit in school—for Life Experience—if I go. *¡O, mi querido Papá—por piedad!*"

Though she was an indifferent student at best, it was important to Héctor that his daughter do well in school so that she might grow up to realize the American Dream, as he had done. Therefore, he relented. Perhaps Máximo would rather take in the dog races in Juárez than a three-day rock concert, anyhow.

Several days before the departure date, the Villa family outing seemed to have fragmented to the point where Héctor felt confident in reserving a single van to accommodate all who wished to travel to

Mexico for the *Día de los Muertos* celebration, after a number of the males in the younger generation decided to accompany Eufemio to Alamogordo instead. Then, only the day before he'd intended to call the rental office, the telephone rang just as the Villas had finished supper and Juana was settling in to watch *Desperate Housewives* in the den, while AveMaría and Contracepción cleared away the table. It was Jesús "Eddie" calling for Héctor from the Taberna Aztlán.

"*Buenas noches.* "A word to the wise with you, *hermano*."

"Anytime, *compadrito.* 'S'up?"

"Are you sittin down?" Jesús "Eddie" asked him.

Héctor had been sitting at the table when AveMaría handed him the telephone receiver at the end of its stretch cord. Now, he stood up quickly. "What is the matter?" he demanded in alarm.

"Plenty," Jesús "Eddie" told him darkly, his voice dropping nearly to a whisper. "The f--kin *An*-glos, man—they're trying to make *trou*-ble for you a-*gain*! This time, on account of all the people you have livin with you, in your own *home*. They're claimin Héctor Villa is in violation of the resi-*den*-tial code; the summons will be mailed out later this week. I heard the news over at city hall two hours ago, when I was puttin a campaign mailin through the postage-stamp machine. (The town clerk, Esteban 'Gordo' Baca, is a buddy of mine, a real *hermano*.) I'm tellin you—it's *ra*-cism, man!"

Barely aware of what he was saying, Héctor thanked Jesús "Eddie" for the tip and broke the connection without cradling the receiver. Then he dialed the rental company's 800 number and reserved two Ford vans, capable of accommodating up to 24 people, from October 31 through November 3.

Héctor lay awake all that night, with the baby Dubya crowded between him and AveMaría on account of the shortage of beds in the combined Villa households. But by morning, he had completed his plan. He felt so sure of it that, even when Contracepción ambushed him in the vulnerable period between arising and drinking his first cup of coffee to announce that Máximo had selflessly proposed to forgo the dog track so as to be at liberty to drive Luz and her to Albuquerque, he did not despair. In fact, he scarcely even flinched. His scheme, he felt, partook of the genius of Pancho Villa in commandeering an empty coal train and using it as a modern-day Trojan horse to smuggle his troops into Ciudad Juárez. Where The Centaur had not failed, he, Héctor Villa, would not fail, either. All he needed was nerve, a bit of luck, and—above all—timing.

Thirty-six hours ahead of the scheduled departure for Mexico, Héctor sprained his wrist in a fall from the roof of his house where he had gone climbing to nail down a few shingles that never needed nailing in the first place. Refusing to visit a doctor, he had AveMaría bandage the arm, starting at the fingertips and going as high as the shoulder, until, it seemed to him, almost his entire right side was swathed in an impressive cocoon of gauze and tape. Then, twenty-four hours before departure, he informed his cousin that, as he himself was clearly incapable of operating a motor vehicle, Eufemio would have to take the wheel of one van, while Máximo drove the other. This announcement, as Héctor had expected, produced noisy protests asserting a preference for Alamogordo and Albuquerque over Juárez. Also as expected, the protests were instantly and effectively suppressed by Juana, as soon as she was made to understand that, absent Eufemio and Máximo, no one would be traveling to Mexico for *Día de los Muertos* at all.

The party made a delayed start on the thirty-first, after Héctor experienced an attack of diarrhea that lasted from breakfast until well after lunch. By the time they reached Canutillo they were running so late he suggested they continue south to the border and pick up the Eufemio Villas' forged documentation papers on the way home, as they wouldn't be required on the trip. In Juárez, the Villas checked in to the Holiday Inn Express and went for dinner afterward at the McDonald's on the Avenida de las Américas, where Héctor tried to ignore the Tarahumara Indian women with their babies and tin cups and the street vendors selling sugar candy in the shape of skulls. Never had Mexico seemed to him so dirty, backward, and miserable—so downright embarrassing, really.

For the next three days, while the families watched the Indians prance in headdress on the plaza before the cathedral and ate their lunches off the tombstones of unknown dead people in neighboring cemeteries, and Eufemio lost all the money he'd borrowed at the dog races, Héctor lay stretched on his bed at the hotel, with the television set switched on. It wasn't, indeed, the documentary about General Huerta's treacherous killing of President Madero that occupied his mind but the final step of the master plan he'd conceived in Belen the week before. At last, when he was quite certain he was doing the right

29

thing, on the afternoon before the return to the U.S. he made a single call from his bedside phone.

At a little past eight o'clock the next morning, two white Ford vans filled with shrieking children left the parking lot behind the Holiday Inn Express and made their way, one following the other, through the rush-hour traffic toward the international bridge. Riders in the police helicopters hovering overhead would have seen the vans pass silently beneath the acre-sized flags, Mexican and American, waving above Chamizal Park and continue on their way across the Rio Grande to the Customs and Immigration inspection station on the north bank of the river where Old Glory waved alone in splendid isolation. And they would have watched tensely as a small squad of agents in uniform surrounded the vehicles that halted at a signal from two of the men, who thereupon stepped forward and tapped smartly on the drivers' windows.

"Documentation?" the agents demanded grimly.

In the instant of his deliverance, the words of a familiar American song, half remembered, occurred vaguely to Héctor Villa. "Free at last! Thank God I'm free at last!" He felt a little remorse, but not much, hardly more than a pang. And Juana, at least, really *had* been a terrorist of sorts, after all.

A Border Surprise

IN THE YEAR OF OUR LORD 1878, on the sixth day of the sixth month of the year, was born to one Augustín Arango and his wife, Micaela Arambula, humble peasants on the Rancho de la Loyotada in Durango State, Republic of Mexico, a son, Doroteo, known to posterity as Francisco "Pancho" Villa: social bandit, indefatigable warrior, military genius, and savior of his country. In his honor, the Hijos de Pancho Villa assemble yearly on the anniversary of the hero's birth in the town of Namiquipa, Chihuahua State, to celebrate the legacy passed down by its owner to his proud descendants, real as well as imagined. Héctor Villa would sooner have absented himself from an election in which George W. Bush was on the ballot than miss the occasion, himself.

Only this year, there were problems to overcome. Several, such as the high cost of gasoline, were relatively small and of little account. Others, like the opening of the annual convention of the Border Lands Association of Artificial Intelligence Service Professionals in Tucson, on the morning of June 9, were more troublesome. (Though, owing possibly to its unpronounceable and highly forgettable acronym, BLAAISP was usually so ill attended as to be hardly worth bothering with, Héctor was a firm believer that failure to present oneself at associational meetings amounted to an un-American, as well as unprofessional, lapse.) More serious still were the prevalent lack of air conditioning in Namiquipa—and another possible source of discomfort, also related to heat. This was his relatives, the Eufemio Villas, still resident (also, presumably, smoldering) in Namiquipa. Eufemio, though formerly a Hijo de Pancho Villa, had been expelled from the society several years before after failing to pay his dues for three years straight. There would be no danger, therefore, of encountering him at the annual meeting. For the rest, Namiquipa was a very small place, where everybody not only knew everybody but encountered him in the streets and shops every day of the week. Eufemio, like most bullies and con men, was essentially a coward, but Juana was a cow of another color, dangerous as a charging buffalo when angered.

If, having had the barn door slammed shut in her face by the American officials and gotten arrested by the *federales* as a suspected terrorist into the bargain, she wasn't simmering with rage still, then (Héctor concluded) Juana must have been touched by an angel in the meanwhile. He had reason to doubt, however, that such a miracle had actually occurred. Therefore, the thought of encountering his cousin-in-law face-to-face, even in the open air and in public, was sufficient for Héctor to consider skipping Hijos de Pancho Villa altogether this year and driving directly over to Tucson, instead.

He came close to doing so when he brought the subject up to his wife across the dinner table, a week before the celebrations in Namiquipa. Héctor realized his mistake almost before the words were out of his mouth, but it was already too late for him. AveMaría, always quick to spot an opportunity, pounced. If Héctor would not be leaving for Mexico June 4 after all, he'd be available to accompany the family to the Mexican Heritage Fair in Albuquerque, sponsored annually by the Mexican Heritage Foundation, that weekend. Héctor nodded compliantly, but inwardly he shuddered. He despised the foundation and everything associated with it as representing the height of un-Americanism and the spirit of disloyalty. Ostensibly devoted to the cause of ethnic self-respect, its true agenda was only too obviously *Reconquista* pure and simple. The Mexican Heritage Foundation was the Nation of Aztlán with a face as innocent-looking as that of Attorney General Gonzales. Almost as bad, in addition to being made a party to treason, he would have to put up with AveMaría's friends on the organization committee, women of a certain age and built like container ships, who held bossy jobs in local government and sang in Spanish choirs in their parish churches. Finally, besides lugging George Dubya around in his arms, he'd have to keep a hawk's eye on Contracepción, forever lusting after the world (as his mother would have put it), lest she slip away unnoticed to a rock concert and discover it there. The more he considered, the more Héctor inclined to the decision to reverse himself and attend the Hijos de Pancho Villa meeting after all.

Having made his mind up at last, Héctor faced two final and inescapable difficulties that must somehow be got round. The first—how to break the news to AveMaría and Contracepción that the original Namiquipa plan was on and the Albuquerque junket off—he concluded to set aside until the last moment, when panic provided its own inspiration. The second—the danger he courted from the like-lihood of running into one or more of the Eufemio Villas in Namiq-uipa—Héctor was determined to resolve at once, if only for his peace of mind. As if in divine reward for his courage, the answer came to him in the middle of the night as he lay sleepless beside AveMaría. At ten the next morning as the stores were opening in downtown Belen, Héctor stood on the sidewalk along Sosimo Pidaloa with his nose pressed against the plate-glass window of a novelty shop. He exited the store a few minutes later, carrying a plastic shopping bag in one hand and looking pleased with himself. And he was equally lucky in regard to the other thing. On the night of June 3, AveMaría and Con-tracepción fell ill together with acute diarrhea after having consumed a large lunch of eggplant parmigiana at the Palazzo Farnese Restaurant in Belen. They were sick all the following day as well, so when Héctor announced, with elaborate casualness, that he guessed they wouldn't feel up to driving to Albuquerque after all, nobody contradicted him. He got an early start for Namiquipa next morning and checked into a motel in Candelaria, Chihuahua State, after dark, having been delayed some hours by traffic gridlock at the border-crossing in Juárez.

Héctor awoke at sunrise to a view of the surrounding Chihuahuan desert, bleak looking even under a late spring sky of milky blue, its naked rock fins oriented north and south on the clay-colored expanse of scrabbled caliche dotted with cholla, greasewood, and mesquite, bisected by the black ribbon of the highway bordered with broken bottles and other trash flung from passing cars. Had this tortured, depressing place called Mexico ever really been his home? He ate a hurried breakfast—*huevos rancheros*, tortillas, and coffee—and drove off from the motel before seven. Though the meetings, scheduled to begin at nine A.M. sharp, rarely got started before one or two in the afternoon, he had 265 kilometers to drive still to Namiquipa, where he would have to find the motel he was booked at and get himself into the disguise he was quite certain not even his sister-in-law would be able to penetrate.

Inspired by the Luz Corral Look-alike Contest, organized in honor of Pancho's favorite "wife" to launch the proceedings, the Hijos had gathered punctually for the first time in memory in their chapter house on the outskirts of town adjacent to the cockfighting arena. To accom-modate the contest, it had been necessary to waive, on a one-time basis, the hard-and-fast rule against the presence of women at meetings, a violation of protocol some of the older members had protested. Already by ten o'clock, the society president and subordinate officers felt themselves vindicated by the spectacular success the contest, fueled by plentiful amounts of beer and tequila, had produced. Never, in the experience of anyone present, had a gathering of the Hijos de Pancho Villa been brought off to such fervent, even riotous, effect. At shortly past ten the new Luz Corral was crowned. Half an hour later, Hijos were pouring into the street, snatching at girls who bore only passing resemblances to Juana Torres, Austreberta Rentería, and Soldedad Seáñez and dragging them into the chapter house to participate in additional contests. In the confusion the arrival, toward noon, of a latecomer to the festivities was not immediately noticed. Wearing a shiny black suit buttoned tightly over his paunch, a white shirt open at the collar, white beard, and wire-rimmed spectacles, the old fellow appeared dazed to discover the party in full swing at so early an hour. But he joined in gamely, working his way around the frenzied dancers through a haze of tobacco smoke to the table where beer chilled in tubs of ice and helping himself to a bottle, a slice of lime, a sprinkle of salt on the back of his hand, and a shot of tequila as a booster.

He was a wallflower at an orgy and almost certainly would have remained that way had he not been spied by Alfredo Terrazas, the newspaper editor and village intellectual. Terrazas, who, when sober, was at work on a history of the Mexican Civil War, was very drunk this morning. In search of beer and a fresh bottle of tequila, he stumbled unexpectedly upon an elderly, potbellied gentleman dressed in black, bespectacled, and whiskered like a goat. Terrazas, in spite of being a journalist and an historian, was also a poet with a poet's imagination, open to the power of suggestion. Steeped as he was in the history of 20th-century Mexico, Terrazas recognized at once the disheveled figure before him.

"*¡Venustiano Carranza!*" he shouted, falling back a step and stabbing ahead of himself with a nicotine-stained finger. "How *dare* you come here—how dare you show yourself at such an affair as this! *¡Canalla! ¡Traidor! ¡A las armas! ¡A las armas!*"

In terror, Héctor tore away his glasses, ripped off his beard, jerked the pillow from under his shirt, and flung everything down on the floor. But the Hijos de Pancho Villa were upon him already, swinging, punching, and kicking, brandishing beer bottles upraised as clubs. Just as he went down beneath the pile-on, he distinguished Eufemio Villa among the crowd, his eyes asquint and reddened like an enraged pig's. Though he was five years in arrears with his dues, the Hijos de Pancho Villa had admitted him, as one of the most enthusiastic organizers of the Luz Corral Look-alike Contest, to the meeting anyway.

IT HAD BEEN A TERRIBLE TRIP and now, already twelve hours late for the BLAAISP convention in Tucson, Héctor arrived at Agua Prieta on the Mexican-U.S. border to discover the northbound traffic backed up for several miles south from the international crossing, on account, a gnarled old *campesino* explained, of a big sale at the Wal-Mart Supercenter in Douglas. (Another waiting motorist thought a free health-fair screening at the Tucson Medical Center was the big draw.) Héctor didn't care if these people were going north to participate in a voter-registration drive by the GOP. At the rate at which the lines were moving, it could be six hours before he passed through Customs and Immigration, with another two-and-a-half hours on to Tucson. The old man, noting his distress, grinned around the toothpick he held between his two or three remaining teeth and gave him a broad wink. A shortcut existed, he confided, into the U.S. only a few miles east of town. The road was stony and rutted, hardly more than a wagon track. Even so, smugglers considered the route too obvious for regular use, and so the *migra* left it largely unpatrolled. If the *señor* wished, he could give him accurate directions . . .

Héctor was desperate. He was a longtime resident of the U.S. of A., bearing on his person the documentation necessary to prove his identity and driving a vehicle duly licensed in the State of New Mexico. Lastly, he was no scofflaw, but an honest person whose only interest lay in returning home in a timely manner to be present at an important professional gathering. Héctor drew a spiral notebook from his coat pocket and, nodding encouragement from time to time to show he understood, jotted down the directions the old man gave him.

The road was considerably farther east and rougher even than he'd been led to believe, winding north through limestone hills covered with pinyon and juniper forest. There were no signs, no markers of any sort, so that the first indication Héctor had that he'd crossed onto American soil was three parked minivans beside the trail two hundred yards ahead. A striped awning had been drawn out from the side of one of the vans to make a strip of shade where three men and two women wearing T-shirts emblazoned with Old Glory across the front reclined in lawn chairs arranged to afford a southward view toward Mexico. At Héctor's approach, the men got out of their chairs and stepped to the middle of the road, holding their hands up to him, palms turned out. They were all of them heavy-set, balding or gray-haired, snowbirds apparently from Minnesota or Michigan who had overstayed their time in the Southwest. Two carried shotguns, and the third wore a pistol strapped to his hip.

Héctor recognized these people at once. They were the ones President Bush had described only recently as vigilantes, extremists with dangerous opinions and un-American values. Goaded by fatigue and frustration, he floored the pedal and pointed his car straight at them. Either they jumped in time, or he, Héctor Villa, would run them all down like mad dogs. It was no more nor less than what Dubya would want—and expect—a man in his position to do.

II

The Draftee

HÉCTOR VILLA did not feel disposed to take phone calls this morning. He was at work outdoors, gilding a large piece of driftwood he and Jesús "Eddie" Juárez had retrieved from a sandbar in the Rio Grande between Contreras and the Sevilleta National Wildlife Refuge and carted home in Jesús "Eddie's" pickup truck for display in the side yard of his house, where he hoped it would not attract too much notice from passers-by. Pleasingly tortured in shape, in which it vaguely resembled a steam shovel with the crane bent backward over the cab, the wood's appearance struck Héctor as significantly enhanced by its coat of gold and bronze paint. Intent on finishing the job, he'd pretended not to have heard AveMaría when she called to him the first time from the back door. She called twice more again before he saw her rounding the corner of the house with Dubya on one arm and the cell phone in her free hand.

"¡Héctor! ¡Te llaman al teléfono! Are you deaf?" AveMaría protested, between low gasps for air.

"¿Quién es?"

"Some Anglo, a Mr. Domenici."

"Tell him I'm not at home."

"I can't; I already told him you *are*."

Héctor, seeing she'd left the line open while they spoke, gave up and snatched the phone from her hand.

"Hello, Mr. Villa? Pete Domenici here. ¿Cómo está?"

Pete Domenici . . . ? The name had a familiar ring, like Tommy Hilfiger or Chef Boyardee.

"That's *Senator* Domenici, calling from Washington. ¿Ingles o Español, compadre?"

"English is okay," Héctor replied, confusedly, before he remembered Pete Domenici was Mexican on his mother's side. Or would that be Bill Richardson, the governor?

"English it is, then," the senator assured him. "Listen, *hombre*, I'm not the *hombre* to beat around the bush. I'm sure you heard of the tragic death in June of Alberto Torres, the incumbent Republican U.S.

representative renominated in the primary for New Mexico District 1, when his car was T-boned— one of those Mexican semis up here driving without brakes or lights, you know. Well, the state GOP wants to appoint *you* to run for his seat in November! How about it, *compadre*? You got name recognition like César Chavez—or, for that matter, Pancho Villa, ha-ha! Your opponent would be Tomasina Luna, a schoolteacher from Los Lunas who's in like Flynn with the American Federation of Teachers-New Mexico and once invited Hillary Clinton to her house for homemade *chiles rellenos*. You can't lose for winning, *amigo*. You aren't going to let us down in a crisis, now—are you?"

Héctor, as he listened, felt his initial astonishment turning to anguish and despair. Since his run-in on the border with the Minutemen the previous June, his hitherto quiet life had been transformed by publicity and other unwanted attention into that of a minor regional celebrity. The story of an innocent Mexican-American citizen harassed and threatened on reentry into his adopted land by a gang of white-skinned, gray-haired, potbellied, racist vigilantes with guns had made him a victim-hero overnight, an emblem of persecution throughout the Southwest—the Borderlands area, in particular. Héctor wasn't enjoying the life of a celebrity, while the manner in which his unfortunate experience had been exploited seemed to him basically un-American. Besides—

"I'm authorized to say the White House is asking you to run as a personal favor to President Bush," he suddenly heard Senator Domenici saying. "By the way—are you *really* a descendant of Pancho Villa?"

"ASK NOT WHAT YOUR COUNTRY can do for you, but what you can do for your country." A Democratic president had said that, but it seemed to Héctor it might as well have come from the mouth of Dubya himself, who only recently had pleaded for Americans to make sacrifices on behalf of the Iraq War. The fact that he himself was not really, in the technical sense at least, an American citizen seemed finally irrelevant. Certainly nobody (including the President of the United States) seemed to know, or care, if Héctor Villa were an illegal immigrant. And so, though feeling like a sacrificial goat, he'd agreed in the end to run for office against Tomasina Luna, who'd been Contracepción's homeroom teacher last year at Belen Junior High.

The Villa women, somewhat to Héctor's surprise, had reacted enthusiastically to the news of his candidacy. Contracepción crowed that she'd get even at last with Mrs. Luna—the old bag who'd refused to allow her to sit in class until she removed the SUPPORT OUR TROOPS ribbon pinned to her T-shirt—when Papá kicked her butt in the election, and AveMaría immediately announced her determination to lose 25 pounds and refurbish her wardrobe entirely before the campaign got under way after Labor Day. And when Contracepción understood that her parents were going to be involved in a major multimedia campaign, including statewide TV appearances and candidate tours with rock bands along, she demanded to be withdrawn from school for the entire fall semester. In the face of all this, Héctor kept his peace, though he could have wished for a better start to a long and tiring campaign that everyone seemed to expect would be ugly as well. He was acquainted with Tomasina slightly, which was all he'd ever aspired to be. An oversized, bossy woman, with an appetite for power as well as *chiles rellenos* and a brassy voice that was reputed to shiver the plaster saints each Sunday morning at Our Lady of Belen Church, Tomasina was not the sort of woman Héctor looked forward to having as an enemy. In fact (the thought occurred to him), he'd rather have the formidable Luz Corral mad at him, any day—maybe even The Centaur himself.

For better or worse, Héctor was now a candidate for a seat in the U.S. House of Representatives and as such (so he'd been led to believe) in dire and immediate need of a campaign manager. The party functionaries in Santa Fe had promised him they were trying to find a suitable replacement for Torres' man who'd been killed in the crash along with his boss, but Héctor was convinced he could do better himself. Less than 48 hours after his conversation with Senator Domenici, he phoned Jesús "Eddie" and offered to treat him to as many beers as he could swallow at a sitting if he'd agree to meet with him that evening after supper at the Taberna Aztlán. He was facing the crisis of his life, Héctor explained, and stood in need of the kind of advice and help that only the closest of friends could give. Jesús "Eddie" had planned on accompanying his wife to a bingo game in the basement of Our Lady of Belen that evening, but he loyally assured Héctor he'd be present at the *taberna* in half an hour's time. The only crisis he could imagine likely to befall the Villa family was Contracepción's getting pregnant, and Jesús "Eddie" was keen to hear the salacious details of her fall from virtue.

When Héctor arrived at the Taberna Aztlán, Jesús "Eddie" had been waiting a quarter of an hour already while he drank beer, ate buttered popcorn, and watched a baseball game on one of three wide-screen TVs. The set was surrounded by a halo of popcorn Jesús "Eddie" flung at the screen each time a player for his team struck out or missed the ball. Héctor, who had no interest in baseball (guiltily, he much preferred soccer), led him away to his favorite table by the window overlooking Highway 47, where he half expected to witness one of the fiery head-on collisions graphically described, every week or two on average, in the *Albuquerque Journal*. He noticed Jesús "Eddie" brought his bar tab along with him to be added to the overall bill when Héctor was ready to pay up at the end of the evening.

"So, what's your *cri*-sis, *amigo*?" Jesús "Eddie" demanded, as soon as the girl had left to place their order.

Héctor, attempting President Bush's *gravitas*, felt he'd achieved John Kerry's constipated look instead.

"I've decided to run for the U.S. House of Representatives," he said.

Jesús "Eddie" stared like a dog that's just heard a tomcat roar like a lion.

"*!!¿Cómo?!!*"

"I'm running for Congress, District 1, here in Belen."

For all his astonishment, Jesús "Eddie" was more disappointed still. So he wasn't going to hear about the impregnation of Contracepción, after all.

"You *loco*, or *some*-thin?" he demanded.

Héctor had been impressed by Senator Domenici's directness on the telephone. Big-league politicians, apparently, did not beat around the bush.

"I'm not the kind of *hombre* to beat around the bush, *hombre*," he said in a stern voice. "I want you to serve as my campaign manager, starting in September after Labor Day."

"You *are loco, compadre*," Jesús "Eddie" told him, pityingly. "You don't know no more about politics than the Pope knows about love."

"But *you* do! You ran for school board last year."

"And just look how *that* turned out!" Jesús "Eddie" was about to say, but didn't. His defeat in that election by the Anglo candidate was still, ten months later, a sore point with him.

"Even if you did get creamed, you have experience now. Plus, you have a friend at city hall—you know, the guy that let you use the postal-stamp machine for nothing."

But Jesús "Eddie" heard his friend with only one ear now. He was thinking. This whole business of Héctor running for election in the First District didn't add up for him. Something was out of kilter—wrong. And then, suddenly, it came to him.

"You *can't* run for the First, *hombre*! They already *have* a candidate—Tomasina Luna! She won in the prim-*ary* last month. Anyway, you don't want to get crossways with Tomasina, the fat *bruja*! That one could eat Bill Clinton for breakfast and pick the scraps from between her teeth with a tooth-*pick*! Just think what she'd do with a babe-in-the-woods like you, *amigo*!"

Héctor sighed. He was trying hard to be patient. "Tomasina is the Democratic candidate. I'm the Republican one."

Jesús "Eddie" set his bottle down with a bang on the formica tabletop.

"*You?* A His-*pan*-ic? A Re-*pub*-lican? In New *Mex*-ico?"

Héctor, to his surprise, found himself suddenly on the defensive. "Well . . . you know how I feel about President Bush . . . I'm doing this, really, as a favor to *him*."

Jesús "Eddie" was out of his chair already, standing with the neck of his beer bottle pointed down his throat.

"The Republican Party is for the *An*-glos," he shouted; "the f--kin movie stars in Santa Fe, the environ-*men*-talists, PETA! Bush is for the *An*-glos *and* the Mexicans, the f--kin wetbacks—not for us who've lived here in New Mexico for five hundred years, the *nuevomexicanos!* The Republican Party is the party of cultural *gen*-ocide, man! You wait, you'll see! They'll geno-f--kin-ciadize you too, *hombre*—if Tomasina Luna don't eat you first! *¡Viva Villa!*" Jesús "Eddie" concluded (somewhat illogically, it seemed to Héctor).

"Panchito! What's the matter with you?" AveMaría exclaimed when she saw her husband twenty minutes later. "Did you see the *fantasma* down along the river by the bridge? Teresa Aguilar was telling me about it only the day before yesterday! It seems like some Indians ambushed a Mexican family there many years ago, and—"

But Héctor paid her no attention. Instead he went on to the bedroom where he pulled off his jacket and shoes and lay down on the bed with his clothes on. Never had he been in such a quandary, so divided and confused in his loyalties, so uncertain where his duty lay. The United States, Mexico, New Mexico—wasn't it a part of the United States, after all? He could not comprehend why his good friend, Jesús "Eddie," had to make everything so complicated. Héctor called for AveMaría to bring him the tequila bottle and a glass and drank something. Afterward he tried to think, but thinking would not come to him this evening, and, in a little while, he fell asleep.

Héctor was still not himself by morning, and his wife, now seriously alarmed, sat him down after Contracepción had left for school to learn what was troubling him. AveMaría listened intently while he explained the situation for her and sat in silence when he'd finished, considering. At last, she spoke. She was a woman, AveMaría reminded him, and therefore ignorant of politics. It appeared to her, however, that her husband's dilemma was not political at all, but spiritual. Therefore she suggested they call Brother Billy Joe and ask him to pray with Héctor, begging the Lord to help him find a solution to his problem.

Brother Billy Joe visited the house that same evening, arriving just in time for supper. When he smelled the *carne asada* AveMaría had prepared, the preacher suggested they should eat first and pray later. Héctor, in an attempt to play the good host, agreed, though Billy Joe's presence at table meant having to deny himself the two or three Coronas he'd looked forward to with the meal. The pastor ate three large helpings of *carne asada*, plus dessert. Then he and Héctor adjourned to the den for prayers.

To Héctor's enormous surprise, Brother Billy Joe failed to perceive a dilemma in his situation. President Bush, the preacher avowed, was a true Christian and the greatest president the United States had ever had, dedicated one hundred percent to Values, the War on Terror, and the coming Rapture. If Héctor had been requested by the President to play a part, however modest, in the fulfillment of his calling, then it was his clear obligation as a Christian to cooperate in the Divine Plan.

As if in afterthought, the pastor wondered out loud whether Héctor supposed the President might agree, following his election as congressman, to address the congregation of the Assemblies of God church, right here in Belen? It would be a huge step toward putting a new roof on the meeting hall, Brother Billy Joe explained.

The Candidate

A POLITICIAN'S LIFE (Héctor was discovering) is, like that of any celebrity, not a happy one.

Even before he'd declared his candidacy for the open seat in New Mexico's First Congressional District, Tomasina Luna issued a campaign statement announcing her endorsement by the National Council of La Raza, accusing the Republican Party of racism (amounting possibly to genocide), and charging her opponent with willful violation of city zoning and state environmental law by creating a junkyard around his house. After dragging its feet for weeks a hundred miles away in Santa Fe, the New Mexico GOP at last sent Héctor a campaign manager he wouldn't have asked to serve with him on a church committee. Haníbal Aragón had a degree from the University of New Mexico School of Law, where he'd been elected secretary of the UNM Campus Republicans. Having exercised his J.D. for two or three years, Haníbal abandoned the practice of law to become a lobbyist in Santa Fe for the state tourism board and the city of Roswell, in his capacity as president of the New Mexico chapter of the National Association of Paranormal Americans. In addition to politics and extraterrestrials, Haníbal's other great interest was the classical guitar on which he performed regularly in coffeehouses around New Mexico, dressed in a black beret and a black cape with a scarlet lining as he fumbled isolated bars of Ponce, Rodrigo, and Lopez-Chavarri. At their first fundraising event together, Haníbal, to Héctor's embarrassment, had produced his guitar with the apparent intent of serenading the assembly of cattle ranchers, bank branch managers, and chambers-of-commerce officials before Héctor could discourage him from doing it. Also at several early appearances, he'd passed out brochures for the International UFO Museum & Research Center, thus giving Héctor's would-be constituents the impression that the gray Roswell alien, not Héctor Villa, was running for Congress. And as if Tomasina and Haníbal weren't cross enough to bear, Héctor had problems at home, where AveMaría and Contracepción conspired—so it seemed to him—to make his domestic life as miserable as his professional one already was. Even before he learned his wife had opened an account there, Héctor received a bill from the Neiman Marcus store in Albuquerque amounting to nearly $6,500 for items purchased in the Ladies' Clothing Department. In the evenings, his phone rang off the hook with calls from the managers of rock bands Contracep had promised she'd ask her father to book for campaign appearances throughout the district. Héctor's computer-service business was beginning to suffer, as the desperate parents of children deprived of their favorite video games by crashed systems found their emergency voice messages left unresponded to among the scores recorded by inquiring radio, TV, and newspaper reporters. Finally, little Dubya was growing querulous and fretful from being left so much at the neighbors' house. Héctor, who'd had no notion of all that a political campaign involved, found his already sizable respect and awe for George W. Bush increased exponentially. If this was what you had to go through to get yourself elected a lowly U.S. representative, it must require real genius—and in heroic degree—to make a grab for the brass ring, and seize it.

Though the thought shamed Héctor, he couldn't help envying the President, his reticent First Lady, and their two well-behaved daughters, both of whom knew enough at least to *try* to keep out of the limelight. By contrast, AveMaría—who insisted on joining him on the platform whenever it was at all possible—never missed an opportunity to put a word of her own in, to the approbation of the media who made a point of reporting her comments. Almost as bad, the stylish Neiman Marcus career woman's outfits she'd put on the new card in the mistaken belief they could be charged to campaign expenses made her look 25 pounds heavier. As for Contracepción, who tagged along with her mother when she wasn't in school and seemed to make a point of dressing (Héctor thought) like a Juárez *puta*, nothing he had to say could prevent her from climbing onto the platform after he was through speaking and flinging herself about with a microphone gripped in her hand, shrieking like Jennifer Lopez to the accompaniment of whatever band she'd talked her father into hiring for the event. Once a week at least, Héctor remonstrated with the Villa females— without getting anywhere in the slightest.

"This is America, not Namiquipa!" AveMaría protested. "You're so *old-fashioned*, Panchito! Here, people *care* about politicians' wives. I go to the supermarket—what do I see in the tabloids at the checkout?

Not President Bush! *No!* I see the Bush twins! Senator Kerry? No—they have a picture of Teresa Heinz Kerry instead! Did you know she's gained a hundred pounds and shaved her head since the election?"

He had no better success with Contracepción. *"¡O papaíto!"* she'd wail. *"Nobody* wants to listen to some boring politician! It's the live entertainment everyone *really* cares about! I'm famous already. Just yesterday, some guy says he's a talent scout from Brazil promised he could make me a star if I'd only go to his house with him and let him take a few pictures!"

So Héctor gave in finally, while keeping his eyes peeled and a switchblade in his pocket for the talent scout, in case the *tipo* showed his face again on the campaign trail.

Meanwhile, he had to endure cameramen in his front yard, GOP strategists and ethnic activists on the phone from Santa Fe and around the Southwest, calls from the office of the president of the Mexican Republic in Mexico City and the Mexican consulate in Albuquerque, and the inevitable campaign-finance problems and threatened scandals. (In one instance, the powers that be in Santa Fe panicked when it came to light that the promoter of one of Contracepción's rock bands was a certain Sid Abramoff. Fortunately, the fellow was found to be no relation to the famous lobbyist in Washington.) There was also the incessant stream of carping, negative, and criminally unfair attacks from Tomasina Luna, and the consequent drop in the Republican poll numbers—which in turn produced more phone calls, alternately worried and angry, from Santa Fe, demanding that Héctor respond with negative and unfair attacks of his own. Héctor did his best to comply, but Haníbal Aragón proved worse than useless in drafting a campaign speech (twice he wanted to suggest that Tomasina was from Mars), and he himself, while fluent enough in English in a conversational way, lacked the necessary rhetorical skills in what was, after all, for him a second language. In despair, Héctor approached Brother Billy Joe—by far the most literate man of his acquaintance, whose Sunday sermons he greatly admired—for help, and got it. Indeed, the preacher's suggestions, which consisted of florid attacks on the Party of the Antichrist and anticipations of the Rapture in which papists like Tomasina Luna and other unbelievers and idolators would be left behind, were overwhelmingly effective. The immediate result of the Billy Joe-Héctor collaboration was a further decline in the polls, increasingly agitated calls from party headquarters, and a significant decrease in contributions to the Villa campaign. In desperation, Héctor considered dropping out of the race, but found himself unable in his heart to let George Dubya down. If only (he anguished) the President would endorse his candidacy in a public announcement—better still, come out to New Mexico to campaign with him! Héctor had no doubt whatever that a visit by President Bush would cast the Luna woman into outer darkness and clinch his own election overnight.

By mid-October, with the election less than three weeks off, catastrophe loomed for the New Mexico Republican Party in District 1. Clearly, the situation called for drastic measures, but no one could think what. So far all the best ideas had failed, including attempts to portray Tomasina as a descendant of the *conquistadores* (therefore, an oppressor of the indigenous peoples of North America) and a lukewarm supporter of the Iraq war (a charge she deftly fielded by citing her long-standing friendship with Senator Clinton, well known for having voted for the war and staunchly defended it in Congress ever since). All seemed hopeless when, as if by a miracle, hope struck at last, overnight and in the most unexpected manner.

It came through the heroic efforts of an embedded "journalist" with the Luna campaign posing as a reporter for a granola paper in Taos at the behest of a top strategist in Washington. (Rumor had it that this was actually Karl Rove himself.) By a brilliantly inventive and daring stratagem, the Republican agent had managed to gain entry to Mrs. Luna's personal computer. As soon as the screensaver flashed on, the agent knew he need look no further for the efficient means of Tomasina Luna's political effacement. He simply took a photo of the screen with his cellphone and downloaded the image later at home. Even before Héctor himself was told, the entire New Mexico GOP establishment had learned the nature of that image: Vice President Cheney, stark naked save for a Roman general's helmet on his head and in his hand a sword that drooped as if formed of India rubber in a shape vaguely suggestive of the flaccid male member. At last, the evil Democrats had gone too far. The desecration, the *lèse-majesté* was simply too enormous—immeasurably worse than setting a match to a piece of red-white-and-blue linen with a pattern of stars and stripes printed across it. All that was necessary now was for the Horror to be unveiled publicly at the earliest possible moment—at a Villa rally, with the media standing by and a large crowd assembled (by the promise of free drink, if necessary).

Santa Fe determined upon the Willie M. Chavez State Park in Belen at six o'clock in the evening, when the Santa Fe Burlington Northern workers would be off work and the day commuters arriving home from Albuquerque. Héctor was like a man brought back from the dead. He felt absolutely assured now that Washington, D.C., was his future—for the next two years, at least, and after that, who knew? Filled with a brimming self-confidence, he wrote his own speech for the occasion, politely refusing help from Haníbal Aragón and Brother Billy Joe both. And this time, Héctor positively insisted on the presence of AveMaría and Contracepción with him and other GOP dignitaries on the speakers' platform. He even sent out an emergency request for the Abramoff band, which he installed in a prominent place next to the free beer and *chorizo* stand, immediately to the right of the platform.

It was a beautiful fall evening, the great riverine cottonwoods along the Rio Grande raising their golden crowns against a cobalt sky, the lion-colored mesa stretching east to the edgy green barrier of the Manzano Mountains. And the crowd, too, was a good one. At least, there were a lot of people. Right from the start, however, something felt wrong to Héctor. The crowd was *too* large, for one thing. And too many of the faces upturned toward him looked like Democratic, not Republican, faces. (Twenty years in the U.S. had taught him that a liberal face always looks different from a conservative one, as if the two belonged almost to members of separate species.) Even so, Héctor felt assured that most of those assembled to hear him were his people.

In any event, he had to get on with the business, and so he did. It wasn't until his first three or four applause lines met with scattered poolings of laughter rather than the universal marine roar he'd expected that he began to think there must be something wrong after all. Perhaps the Luna had got the wind up, somehow. For reassurance Héctor glanced behind himself, where the big video-projection screen awaited the damning image prepared for it. Then he went on with his speech.

He had just come to the part where, for the first time, he linked Hillary Clinton's name with Tomasina's when a woman stood up, very near to the projector itself, and shouted at him, waving a piece of paper above her head. Héctor tried to ignore her but found that, refusing steadfastly to shut up, she could not be ignored. In the next instant, he recognized the woman for Tomasina Luna herself. Shocked into momentary speechlessness by her wholly undemocratic and un-American tactics, Héctor gave Tomasina the opening she wanted.

"You dare throw Ms. Clinton up at *me*, do you?" she yelled. "Well, let me tell you, *Señor* Villa, there's something else Hillary's against, and that's illegal immigration! And that means you, *amigo*! Don't try and deny it! I have, right here in my hand, a letter written to me, personally, by your own cousin—Eufemio Villa in Namiquipa, Mexico—telling the whole story of how you and your wife snuck across the border twenty years ago in an undocumented state! Let's put it up on your projector, *Señor*, so we can all have a look for ourselves!"

The Villa family, pursued by loud jeers issuing from open-mouthed Democratic faces and a scattering of flung *chorizo*, had nearly reached the safety of AveMaría's Subaru when Héctor's cell phone rang. As a man clutches at a straw, he grabbed the thing from his pocket and clapped it to his ear.

"Hello—Mr. Villa? This is the White House calling. Please hold the line for President Bush. The President wishes to congratulate you on a major campaign speech today, Sir!"

A Desert Idyll

FOR **HÉCTOR**, Las Vegas was *the* American city. The Strip at night suggested (he thought) an explosion in a fireworks factory—all the flashing, soaring, running, bursting lights in every color of the universe; the gaudy hotels, like upended cruise ships; the fancy stores, luxurious casinos, and romantic cocktail lounges; his compatriots crowding everywhere and jabbering at one another in every dialect known to Viejo México. Vegas was his dream town, a cornucopia of everything he'd sought in coming to the United States in the first place. Las Vegas, Héctor felt, soothed his soul—which very much wanted soothing in the wake of his political disgrace and the Democratic Party's landslide victory when Tomasina Luna crushed his emergency replacement as the Republican candidate for District 1. (That, at least, had not been his fault, as he'd warned Santa Fe in the strongest terms against running his former campaign manager, Haníbal Aragón, in his stead.)

Besides embarrassment to contend with, Héctor now found the Department of Homeland Security, the Minutemen (once again), and *VDare.com* (a viciously anti-immigration website) breathing down his neck. (True, President Bush had praised him, publicly and by name, as a selfless Mexican immigrant seeking only to take upon himself the responsibility of high public office Americans won't accept for themselves anymore—but that had been on the President's weekly radio address, which, in New Mexico as everywhere else, went completely unnoticed.) Thus Héctor considered he had a compelling excuse to get away with his family for a week. The MGM Grand Hotel was offering a fall discount rate he couldn't pass up, especially since he'd been able to discount it further by offering to help service the hotel's computers where needed.

Héctor felt too exhausted following his ordeal to wish to drive the distance to southern Nevada and back. And the airfares between Albuquerque and Las Vegas were dirt cheap, he discovered. The Villas left home in Belen at a quarter to eight in the morning and landed in Vegas shortly before noon, Pacific Time, not over half an hour late after their flight was nearly diverted to Phoenix when a stewardess observed

Dubya pulling a small, orange plastic machine gun from his play bag. The incident caused some further ado on debarkation—certain questions to be answered, and so forth—but for Héctor, twenty minutes later, the sight of the famous Las Vegas Strip lifted his heart in a way that more than made up for the routine unpleasantness of modern air travel. He checked in at the hotel desk and rode with the bellboy and the luggage to the fourteenth floor (the thirteenth had apparently been overlooked by the construction company), while the family remained below to investigate the marvels of the MGM Grand.

In his expansive mood, Héctor tipped the boy twenty-five bucks, kicked off his Adidases, took a beer from the courtesy bar, and propped himself with fat pillows on the bed to watch TV. From this position, he could also admire, through the window, the towers of the city rising around like grand sequoia trees wreathed in mobile Christmas lights and beyond them, vaguely through the smog, the sere desert mountains that reminded him less pleasantly of the landscape surrounding Namiquipa. Almost an hour passed before it occurred to Héctor to wonder what AveMaría and the kids had been up to all this time, just as a sudden commotion sounded outside in the hall and impatient fists thumped the door.

"*¡Papaíto!*" Contracepción shouted. "Let us in—*quick!* I have to pee *so bad!*"

Héctor opened the door—and promptly fell back into the room, away from the shaggy-maned lion, so realistic it appeared to him full-sized though, indeed, it stood no taller than about two feet at the head. "*¡León! ¡León!*" Dubya roared, while Contracepción, over her shoulder on a run to the toilet, screamed, "We visited the *Lion Habitat, Papaíto!*"

Héctor was considering there must be plenty less innocent places for a young girl than the Lion Habitat in the MGM Grand, when his daughter came tearing back from the bathroom and AveMaría thrust Dubya unceremoniously into his arms. "Here! He wants to go see the lions again. *You* take him this time, Panchito! Contracep's got an appointment in five minutes at the Grand Spa, and I have one with Christophe—you know, the famous Hollywood beautician!"

Hanging around with a child in his arms to observe a collection of mangy oversized cats wasn't what Héctor had had in mind to do on his first afternoon in Las Vegas. He tried, however, to be a good sport about this.

"OK," he told his wife, shortly. "Try not to make it longer than necessary, though. You know how cranky Dubya gets without his mother. And take that damn lion out of the doorway before someone trips over it."

"His name is Metro," Contracepción corrected him, in a reproving voice. "He's a *nice* lion, *Papaíto*."

The women vanished like magic as soon as they'd retouched their makeup, leaving Héctor alone with his son and the stuffed lion. A boxing match had started on the closed-circuit TV. He switched it off reluctantly, tied his Adidases back on, and descended with Dubya on his shoulder to the lobby, in search of the Lion Habitat.

The Lion Habitat was inside the Grand Hotel Casino, close by the entertainment dome. To Héctor it resembled a vast terrarium thirty-five feet high, with waterfalls and a pond, rock ledges, and thick East African foliage, including acacia trees. Eventually he was able to make out five lions, barely visible over the heads and packed shoulders of a hundred times as many visitors. Though the crowd made it hard to approach the inch-and-a-half-thick plate glass, Héctor felt reassured by its massed presence as he pushed his way with Dubya along a see-through tunnel, while a glaring lioness paced on either side of him and a huge male lion lay stretched on his side for a nap overhead. Dubya, Héctor was aware, was a somewhat obsessive child. He hoped very much that lions were not about to become another of the kid's obsessions.

When Héctor learned that evening how much money AveMaría had paid Christophe to do her hair, he decided they couldn't afford to eat at the Wolfgang Puck Bar and Grill after all but would order in pizza from Domino's instead. After supper, Contracepción wanted her father to take her to see Céline Dion at Caesar's Palace. But Héctor, pleading fatigue after a long day, promised to take her the following night—and AveMaría, too, if a sitter could be found at the hotel for Dubya.

"I'm going down to the casino for a beer and a game of blackjack," he added. "I won't be gone long—not over an hour or so, is all."

His wife gave him a suspicious look.

"Remember, Héctor—you're to say nothing to those *putas* in miniskirts they call cocktail waitresses here."

"*¡Quiero visitar los leónes!*" Dubya yelled from the bathroom, where

Contracepción was giving him a tub bath.

As Héctor had feared, a single visit had been sufficient to hard-wire the boy's brain so far as the Lion Habitat went. For most of the next day, and the day after that, he found himself nearly as much a prisoner as the lions while AveMaría and Contracepción shopped and took themselves to lunch in exotic restaurants featuring cuisines from all over the world. Héctor and Dubya would watch the dozing lions from various angles for an hour or so, after which Dubya demanded to be taken to the adjacent gift shop to purchase another stuffed one. They would then return to view the lions again. After two days of this, relieved only by an outrageously expensive evening courtesy of Céline Dion, Héctor was in a rebellious mood. From having read Dr. Spock in Spanish translation years before, when Contracepción was a baby, he knew he should be less selfish and more understanding of the kid's needs. Only, this was *his* vacation, after all!—God and President Bush knew how well earned. He should have left the whole kit and caboodle of them at home, he told himself. AveMaría, however, would never have believed he hadn't spoken a word to those cocktail waitresses the whole week.

The third morning at breakfast Contracepción offered to take Dubya at eleven, following her belly-button ring implant appointment. Héctor sniffed a rat—he'd noticed the way she and the Mexican kid who worked the cash register at the gift shop ogled each other—but he was so fed up and frustrated with the way his week had gone as to be almost beyond caring what his daughter was up to. He therefore accepted her offer, hoisted Dubya onto his shoulders, and took the elevator down to the Lion Habitat. The crowd was denser even than usual, people lined up three deep to gawk at two big lionesses, shiny from a fresh shampooing and lying back-to-back on a flat rock with their black-tipped tails hanging over the edge. Only the thought that, just two hours from now, he'd be free to buy himself a cold beer and head for the blackjack tables gave Héctor the strength he needed to get through the ordeal.

"We don't want to see any more girl lions, do we?" he asked Dubya in a coaxing voice. "Why don't we look around for the daddy lion—the King of the Jungle—instead?"

Away from the lionesses, the crowd thinned considerably until Héctor found himself standing almost with his nose against the glass, staring at a pond surrounded by bushes and the mouth of a cave yawning behind it. "Come on now, get down and give *Papá* a rest," he said firmly, swinging Dubya off his shoulders and setting him on his own two feet on the concrete floor.

The boy stared at the isolated pond. Then he snuffled and rubbed his eyes. *"No hay leones,"* he protested. *"¡Quiero ver leones!"*

Héctor, looking about, spied a man in a keeper's uniform approaching with a bucket in one hand and what looked at a distance like a carpet sweeper in the other. Watching the keeper draw closer, he saw that the man was either Mexican or of Mexican descent.

"Maybe you can help us," he said. "We want to see a *real* lion—you know, like, with a mane. Are they off somewhere hiding, or what?"

The keeper, who had been staring intently at Héctor, never answered him. Instead, he inserted his index and forefingers into his mouth and produced a long whistle. Seconds later, a hairy leonine head in which a pair of amber eyes glowed appeared in the door of the cave. *"¡Eh-eh! ¡Leo!"* the man shouted. The lion, his curiosity satisfied and seemingly unimpressed, lay down, half-in and half-out of the cave, and commenced licking his broad spotted paws.

"You don't count for nothin with them, 'less you're one of the ones feeds them," the keeper said. "I'm just the Poop-scooper-upper, is all."

Héctor was flabbergasted. "You mean, you climb in there with the lions and just, like, follow around cleaning up after them?" he demanded.

The fellow laughed. "You *loco* or something, *hombre*? The owner takes them back out to his ranch in the desert ever evening. *That's* when I get to work, with *this*." He raised the sweeper off the floor as he spoke, and Héctor saw that the thing was indeed a giant pooper-scooper. "Rest of the time, I'm the *tipo* carries out the trash and stuff around here." He winked. *"You* know—one of them jobs only poor Mexican folk like us will do. *Por cierto, compadre*—ain't I seen you on television once? The *hermano* got beat up by the *migra* down on the border somewheres?"

Héctor blushed. After living for so many years in the United States, the publicity every American seemed to crave only made him uncomfortable—a totally un-American reaction, he knew.

"It was the Minutemen, not the Border Patrol. And they didn't beat me. They called in a couple of agents, who took me in to the station. No big deal, really—I was out of there in half an hour at most, after they'd checked my residency claim."

The Poop-scooper's face suggested he wasn't buying Héctor's story.

"Hokay, *compadre*, hokay! *Now* I remember—you're into politics, too, over in Arizona."

"New Mexico. And I'm not running for office now, and never will again."

The Poop-scooper looked sorrowfully at Héctor and shook his head, as if disappointed in him.

"*Mira, 'mano*, it is no good pretending. You are a big man, a real *pez gordo*—an American success story! You have made good in this country. But you were not born in America, no? From where in México do you come, then?"

On learning Héctor to be a native of Namiquipa, the Poop-scooper rolled his eyes in amazement.

"And I am from San Lorenzo! Imagine! Only a few kilometers away. *Compadrito!* You must allow me to buy you a drink while you are in Vegas. It is Juanito Villalobos who insists. I will not take no for an answer, my friend."

Against his better judgment, Héctor gave the fellow his room number. So far, AveMaría and Contracepción had nothing scheduled for the following evening. It seemed to him prudent he should tie himself up, here and now—if only for an hour or two—before they did it for him.

Noche de Desastre

THE MORNING AFTER MEETING Juanito Villalobos, Héctor threw Dr. Spock's strictures to the wind and put his foot down when Dubya demanded to be taken to the Lion Habitat immediately after the family's return from breakfast at McDonald's. His patience was abruptly at an end. Although the Habitat itself was free, the Villas' suite by now was overpopulated with a collection of expensive stuffed lions in varying sizes, from Metro to something hardly bigger than a rat. AveMaría and Contracepción, both of whom had plans of their own for the day, were similarly disinclined to spend it hanging around a zoo exhibit, however elaborate. In response to being denied lions, Dubya threw a temper tantrum and had to be shut in the bathroom until he got control of himself, while Héctor made his escape under cover of the confusion. Let the women trade the kid off between them for the rest of the day: *He'd* done *his* duty, and more, since their arrival in Las Vegas. *¡Viva yo!* Héctor assured himself happily, as he strode from the elevator and across the hotel lobby in the direction of the casino, close by the entertainment dome.

He was hurrying past the entrance to the Lion Habitat when an unpleasantly familiar voice called his name. Héctor turned and saw Juanito Villalobos following behind him, in uniform and carrying a broom on his shoulder. He considered cutting him and found he hadn't the heart to be rude to the *tipo* after all, despite having determined overnight to decline the offer of drinks this evening.

"*¡Eh, compadre! ¿Cómo le va?* And where is your little boy today, *amigo*? He has lost interest so soon in my beautiful lions?"

Héctor sighed. Would he never have time alone in which to enjoy his much-needed and better-deserved vacation?

"The kid's with his mom this morning," he said shortly, "and I'm on my way to have a little fun, myself."

Juanito's sly grin spread nearly as wide as his broad, pockmarked face. "*Cómo no, hermano.* It is safer that way than to hire a babysitter—much. You know where your wife is, but she knows nothing of where *you* are!"

Héctor began to be nervous. The thought of what Juanito implied made him feel compromised, dirty, and insecure, at risk of some vague catastrophe.

"My wife doesn't care what I do," he said defensively, "so long as I don't go in the hole more than a couple hundred bucks."

"It seems you have a good wife," Juanito observed, knowingly. "Better than most. For some women, even a cocktail waitress is cause for jealousy. And so, tonight, we have a good time together! Guys' night out—eh, *compadre*?"

"Sure," Héctor agreed, helplessly. It was the only thing he could think of to say.

In the casino he won $105 at blackjack and forced himself to quit while he was ahead. For some reason—the Poop-scooper from the Lion Habitat perhaps had something to do with it—Héctor did not feel justified in trusting his luck today. Also, he was anxious not to be away too long: AveMaría and Contracepción by now would be wanting a break from Dubya, so they might go shopping in the Grand Canal Shoppes at the Venetian. (Anticipating an SOS from his wife before now, he'd turned off the cell phone he wore on his belt.) There was just time, Héctor decided, for a stroll along the Strip and a quick lunch (he ordered a reuben sandwich and a margarita) at New York, New York before he returned to the hotel room, where Contracepción was minding Dubya while she watched *The Bachelor* on TV. "I can't believe *he* gave *her* the rose!" she was shrieking as her father let himself in. "*Papá*, where have you *been* all morning? *Mamá* went out two hours ago to play the slot machines, leaving me all by myself with Dubya, who's been such a *brat*! Nothing but lions, lions, lions—you'd think we were on a safari or something! *Please* can I go *now*, *Papá*? We're going home in only four days, and I haven't got to see or do *any*thing I wanted yet in Vegas! I feel like it hasn't been any vacation for me at *all*, hardly! Puh-*lease*, *Papaíto*!"

So Héctor passed yet another afternoon with Dubya at the Lion Habitat, keeping his eyes peeled the whole time for Juanito Villalobos. Nothing but trouble could come from associating with a *hombre* like that. It was Héctor's firm intention to confront Villalobos and tell him face to face he preferred to spend the evening in the company of his wife and family. But the keeper must have had the afternoon off, or perhaps he was away poop-scooping behind the scenes somewhere. One way or another, Héctor went upstairs at five without having caught a glimpse of Juanito Villalobos.

That evening, the Villas ate an early supper at the International House of Pancakes. Back at the MGM, they held a family conclave to decide how the rest of the evening should be spent. To Héctor's disgruntlement, the hotel failed to offer childcare facilities, meaning Dubya would have to go everywhere with the adults (when *they* were not going everywhere with *him*). Héctor was greatly relieved not to find a message waiting from Juanito Villalobos, and he was beginning to hope the keeper might fail to follow through with his offer of a drink. Contracepción was clamoring to be allowed to attend a Bon Jovi concert in the Grand Garden Arena, while AveMaría was keen on seeing David Copperfield at 7:30 at the Hollywood Theater, provided they allowed Dubya in with her. Héctor himself would have liked to take in a boxing match between Jesús Chavez and Marco Antonio Barrera farther down the Strip. When, however, he learned that tickets to hear Bon Jovi began at $52 and David Copperfield cost a flat $97, Héctor determined to deny himself the indulgence ($450-$475) and apply the money he'd made at blackjack that morning to subsidizing the girls' evening on the town. Indeed, the more he considered the matter, the more it seemed to him the responsible thing to return to the gaming tables that evening and replenish his depleted, if not quite empty, pocketbook. This meant hiring a babysitter through the front desk, which would cost him big bucks. On the credit side, it would free him up to *make* those bucks. It was a gamble, of course. But what was he here to do, in the first place, if *not* to gamble?

On learning she was going to be allowed to hear Bon Jovi after all, Contracepción threw her arms around her father and kissed him on both cheeks, Mexican style, squealing with delight at the prospect of getting to display her new belly-button ring at a Vegas rock concert. AveMaría, stricken with guilt at the thought of abandoning her baby to a stranger for the evening, was more subdued in her enthusiasm. ("At least, she's sure to be *mexicana*," she consoled herself.) In the end, Héctor phoned the front desk and arranged the procurement of a babysitter at the rate of $15 per hour ($20 after 10 P.M.). Then, after instructing them to look for him at the blackjack tables in the casino after the shows let out, he left the women to primp and preen in the bathroom while he descended to the lobby. Héctor was eager to make an immediate start in his quest for financial solvency. Walking out through the elevator doors, he collided frontally with Juanito Villalobos walking in.

"*¡Ay, compadrito!*" the Poop-scooper exclaimed. "*¡Vaya casualidad!* I was just on my way up to your room in search of you. You had not forgotten I have promised to buy you a drink tonight—no? You have eaten already I think? *¡Bueno!* So have I, *hermano*. We can drink all the more now, without getting picked up by the *policía*, or the f--kin *migra—pinches cochinos!*"

Holding Héctor under the elbow in a familiar way, Juanito steered him into the casino and between the tables up to the bar, where the two men seated themselves on tall stools facing the long array of bottles and taps presided over by two strong-looking tawny blondes, alike enough to be sisters and with the bold predatory faces of a pair of exceptionally handsome lionesses. Juanito Villalobos pulled a leather trucker's wallet, attached by a chain to his hand-tooled belt, from a back pocket of his jeans and fingered out a few grimy dollar bills.

"Héctor!" he invited, in the grandiose manner of an *alcalde* bestowing upon an illustrious visitor the keys to his city, or a mafia don exhibiting his kingdom to a favored lieutenant, "I will treat you to anythin you care to drink—beer, whiskey, tequila, whatever! Please order freely, *compadrito*! You are a big man in America, after all—a success story! I feel honored just to share a drink with a *hombre de categoría* like you, *Señor* Héctor Villa!"

Héctor felt slightly sickened. He was trapped, unless he had the stomach to refuse the man's generosity, however unwanted—and he didn't have it, he knew. All he could do, in the circumstances, was accept the offer of a drink with as good grace as he could muster, leave Villalobos with a reciprocal round, and find himself a place at the blackjack tables as quickly as possible. It was all very embarrassing and annoying, *ciertamente*. Also, it was the civilized thing to do.

For a sub-keeper, or maintenance man, at what was basically an upscale zoo, Juanito Villalobos was a sharp dresser, Héctor thought, taking in the polished yellow cowboy boots and pressed powder-blue pants, the black-and-white checked shirt with its spread collar, and the Indian silver necklace weighing heavy on his brown collarbone. He was tempted to order Napoleon brandy but compromised with Crown Royal instead. Villalobos nodded approvingly.

"You know how to live, *compadrito*—anyone can see that," he said. "So, Héctor! What you do for a livin when you ain't fightin the *gringos* or gettin yourself elected to somethin?"

When Héctor explained that he owned a computer-repair company, Villalobos became attentive.

"How many men you got workin for you?" he wanted to know.

"Just me. My wife helps with the billing some."

"Maybe you need a bodyguard, next time you run for office?"

"I'm through with politics. I thought I mentioned that."

Juanito Villalobos nodded. "That's what they all say. I'm goin to go ahead and write down my address and phone number, *hermano*," he added. "You think you can use me, just let me know. Us *mojados* owe it to each other to stick together, up here in El Norte. I don't want to spend the rest of my life pickin up behind the ass-end of a bunch of mangy, flea-bitten cats. Can you believe they f--kin *shampoo* the goddamn things ever single day?"

Héctor, impatient to get down to work at the tables, called for a second round of drinks so as to leave the bill even-steven. When one of the lionesses came with them, Villalobos asked her to bring the cigar box, from which he carefully selected two thick and long Bances.

"One for me, one for you," he explained, laying one of the cigars on the wood beside Héctor's balloon glass. Then he beckoned the girl closer, leaned across the bar, and whispered something in her ear. She nodded distantly and went away again.

"This is a night to celebrate," Juanito Villalobos proposed, holding a plated lighter under the end of Héctor's cigar. "Tonight, I have found my *compinche* for life."

Héctor had smoked half his cigar already before he remembered cigar smoke gave him a headache. The smoke, combining with two stiff Crown Royals, made a vague space where his brain ought to be—tonight of all nights, when solvency depended upon its utmost strength and capacity. In his distraction, he scarcely noticed when a pair of young women approached the bar and took a stool on either side of himself and the Poop-scooper. Both girls had on hip-huggers exposing their beringed navels, flimsy camisoles, and so much makeup they looked like patrons who'd forgotten to remove their facials before leaving the spa.

"Hi," the girl next to Héctor said. Startled, he turned sideways in time to see her take a sip of his drink. "I have a thing for Crown Royal guys," the girl said. "But I always drink Napoleon, myself," she added to the hovering lioness.

Héctor was too astounded to speak. On his opposite side, Juanito Villalobos and the other girl were already getting to know each other while her drink was being poured.

"You don't need to be shy just because you're Mexican," his girl said. "I wasn't raised to be prejudiced." As if to prove it, she hitched herself onto his lap, threw one arm about his neck, and reached with her free hand to accept her balloon from the lioness.

A piercing shriek from across the room was sufficient to penetrate Héctor's mind, even in its present condition of shock and befuddlement. Looking around the girl in his lap, he saw AveMaría plunging toward them across the room, her capacious handbag brandished above her head. His first thought was that the thing was impossible; David Copperfield could hardly even have started yet. He had no other thought beyond that one, and no memory later of bucking the girl off and dashing headlong between the card tables and the astounded dealers in the direction of the nearest EXIT sign. The house police caught up only a few yards from the doors, bringing him down with a flying tackle on the carpeted floor among the discarded bar tickets and cigarette butts.

III

Government for the People

"I OWE YOU AN APOLOGY, *compadrito*," Héctor Villa was telling Jesús "Eddie" Juárez.

Jesús "Eddie," who hadn't the foggiest idea what his friend was talking about, nodded his head and attempted a forgiving smile anyway, on the off chance it might prompt Héctor to clinch his apology by buying another round.

"I never understood all you had to go through, losing that school-board election and all, until I had to walk a mile in *your* shoes last fall," Héctor explained.

The two men were seated at "their" table by the window at the Taberna Aztlán, watching Saturday-afternoon football on the widescreen TV while automobile horns blared and brake drums screeched outside on Highway 47. Since the Villas' return from Las Vegas some weeks before, Héctor had taken to spending more time away from home on evenings and weekends than had previously been his custom. He'd found it easier by far to make satisfactory explanation to the house police at the MGM Grand Hotel than to AveMaría, and his nights the first week home had been spent on the new Castro Convertible in the den.

Jesús "Eddie," recalling his own humiliation at the polls, scowled and chucked a handful of popcorn toward the players. "The f--kin *Anglos*," he agreed. "I tell you, *'manito*: There ain't been an honest election in the Rio Abajo since the Mexican War!"

Héctor sighed. His friend's cynicism about the United States upset and depressed him. The fact that he and Jesús "Eddie" had been unlucky in electoral politics hardly proved the overall corruption of the American system. George W. Bush, like George Washington before him, had got himself elected President without ever telling a lie. In the two months since his own loss to Tomasina Luna, Héctor had suffered acutely from intimations of political inadequacy, the knowledge that he'd let his country and his President down in their time of need. Not even recent domestic strife and misunderstanding had eclipsed his suffering. God alone knew what damage the Luna woman would do when she got to Washington in January. And how happy Hillary Clinton would be to see her there!

"Tomasina isn't an Anglo," he objected mildly.

Jesús "Eddie's" fist struck the table so hard the popcorn jumped in the bowl.

"She *works* for the *An*-glos, *hombre!*" he shouted. "She supported my op-*po*-nent for the school *board*—the fat bitch!"

Héctor decided to give it up. "Anyway—I'm sorry, *amigo*. I'm taking the tab tonight, okay?"

A few evenings later, he arrived home to discover AveMaría and Contracepción tearful and nearly incoherent with rage and indignation. Fortunately (Héctor reflected), female hysteria was among the many things that went better with beer. He took a bottle from the refrigerator and went on to the living room, where the women sat waiting to describe the outrage for him in hideous detail.

The thing *was* outrageous, he had to agree after he'd heard his wife and daughter out. It had begun when Contracepción submitted a passionate defense of the Iraq war in fulfillment of a one-page writing assignment in English class the week before. The teacher, a Mrs. Ahmadinejihad, having marked up the page with red-penciled underlinings and *sp*'s beside the offending words, inscribed an emphatic scarlet "D" above the top line beside the author's name. Since Mrs. Ahmadinejihad, an Iranian lady who'd lived in the United States less than two years, was no great shakes in the spelling department herself, Contracepción had looked up the words in her pocket Webster's dictionary and discovered that she'd spelled all but one of them correctly. Mrs. Ahmadinejihad was guilty of decorrecting her essay! Confident of success, Contracepción had approached the teacher the following day, presented her evidence, and politely requested a mark upgrade to A- or B+. To her horror and astonishment, Mrs. Ahmadinejihad, rather than admit her error, had explained that the low grade reflected not the essay's relatively unimportant spelling errors but its basically irrational and self-contradictory argument. Stung to retort, Contracepción had countered unthinkingly by calling Mrs. Ahmadinejihad unfair and un-American—for which she'd been sent to the principal's office and suspended from school for an entire week. By the time she'd finished recounting the story to her father, Contracepción had reconciled herself somewhat to the prospect of missing a week's worth of classes. Her resentment at the injustice done her, however, burned stronger than ever.

"Panchito, what to do?" AveMaría wailed. "It is not just what this *bruja* has done to poor Contracep—we have communist foreigners teaching at our schools, right here in Belen!"

Héctor did not answer her at once but sat very still and rigid on the overstuffed sofa, too appalled even to finish his beer. "I must call the FBI in Albuquerque," he said finally, "and let them know about this thing that has happened, the evil situation that exists here."

"Oh, and *Papá*, I almost forgot!" Contracepción cried. "Mrs. Ahmadinejihad is, like, good friends with Mrs. Luna! I see them together all the time around school, talking with their heads together so you can't hear a word they're saying! Do you think they could really be terrorists or something, *Papaíto*?"

Once the connection had been made for him, Héctor had to wonder why he hadn't seen it from the beginning. Tomasina had run for the House on an antiwar platform. The Ahmadinejihad woman was an Islamist from Iran, a country President Bush had identified as part of the Axis of Evil. At once, the whole business came together for him. He must, of course, inform the FBI as soon as possible. But not before he'd faced the English teacher down and seen the Enemy for himself.

"Take care that you do not discuss this matter with anyone," Héctor told his daughter sternly. "I will call tomorrow for an appointment with Mrs. Ahmadinejihad at the school and hear what she has to say for herself. After that—well, we shall see what we shall see! I am not the *hombre* to beat around the bush in situations such as this one, I promise you."

Mrs. Ahmadinejihad was, apparently, a very busy woman. Contracepción's suspension was nearly up by the time Héctor succeeded in getting an appointment with her. He quit work early that afternoon, drove home, and left his van parked in the street in front of the house. Already by 3:15 nowadays, the Belen rush hour was terrible, and he preferred AveMaría's Subaru when maneuvering in heavy traffic. On the drive between home and the school, Héctor strove to get his temper under control, partly by paying scrupulous attention to the posted speed limits. He was quite aware of his tendency to speed when driving under the influence of righteous anger.

Héctor was approaching the downtown district on the Jarales Road when he caught sight of bar lights flashing red, blue, and yellow in the Subaru's rearview mirror. He glanced at the speedometer: 28 in a 30 mph zone. What in hell were they pulling him over for? He couldn't believe his bad luck. His appointment with Mrs. Ahmadinejihad was just fifteen minutes from now, and the school was still a good five minutes away. The police cruiser pulled in behind him on the shoulder. Héctor was about to get out of the car and walk back to it when he recalled that he'd done this the last time he'd been stopped and come close to getting himself shot when a robotic voice roared "GET BACK IN THAT CAR!" through the bullhorn mounted on the cruiser. So he sat tight on the seat, watching the side mirror as the cop—a fat man with womanish hips and a shaved bullet head—stumped forward carrying a ticket book in his hand. Héctor looked up at him through the open window with what he hoped was the patient, slightly hurt expression of a solid citizen unfairly wronged.

"So what did I do?" he asked the officer. "I wasn't speeding, was I?"

The look he received might have been directed at a child molester caught with three children bound hand and foot in the trunk.

"Operating an unregistered vehicle," the cop informed him. "I called in to Dispatch. Registration expired over three months ago."

Héctor felt dismay, humiliation, and anger all at once. How like a woman to forget to reregister her car! He usually thought to remind AveMaría to have the oil changed every 3,000 miles, but a man couldn't think of *everything*. "Is it?" Héctor asked. "It's my wife's car," he explained lamely.

The cop acted as though he hadn't heard him. "License and proof of insurance, please," he demanded.

He waddled back to the police cruiser with the license, while Héctor consulted his watch. He had twelve minutes to make it to the school, and he'd never known even a routine stop to take less than ten minutes. How could AveMaría have been so careless? Now *his* name would go on the ticket, and he'd have a second citation in less than two years on his municipal-court record—in addition, of course, to the ongoing trouble with Homeland Security. Now, he'd never be allowed to run for office again, even if he wanted to someday. Without really thinking about what he was doing, Héctor reached across the seat, punched the glove-box button, and withdrew the registration and insurance packet. Of course, Dispatch knew what it was doing—you can't argue with electronics—but it did no harm to check anyway, while he waited. Here were the operator's manual, proof of insurance, and what must be last year's registration slip. He pulled this free of the little bundle and looked it over. "EXP 09/23/06" he read in an upper right-hand box. So there *had* been a mistake, after all! It seemed too good to be true. Though, truth be told, Héctor was inclined to give Police Dispatch benefit of doubt ahead of his wife.

Nevertheless, when the officer returned with the written-out summons for a court appearance and a fine amounting to fifty dollars in his hand, he thrust the document at him through the window.

"So what's this?" he asked the man politely.

The cop held the slip at the end of his nose, and then nearly at arm's length.

"See?" he demanded, pointing with a fat finger to another set of numbers in a different box. "Expired. What I said. Dispatch is always reliable. You can't argue with electronics."

So Héctor signed the ticket. Well, it had been worth a try, anyway. And there went fifty dollars AveMaría was *not* going to spend on the new pair of sandals she wanted from Neiman Marcus.

He arrived at the school nearly ten minutes late, and three minutes later knocked on the closed door of Mrs. Ahmadinejihad's classroom.

"In America is always late, late," the teacher said, frowning, as he entered. "Is not like in Iran, where the watch hand of the late one is cut off—*whack, whack! Allahu Akhbar!*" Héctor couldn't tell whether she intended this to be a joke, or not.

Within her *burqa* and robes, Mrs. Ahmadinejihad appeared to be a slight, wiry woman with a brown hatchet face. A small oriental carpet Héctor supposed was a prayer rug lay on the linoleum floor beside her desk, and the bulletin board above it was papered with color photographs of golden-domed mosques rising against forbidding desert backgrounds like brown moonscapes. Without asking permission, Héctor seated himself on the chair set close against the desk to face the teacher—the hot seat, obviously, for generations of unruly children.

"I am here," he explained, "to discuss my daughter, Contracepción, with you."

"Ah yes. Contra—in Iran, we do not use such words as that one. It is a shame and a crime even to speak of it. But *here*—"

Héctor felt determined to put this bigoted woman in her place. "In America we are Protestants, not Islamists," he said firmly. "Americans are not afraid to speak plainly. That is why I must tell you, Mrs. Allah-*uh*-jihad, that you have treated my daughter very unfairly. First, you marked her down for spelling mistakes that weren't mistakes at all. Then, you said the low grade wasn't for spelling in the first place, but because her paper was not good sense. Is that correct?"

"Yes, yes, of course, very—*more* than correct!"

"What would you say if I told you everything Contracep wrote in that paper was *exactly* what Vice President Cheney said in his TV address two weeks ago?"

"Cheney? But he is a war criminal! An enemy of Holy Islam! He makes no sense at all!"

Héctor knew he was dealing with a madwoman.

"So you won't change my daughter's grade to A-? Or even B+?"

"Me? *No!* I am not heretic, I am not *kaffir!* Islam is Truth! Islam does not compromise! Islam conquers by the sword!"

Héctor arose with dignity, holding his cap in his hand.

"Then I'm afraid, ma'am," he said, "my next stop must be the principal's office. Can you tell me how to find my way there, please?"

Government by the People

HÉCTOR VILLA was by nature a patient, long-suffering man. Even so, he arrived home in a cross mood that evening, at the end of an unusually frustrating day. First, there had been the traffic ticket; next, his unproductive meeting with Mrs. Ahmadinejihad. Finally, he'd been unable to meet with the school principal, after waiting for better than an hour for him to be through with what his secretary described, in an awed voice, as a meeting with the football coach and the head cheerleader. When, at last, the principal emerged from his office, he and the secretary had held a rapid conversation in whispers, ending with the principal striding off without a word to Héctor. He had, the secretary explained, a seminar on educational democracy to attend at the Valencia Branch of UNM.

"Panchito, what is the matter?" AveMaría exclaimed when she saw him. "That creature in *demonia*'s form agreed to give Contracep a B at least, didn't she?"

Héctor waved her off impatiently on his way to the fridge for a beer.

"I'll tell you about all that in a minute," he said. "I got a fifty-dollar ticket on the Jarales Road this afternoon driving over to the school."

"A ticket? Driving my car? What for, I'd like to know?"

For the first time in his life, Héctor felt the urge to strike a woman.

"For driving an unregistered vehicle! You forgot to register the damn Subaru last summer!"

"I did not! *¿Quién dijo tal cosa?* I mailed the check and registration myself, two days before the two-cent postal increase! I can show you the canceled check right now, if you want to see it!"

Héctor did not know what to think. On the one hand, it was good news to learn he hadn't deserved a ticket, after all. On the other, it disturbed him profoundly that such a mistake—if it was a mistake—could happen in the United States. New Mexico wasn't México, where you were all the time being gouged with the *mordida* by one public official or another. He fished the ticket from his shirt pocket and sat down at the kitchen table with a bottle of Corona.

"Either I mail them a check for fifty bucks or show up at Municipal Court a week from Monday for arraignment," he told his wife gloomily.

"But you are innocent! Did you not show them the registration form—in the pocket in the *tablero*, with the other papers?"

"Of course, I showed it to him. Am I a *tonto*? He said it was *caducada*—no good."

"Then it is the *guardia* who is *tonto*, not you."

Ever since he'd received the summons from the zoning board, Héctor had avoided city hall the way a man avoids the neighborhood of a hospital where he was once treated for a deadly disease. "I need to phone the department right now and explain it all to them," he said.

"But first, I want to hear—did Mrs. Abomina-Jihad change Contracep's grade to an A-, or not?"

To his surprise, the cop himself—an Officer Maldonado—was at the station when he called. "So maybe a mistake was made somewhere," he said finally, when Héctor had finished his explanation. "You never know with computers. Anyway, once I write a ticket, I've wrote it—that's the law. You got to go to court and tell the judge what you told me. Or just send the fifty bucks—it's whatever you decide to do, sir."

When Contracepción returned half an hour later from the minimall where she'd spent most of her week off from school, she was as outraged as her mother had been by Héctor's account of his interview with Mrs. Ahmadinejihad. "How dare her!" she cried. "She's not even American! Why don't they send the raghead back to Iraq where she belongs!"

"And as if that wasn't enough for one day, one of those *nuevomexicano* cops gave your father a fifty-dollar ticket for driving an unregistered car I registered myself more than three months ago!" AveMaría put in. "We might as well never have left México in the first place!"

"Don't talk that way, AveMaría!" her husband corrected her sharply. The truth was, Héctor, in his heart, felt troubled and confused. He was witnessing an arbitrary aspect of his adoptive country he'd scarcely known existed before today. The business of the zoning board eighteen months ago had not, it seemed, been the thoroughly anomalous affair he'd assumed it to be. "In America, we have government of the people, by the people, and for the people. You will see, both of you! All this will come right in the end."

Driving to his first job next morning, Héctor used his cell phone to inform the FBI office in Albuquerque of his suspicions regarding Mrs. Ahmadinejihad and Tomasina Luna. Next he phoned the principal's secretary to make a formal appointment for an interview with her boss. The woman's manner was strange, he thought, and she kept him on hold a long time. When she came back on the line the secretary explained that, from the principal's viewpoint, he and Héctor had nothing to discuss: Mrs. Ahmadinejihad had merely been applying a valuable multicultural perspective to his daughter's essay. Héctor was starting to reply that, for an American school, the only appropriate teaching perspective was an American one when the woman, pleading an important incoming call, broke off the conversation without telling him goodbye. Offended by her lack of manners, Héctor reflected that it would be easier to procure an audience with Vicente Fox at Los Pinos than to make an appointment to see Dr. Virgilio Gallegos, principal of the Belen High School—and was instantly ashamed of his unpatriotic thoughts. The school situation, he decided, must be deferred until after his arraignment, only four days away. It would, Jesús "Eddie" Juárez had advised him, take most, if not all, of his morning.

"The judge, he is *An*-glo," Jesús "Eddie" had added. "Red hair, one of them spotted-all-over faces like a flea-bitten horse—name's McCorkle, the skinny sonofabitch, from Catron County where the Anglos run *ev*-erthin. Ex-Confederate racists, come into New Mexico when the Yankees chased them out of Mississippi and Texas after the Civil War."

In fact, Héctor was detained half an hour in municipal court. Together with his fellow miscreants, he sat waiting on one of the folding chairs arranged in careful rows as armed policemen led in four shackled men wearing prison garb and stood them before the black-robed judge. The first prisoner pled guilty to cutting a man with a knife in an altercation in the Belen movie theater, the second to public intoxication, and the other two to DUI and operating an unregistered vehicle.

When Héctor's name was called, he rose and approached the bench with alacrity, feeling confident in his innocence and his best business suit. In addressing the previous defendants, the judge had assumed a peremptory, even contemptuous demeanor suggesting that, no matter how Lady Justice might decide, he considered all of them guilty until proven innocent (and perhaps not even then). Héctor found his manner distinctly off-putting. Still, he fully expected Judge McCorkle to recognize him for the innocent man he was and adjust his manner accordingly. To his discomfiture, the judge appeared unable to distinguish between Héctor Villa and some knife-wielding *matón* in jail pajamas. Nevertheless, Héctor remembered to say, "Yes, Your Honor" and "No, Your Honor," and answered, "NOT guilty, Your Honor," in a strong, assertive voice when asked how he pled.

"Are you aware all the prosecution has to do to prove this charge is establish valid tags were not in fact in place on your vehicle at the time of the arrest?" McCorkle demanded. Héctor responded in the affirmative and was starting to add that the tags had been affixed to both the front and rear plates of the Subaru, when the judge interrupted to warn him sharply that an arraignment was not the proper place to offer evidence. To Héctor's dismay, instead of dismissing the case, Judge McCorkle set a trial date. Then Héctor was free to go.

The mood around the dinner table *chez* Villa that evening was grim. To the subdued family, Héctor's arraignment came as an added blow in a week in which AveMaría had been rebuffed in her attempts at going over Dr. Gallegos' head by securing an appointment with the school superintendent and Mrs. Ahmadinejihad had responded to the open letter of protest posted by Contracepción on the school Information and Coming Events Board by assigning her a two-page paper on the contribution of Islam to the making of Western civilization. America, as a country of laws and free speech, was plainly being replaced by a new, un-free America—a conclusion reinforced for Héctor by a FOX News segment concerning a former Taliban member, now a scholarship student at Yale University, who was demanding (evidently with some success) the construction of a minaret overlooking the quad to allow a *muezzin* to sound the call to prayer seven times daily across the campus. The upshot of all this, so far as it concerned Héctor Villa, was that he needed now to retain an attorney to defend him in municipal court.

"I'm going to get even with that Jihad woman," Contracepción boasted. "She's going to wish she was back in Iraq with all the other Swamis and Swahilis before I'm through with her."

"You will do no such thing," her father told her sternly. "If I ever hear of you making trouble at school, I'll send you to live with your grandmother in Namiquipa where you'll learn what a tough teacher really is like. When I was at school, Señor Arias used to beat us black and blue when we couldn't remember the words to 'Mexicanos, al grito de guerra.'"

At the risk of offending Jesús "Eddie," who'd recommended Miguel Castro, a local attorney specializing in antidiscrimination law, Héctor decided to retain Francisco Madrid, a dreamy man who practiced law part time while devoting the rest of his days to classical guitar and the construction of an environmentally friendly house from chicken wire, crushed aluminum cans, and old tires. Madrid tried at first to dissuade him from wasting his money on a lawyer. It was an open-and-shut case in Héctor's favor, he insisted. As soon as the judge learned that Officer Maldonado couldn't read an auto registration form when it was shown him, he'd be certain to dismiss the charges. Héctor considered this advice carefully and decided to reject it. After more than twenty years in the United States, he was learning to proceed more cautiously in respect of the powers that be.

The day of the trial, Héctor, resisting the superstitious temptation to stop by Our Lady of Belen to offer up a Hail Mary on behalf of the cause, drove with AveMaría and Dubya to court, where Francisco Madrid awaited them. His case was stacked first in the afternoon session, so they didn't have to wait long. Judge McCorkle entered in his black robes, and everyone stood up. He sat down, and everyone sat after him. The few people in the courtroom seemed to be the miscreants themselves and their guardian angels holding their briefs in their laps.

The proceedings passed for Héctor in a rapid blur. The prosecuting attorney argued that the defendant, having originally neglected to attach current registration tabs to his license plates, had affixed them following his arrest. Cross-examined by Madrid, Officer Maldonado testified that he had not checked all the several expired tabs left on the rear plate, as Dispatch had already confirmed an unregistered vehicle for him. Here, the prosecutor pounced, asserting the reason Maldonado had failed to identify the valid tag at once was that the defendant had placed it in the lower-right, instead of the upper-left, corner of the plate, where it belonged. The legal understanding of "in place" was "in the right place," the prosecutor urged. Therefore, he concluded, the defendant was indeed guilty as charged. Judge McCorkle found for the City of Belen and fined the defendant fifty dollars. The entire business was over in under ten minutes.

Francisco Madrid was too embarrassed for a postmortem. He left the Villas outside the courthouse and headed directly for his car. Héctor followed him toward the parking area, walking slowly and unconsciously like a somnambulist. The family had just reached the Subaru when the cellphone AveMaría carried in her handbag went off, sounding the refrain of the golden oldie "It's My Party." She made a grab for it and stood listening as if transfixed, her eyes widening in horror.

"¡*Panchito!*" she gasped.

"Who the hell is calling me at a time like this?"

"It's the school! Contracepción is in trouble! They've already called the juvenile officer. Something about Muhammad in a bottle of tequila found in the Abomina-Jihad woman's desk!"

Héctor, exercising his Second Amendment rights, kept a loaded pistol under the driver's seat of his van. Fortunately for everyone concerned, neither truck nor pistol was to hand just now. For the first time since he'd purchased it several years before, he felt an irresistible urge to use the gun on someone (he knew just whom). Worse than anger, though, was the overwhelming sense of disillusionment he was experiencing. Héctor had learned for himself the truth of the hoary American saying: "You can't fight city hall."

American Parenthood

OVERWHELMED BY THE SHAME of having a juvenile delinquent for a daughter, Héctor could almost forget that he himself was a convicted law offender and the subject of an ongoing investigation by the Immigration and Borders division of the Department of Homeland Security.

The entire business had been a father's worst nightmare, as well as a major multicultural scandal. The Southwestern media, like ravens on the city dump, had been all over the story of how the daughter of an illegal Hispanic immigrant politician deliberately and gratuitously insulted Islam and Muslims the world over by immersing a plastic figure marked "Mohumud" in a bottle of alcohol. Al Jazeera picked up the incident, and for weeks after Héctor lived in terror of a *fatwa* issued against Contracepción. (In the event, his plan had been to flee with the family into Mexico, where he counted on the nasty reputation enjoyed by the Federales to deter even the toughest Al Qaeda hit team.) The *Valencia County News-Bulletin* and the *Albuquerque Journal* ran front-page stories featuring Contracepción's photograph and drawing death threats from the Muslim community, and proposals of marriage (among other things) from the Hispanic one. The school canceled Héctor's computer-repair contract, and the superintendent addressed a specially convened student assembly to reiterate that the Belen Consolidated School District expected its students to "deal effectively with change, value diversity, become life-long learners, and develop into responsible citizens who will have a positive effect on their community, country, and world." Most wounding of all was a letter from the White House, reminding the Hon. Héctor Villa that a good Republican speaks ill neither of another Republican nor of the Prophet Muhammad, founder of a religion of love and peace, and signed "W." Excepting Jesús "Eddie" Juárez, who loathed Middle Easterners almost as much as he despised Anglos, the only quarter from which the Villas received support was the First Assembly of God, where Brother Billy Joe preached a fiery sermon attacking Mohammedans and papists as Jesus bashers and invited Contracepción to stand and be acknowledged by the hysterical congregation.

Since her suspension from school for the remainder of the semester, Contracepción was also under sentence by the juvenile court to perform six months of community service with a faith-based outreach program run by the shiny new mosque founded in Belen the year before. The ruling further made her a prisoner of the State of New Mexico until the following spring. What to do with their daughter after that was a matter of endless discussion for her parents. Héctor argued for sending the child to her grandparents in Namiquipa, where she could learn discipline at home and at school. But AveMaría steadfastly refused to hear of this. She insisted that, instead, Contracep should learn responsibility by staying home and helping to care for Dubya. Secretly, she'd determined that what the girl really needed to teach her maturity was a boyfriend. In Mexico, thirteen was regarded as being about the appropriate age; in America, it was apparently even lower. (Only recently, a neighborhood friend had been boasting about her daughter, aged eight, who'd just found a new boyfriend, a kid of about nine. "Oh," the girl's mother had exclaimed proudly, "he's hot!") Indeed, AveMaría had someone in mind: Mañuel Orozco, sixteen years old, the son of an immigrant family from Ciudad Chihuahua who also attended Brother Billy Joe's church. Maybe by summer, she thought, with Contracep on the verge of turning fifteen herself, Héctor would be agreeable to the suggestion. Or perhaps the girl would have discovered romance for herself.

Besides Contracepción, the Villas were preoccupied by much else in late fall, and time passed quickly. AveMaría, in addition to her other responsibilities, had Contracepción to chauffeur to and from the mosque, and Héctor was preoccupied with his business troubles and the bureaucratic inquiries and forms that arrived almost daily from the U.S. Citizenship and Immigration Services, all of which required completion in excruciating detail. Though he'd understood early on that USCIS was simply going through the motions, the process occupied much of his valuable time, while creating in his own mind the humiliating impression that he was some kind of petty criminal, well beneath the attention of (for instance) the IRS. What with one thing and another, it seemed no time at all before the *ristras* were up, the *candelarias* glowed in rows along the flat roofs of the faux-adobe houses, and the Visa and MasterCard billing statements ran three and four pages long.

Owing partly to Brother Billy Joe, Héctor continued to be oppressed by worry in respect of Contracepción. The preacher had been outraged by the juvenile court's action in forcing the girl to work for a mosque, which he claimed was tantamount to slaving for Satan himself. He became obsessed with the court's sentence, and it really seemed at times to Héctor that Billy Joe considered the father morally culpable by acquiescing in the penalty—as though, he reflected indignantly, an ordinary American such as himself had any recourse in the matter. "You can't fight city hall!" was a mantra Héctor had taken to repeating over and over to himself. Though he shared the preacher's distaste for the enemies of God and of the United States, he took comfort, as the weeks passed, from his daughter's improved spirits. And Contracep had made friends at the mosque. Almost every afternoon lately, she'd found a ride home from work.

One evening after supper when Héctor was putting the Christmas tree up in the living room, Jesús "Eddie" telephoned from the Taberna Aztlán to suggest that he join him for "a coupla" drinks. Jesús "Eddie" sounded unmistakably tipsy, and Héctor had succeeded at last in positioning the tree almost exactly upright in the stand when, perceiving urgency in Jesús "Eddie's" voice as well as alcoholic befuddlement, he agreed to drive to the *taberna*. He discovered his friend seated before the wide-screen TV with his back to the entrance to the main lounge.

"*¿Compadrito, qué pasa?*" Héctor asked, clapping Jesús "Eddie" on the shoulder. Though he did his best to sound jovial, the smell of stale beer and the scattering of crushed popcorn over the worn carpet depressed him. "Not good, *amigo*—not good at all," Jesús "Eddie" replied. He sounded like a water buffalo expiring in a tar pit. "How does a friend give a friend bad news, *compañero*? I think I begin by buyin you a drink, that you may have *hacer de tripas corazón* to hear it."

"Of what are you speaking, *hombre*? You have bad news—for me?"

Jesús "Eddie" looked tragic. "I could not do it at home, in the presence of your wife. AveMaría is a wonderful woman, *amigo*."

"*Sí, sí, ya lo sé*—Go on, I'm waiting."

Jesús "Eddie" nodded. "OK then, as you wish. Bad news first.

Drink after."

"*¿Pues?*"

"Contracepción—your daughter—has a boy-*friend!*"

Héctor felt flabbergasted, next confused. The girl was fourteen, after all. But why had AveMaría said nothing to him about this?

"*Pues bien; ¿qué más?*"

"She met him at the mosque. . . . The kid is a rag-*head, hombre!*"

His drink arrived just then, and Héctor downed it in a swallow. The tequila hit his stomach before his brain could register the news. "How do you know this?" he demanded.

Jesús "Eddie" did not meet his eye. The truth was, he'd been stalking Contracepción, infrequently, for the past two months.

"I happened to see him drivin her around town in his car this afternoon," Jesús "Eddie" said at last.

Héctor was not by nature a violent man. Therefore, he did not immediately recognize rage—the towering, blinding, disintegrative rage of his ancestor and namesake—in the emotion that exploded like a firebomb within his brain. In that instant, he could have killed the anonymous young man with all the cruel, fierce, rebarbative relish his distant ancestors had enjoyed. Thoughtlessly he seated himself on a stool beside Jesús "Eddie" and ordered a second drink from the bartender. By the time the man brought it, Héctor had recovered himself somewhat. Accepting a ride from a boy with a car wasn't the worst thing a healthy fourteen-year-old girl could do, he reflected. He felt a sudden and bitter resentment against his friend. What had Jesús "Eddie" meant by exploiting his parental emotions with so trivial an alarm? He was on the point of saying as much when Jesús spoke again.

"She was settin snuggled a-*gainst* him there on the front seat and the sumbitch had his arm round her, drivin with one *hand* like he thought he was Elvis, or somebody." He said it with a snarl, and the hatred in his voice surprised Héctor. "I hate the f--kin *A*-rabs," Jesús added, with equal feeling. "Times, I think they're worse than the goddamn *An*-glos, even."

Before he'd finished the second drink, Héctor was in full control of himself, determined not to discuss the intimacies of family life further with Jesús "Eddie." Something, he felt, was amiss in this business. Certainly, the intensity of Jésus's emotional response to Contracepción's new friend was peculiar, even when you took into account all the beers he'd had to drink that evening. On the other hand, it seemed odd that Contracep, ordinarily an open and confiding girl, had said nothing of her first serious crush to her mother, or that AveMaría had thought it unnecessary to mention the matter to him. Héctor resolved, therefore, to adopt a casually uncommunicative attitude toward Jesús "Eddie" for the rest of the evening and take the subject of Contracepción and her Muslim boyfriend up with his wife in a serious way when he got home. He stayed for one drink more and left, after making it a point to leave his share of the tab, plus a handsome tip for the barman. A light snow was falling, slicking the roads, and Héctor was detained briefly on Highway 47 by a wreck involving a van crowded with suspicious-looking Mexicans and a Cadillac carrying a party of elderly Anglos from the Belen Country Club home to their gated community north of town.

Dubya, who had been put down for the night a couple of hours before, was up again and refusing to return to bed when Héctor reached home. As he passed by her room, he heard Contracepción chatting in a low, confidential voice on the phone behind the closed door she'd recently begun locking from the inside. Héctor went on to the master bedroom, undressed, and lay down in bed to watch the ten o'clock news and await his wife. Tonight, as on other occasions, he found himself wishing AveMaría were a bit more of a disciplinarian—but then, American kids never responded to disciplinary measures the way he recalled Mexican ones doing.

It was a quarter to eleven before AveMaría got Dubya down for good and came to bed herself. She was surprised to find her husband asleep with the bedside light on, the TV muted, and the remote resting in his hand on top of the blanket. Intending to undress in the dark to avoid wakening him, she reached across the bed for the light switch and saw that he was awake still, watching her.

"Panchito, are you all right? Why didn't you turn the light out?"

"I'm not tired, I'm worried. María, I have something to tell you."

Concerned, she bent for a closer look at his face and recoiled from what she saw there.

"*¡Santa María!* Is someone dead?"

Héctor was resolved not to beat about the bush. "Contracepción has a boyfriend—a Muslim kid she met working at the mosque."

AveMaría clutched at her throat and collapsed on the bed.

"A *Muslim*? O Jesus Mary and Joseph!"

"So you didn't know, after all? I was thinking maybe you did."

"You suppose I wouldn't have told you if I knew? How did you find this out, anyhow?"

"Jesús 'Eddie' told me tonight. He saw her with the kid in his car this afternoon."

"But what about Manuel Orozco?" his wife wailed.

"*Ese, quién es?!*"

"You know, from church. I've been thinking, he'd be just the boy for Contracep. She'll be fifteen soon, it's time, and she'd be starting right at the top. It's what the girl needs to keep her out of trouble, Panchito."

Keep her out of trouble, Héctor thought. Good God in Heaven. And women were supposed to know all about such matters. He hadn't understood until now how assimilated AveMaría was becoming, how thoroughly Americanized. In Mexico, things tended to happen to girls of Contracepción's age. That was something else entirely than *arranging* for them to happen, as it seemed parents did in America. Was it really possible to have too much of a good thing when it came to this business of assimilation?

"We can discuss it all tomorrow," he said wearily. "Right now, I am going to sleep."

Mother and Daughter

NEITHER MR. NOR MRS. VILLA slept much that night from worry over Contracepción and her love interest. From time to time, one or the other drifted off—AveMaría into nightmares of a Muslim wedding, Héctor to dream of thrashing the lusty young Islamist within an inch of his life. But they soon woke and lay side by side in the darkness, discussing in hushed tones the measures needed to be taken before Ave-María delivered Contracep to work at the mosque the next morning.

Héctor was for confronting their daughter at breakfast and forbidding her outright to see the *tipo* again. His wife favored collecting Contracep herself after work on pretence of driving her to the Los Lunas mall to shop for new shoes and postponing the unpleasantness until after supper in the presence of Brother Billy Joe, who was expected to drop by for dessert and coffee. Héctor, who considered AveMaría's plan a classic example of weak-minded female indirection, held his tongue anyway. If only his children were reversed in age and it were Dubya he had to deal with tomorrow! For some reason he didn't understand but which had nothing to do (he assured himself) with cowardice, Héctor felt he'd rather face a firing squad than have to lay down the law to his daughter on an issue of romance. And, was she really his daughter anymore? A great part of his anguish, Héctor realized, derived from the fear that he wasn't going to recognize Contracepción when, for the first time since learning the news from Jesús "Eddie," he laid eyes on her at 7 A.M. across the breakfast table.

In fact he avoided her gaze over breakfast, ate almost nothing, and excused himself from the table after ten minutes, saying he had an early appointment in Mountainair, 45 miles away. When AveMaría gave him a significant look, Héctor couldn't help feeling like a coward in spite of himself. The sense of having ignominiously abandoned his post stayed with him as far as Blue Canyon, where he stopped at the roadside café for several more cups of coffee and a sweet roll to avoid having to wait in his truck for forty minutes outside the client's place of business. Thank God (Héctor reflected fervently) he had but one daughter to give to his country!

When her husband had departed for Mountainair, AveMaría called Brother Billy Joe on the bedroom phone to inform him of the current crisis *chez* Villa and enlist his help that evening. After that it was time to drive Contracepción to work. The girl complained all the way of being forbidden makeup and jewelry and having to wear a headscarf on the job, and acted offended when her mother failed to offer sympathy. AveMaría had not, indeed, been terribly surprised to learn that Contracep had a boyfriend, having spotted the telltale signs for herself over the past couple of weeks. But she had been totally unprepared for the news that the young man was an Islamist, a sworn enemy of America and the Lord Jesus. Contracepción had been brought up, at home as well as at Sunday school, to know better. As for what might have gone wrong, AveMaría could not have said, anymore than she'd understood why her youngest sister, Angélica, had run off to Ciudad México at the age of fifteen to work as a call girl. Of course, the money was good, but Middle Eastern people didn't have any money, they were all poor, except for the Jews—and besides, they looked just exactly alike. How could you fall in love with one of them when you couldn't tell the one you loved from all the rest? Brother Billy Joe would have said it was the Devil, but AveMaría knew better. It was just the way young girls were. After all, she'd been one herself, once. And it was true her father had never considered Héctor much of a prize—though at least he'd been *mexicano*, not one of those look-alike Islamists with a bomb under his turban. Thinking of bombs frightened AveMaría to the point where, by the time they arrived at the mosque, she was in near panic from imagining it to be a terrorist religious cell like those she'd seen American troops smashing their way through in Iraq on the evening news.

The place appeared peaceable enough, and AveMaría regained sufficient control to say, in a more or less normal voice, "I'll pick you up myself this afternoon, *¡vida mía!* We'll run up to the mall in Los Lunas and buy you the shoes you've been wanting since *Día de los Muertos!*"

In that instant, the daughter's face told her mother all that she needed to know. For the rest, there was the glimpse she had of a young man peering furtively around a corner of the mosque toward the car, a Moorish Adonis with a black beard and black curly hair—absolutely the handsomest boy, AveMaría caught herself thinking, she had ever laid eyes on.

"¡O Mamá!" Contracepción wailed, "I don't need those dumb sandals! Honest, I don't! And the mall is always so crowded on Friday afternoons!"

AveMaría did not know what to say. If she were in her daughter's shoes, she wouldn't want to visit any mall with her mother this afternoon, either. Contracep, of course, was a beautiful girl and very well developed for her age, who'd attracted admiring glances from men from the time she was ten or eleven. Even so, the mother couldn't help being impressed. She herself had never attracted a boy like this one when she was fourteen—or ever. The kid looked to be just the right age for Contracep, plus—he *was* hot! Anyone could see that, just by looking at him.

"OK," AveMaría agreed lamely, "we'll look for shoes some other time. Only—I want you back by five o'clock sharp, before your father gets home, do you hear me? Otherwise, he's going to be very angry—and so will I." *And be sure and tell me the first time he kisses you,* she wanted to add, but didn't.

"¡O Mamá, gracias—muchas, muchas gracias!" Contracepción jumped from the Subaru and started at a trot toward the corner of the building, from where the gorgeous visage had withdrawn itself. AveMaría watched with a kind of fierce indulgence as she went, her headscarf fluttering on the stiff desert wind. It was the fastest, she thought, she'd ever seen her daughter move. (Contracep, far from being an athletic girl, was really rather lazy.)

AveMaría's first thought on reaching home was to telephone her best friend, Teresa Aguilar, who had a daughter the same age as Contracepción, and confide to her that Contracep had found herself a hunk of fifteen or sixteen. In the end she decided against this, as Teresa was not only a Catholic but an actual practicing one, somebody who could be counted on to disapprove of a Christian girl dating an Islamist, no matter how great-looking. AveMaría had just reached this decision when Brother Billy Joe called to postpone dinner with the Villas until the following evening. A church member's son, he explained, had committed suicide the evening before, leaving behind a note blaming his action on his father's refusal to buy him the BMW sports car he'd asked for for Christmas. Though AveMaría was relieved at not having to put herself out as a hostess on so eventful a day, her brief conversation with the preacher caused her a pang of anxiety, produced by dark foreboding. What, she wondered, would Billy Joe have to say when he learned of Contracepción's conquest? Although she chose not to dwell on the subject for now, AveMaría thought she could make a pretty good guess. Between them, Billy Joe and Héctor would constitute a formidable opposition that was all too likely to carry the day against herself and Contracep. What words would get said on the way to a decision scarcely bore contemplation, she found. Why couldn't the preacher and her husband understand that this boy was just exactly what the girl needed to bolster her self-confidence and help her find the way to maturity? Every talk-show host and advice columnist she knew of would agree with her in rejecting the ignorant and unfeeling viewpoint of two privileged men who shared between them the power to determine a poor adolescent girl's fate.

Her worst fear, that the young man would delay in delivering Contracep to the house until after her now-watchful father had reached home, proved unfounded. Instead, with faultless Oriental tact and prudence, he dropped her off a block away and just on the stroke of five o'clock, a good half-hour before Héctor's van drew up to the curb.

"Where's Contracepción?" Héctor demanded first thing of his wife, even before he'd taken a beer from the fridge.

"In her room, studying her Sunday-school lesson," AveMaría informed him. "And Brother Billy Joe called this afternoon to say he can't make it tonight. He's coming tomorrow night instead."

"*¡Bueno!* I want to know what a preacher makes of this mess, but I'm too exhausted to discuss it with him this evening. And since Billy Joe won't be eating with us, I can drink a beer, or two, with dinner—*¡gracias a Dios!*"

When Contracepción took her place at the dinner table that evening, her father regarded her furtively with eyes from which the scales had fallen at last. How, Héctor wondered, had he failed to see disaster looming? His daughter, not yet fifteen, was what in Mexico is called a *guapa* and in America a piece of ass. He saw it all now. The wonder was not that some starry-eyed Muslim kid had become smitten with his daughter, but that she didn't have a train of Hindus, Buddhists, Rastafarians, Seventh-Day Adventists, Jehovah's Witnesses, Unitarians, Falun Gongists, Mormons, Episcopalians, and Catholics slobbering after her as well. That was the downside of multiculturalism,

Héctor thought bitterly. Perhaps, after all, the Villas ought never to have left Mexico, where life was socially less complicated. He drank more beer than was good for him and went to bed ahead of AveMaría, full of dread. And this was only the beginning! No sooner would he succeed in driving this *tipo* off than the guy would be succeeded by another, and another, and another still—each and every one of them responding to that same primordial urge, each one after that single, so very basic thing that precedes every race and creed in the world. Well, he was going to leave it to Brother Billy Joe—a real professional—to sort things out.

AveMaría, hoping for a second glimpse of Paradise when she drove Contracepción to work the next morning, was disappointed by the failure of Abdul (the girl had shyly confided her suitor's name after the father had gone early to bed the previous night) to make an appearance. All day she fretted, contemplating the coming scene she imagined for that evening when patriarch and prophet joined in righteous wrath against the scandalous liaison contracted between innocent girlhood and ardent youth. At four-thirty, anticipating Abdul's imminent delivery of Contracep, AveMaría swallowed a Lorazepam to quiet her nerves. Then she went on to her daughter's bedroom, selected from the closet the most modest article of clothing she could find there, and laid the dress across the bed with a note pinned to the bosom: "Bro. B. Joe coming to see your Father tonite."

Dinner went off quietly, despite Héctor's glumness and the preacher's excessive volubility regarding his planned "Crusade for Souls" that winter. Immediately afterward, AveMaría sent Contracepción away with Dubya to give the child his bath and followed the men into the den, ignoring their pained surprise at her presence there. But when his wife gave no indication of leaving, Héctor plunged in, and, in less than five minutes, Brother Billy Joe had heard the entire sordid story.

"So, what's a father to do?" he ended in a tragic voice.

The preacher sat dull-eyed, his plump hands crossed on his belly. Having dined heavily at AveMaría's table, he found himself unable to summon his usual alacrity of thought.

"Ah—shotgun marriage?" he suggested sluggishly.

"They haven't done anything yet!" AveMaría almost shrieked. "Contracepción is a virgin—I guarantee you that!"

"It was the boy's family I was thinking of, really. Islamists have a very rigid code of honor—you know, for unbelievers. And the two seem to have been dating for a couple of weeks now."

"My daughter can't possibly marry one of those people!" Héctor informed him passionately. "I'd rather see her dead first—almost. 'Kill the body but not the soul,' and so forth. Besides, the girl isn't fifteen yet!"

AveMaría had a flash of inspiration—as blinding, she thought later, as the light that knocked Saint Paul off his horse.

"What if Abdul converts?" she cried.

Brother Billy Joe's eyelids had drooped as the conversation proceeded. Now they flapped wide open and the preacher pulled himself up straight in his chair.

"Why of course! Our Crusade for Souls! Contracepción must bring the kid with her to the very first meeting next month! First we save him, then we bring along the entire mosque—we convert everyone! It'll be a nationwide story, folks! After that, there's no question we can afford to put that new roof on the old dump! Hell—I mean, heck—we can build a whole new church if we want one!"

To Héctor, his wife looked to be on the verge of swooning—from sheer pleasure, it seemed. His own reaction to the catastrophe was coldly formal, wholly impersonal. If this was how the Man of God proposed to defeat the Archenemy, Héctor thought, the First Assembly of God could not be long for this world. The same went for the Villa family, so far as he could tell.

Daughter and Lover

FOR DAYS AFTER THE MEETING with Brother Billy Joe, Héctor was too angry to communicate with his wife except in monosyllables. During most of this period, the reason for his anger eluded him. It was not until the third or fourth day that he understood the cause of his distress. Whether the kid Abdul converted to Christianity or not, Héctor Villa did not want his daughter taking up romantically with an Afghan—period. And he couldn't comprehend how AveMaría could wish such a thing, let alone facilitate it. Though he was angry with the preacher as well, Héctor tried to be fair: The man's job, after all, was saving souls; AveMaría's was to see that their daughter was properly brought up to make a suitable marriage, at the appropriate time and with the right sort of man—which, in Héctor's view, definitely did not include bearded Central Asians in turbans who rode camels and herded goats back home, while covertly keeping Osama bin Laden and his Qaeda supplied with food, weapons, and (so he understood from reliable sources) a steady stream of voluptuous virgins from Pakistan.

Héctor knew enough popular psychology to understand that *facilitator* is an unpleasant term for a nasty thing. But he couldn't think of another word to describe his wife's behavior in welcoming Abdul into the house every afternoon after he'd delivered Contracepción to the house for cookies and milk. (Though only fifteen, Abdul carried an official-looking laminated driver's license identifying him as being sixteen years of age.) Since the first afternoon, when the boy had announced a preference for goat's milk over cow's, AveMaría had taken care to keep a half-gallon of the stuff in the refrigerator. The children ate their snack in the kitchen to allow the Señora Villa to keep them under her watchful eye. This was the one room in the house devoid of a crucifix, which spared AveMaría the trouble of veiling the Lord Jesus from Abdul's gaze with a handkerchief, as the young Islamist piously insisted she do. (When her husband pointed out a certain inconsistency between converting the boy to Christ and removing from his sight the central symbol of His religion, AveMaría had countered with the argument that, before Adbul could open his heart to Jesus, he needed

to be set at ease and made to feel comfortable and at home.) Promptly at six, Contracepción walked her young man out to the car, where,
furtively observed by AveMaría, Abdul took formal leave of her before
driving off. Her heart aflutter as she watched the affecting scene from
behind a curtain in the sitting room, the expectant mother hardly
knew whether to be reassured or disappointed when he failed to kiss
the girl. How had Jesús "Eddie" got the notion that the couple went
joyriding about town, passionately necking behind the wheel? Not
for the first time, AveMaría wondered whether Jesús "Eddie" might
have a dirty mind.

After Contracep and Abdul had been "going together," as AveMaría
phrased the situation for herself, for two weeks, she decided to let Teresa Aguilar in on the romance. After all (she reasoned), the relationship, having behind it the honorable Christian purpose of salvation,
could hardly be called a pagan one—not even by a devout member of
the Roman Catholic Church, which AveMaría recalled from her girlhood as being unpleasantly judgmental and irrational. Though only
four or five years her senior, Teresa herself had seven children, the first
two of whom were grown and already married with children of their
own, while the second-youngest—Castidad, a year older than Contracepción—certainly didn't look like a girl who'd ever been kissed by a
boy. AveMaría was not given to boasting, and she certainly had never
been one to take pleasure in making someone else feel envy. Still (she
couldn't help thinking), Teresa was bound to be impressed by Contracep's success with a serious young man of Christian intention—even
to the point, perhaps, of giving poor Castidad a nudge in that direction herself! You just never knew, AveMaría reflected, how sharing an
inspirational story with someone could change that person's whole life,
and perhaps the lives of countless others as well. And, naturally, what
goes around, comes around. The life you save may be your own!

AveMaría called her friend late one morning when Héctor was
away on a job in Quemado, after she'd dropped Contracepción at the
mosque. (Oddly, Abdul never offered to drive her *to*, only *from*, work.
She must ask her daughter about this sometime, AveMaría reminded
herself.) Teresa Aguilar picked up on the fifth ring, just as AveMaría
was about to hang up to forestall the mailbox playing the introductory
bars of Franck's "Panis Angelicus." It was her turn to host the Catholic
reading group, Teresa explained; this week, they were considering *The*

Exorcist, in Spanish translation. Teresa promised to phone back in fifteen minutes after the girls had gone, and AveMaría sat in her favorite armchair with the phone in her hand, awaiting the call and treasuring in her heart the miracle of love between her daughter and Abdul Agha, the Afghan boy.

When, at last, the telephone did ring, she fumbled and nearly dropped the receiver in her excitement.

"*¡Diga!*"

"*¡Oye!*" The voice was, indeed, Teresa's. "Finally, we can talk. I thought the girls never would leave! We get together to discuss the Great Catholic Books, and all they want to talk about is their husbands. But what's up with you, AveMaría? You sounded as if you'd won the lottery a half-hour ago."

"Oh, nothing much." AveMaría was doing her best to sound casual. "Héctor's gone for the day, so I did a little shopping at the mall, just a few odds and ends, including a gorgeous Donna Karan suit I found on sale—in case Héctor decides to run for office again, you know. And Dubya's been talking a blue streak all week—something he must have learned from the neighbor's parrot, I can't understand a word!" She paused, casting about for more trivia in the attic of her mind and not finding any. "Oh, I almost forgot to mention: Contracep has an admirer, her very first—isn't that sweet! Fifteen years old and such a *guapo*, too! You know, Teresa, if I was ten years younger—and didn't have Héctor, of course—I think I'd be halfway interested myself."

Teresa's voice sounded dubious, and perhaps a little cold. "Your girl's just fourteen, isn't she? Don't you think that's a little young for . . . that sort of thing?" Teresa always avoided speaking the name "Contracepción," whenever politeness allowed.

"She'll be fifteen in May. And they've never even kissed, they're so content just to be together! You remember, Contracep had a little . . . problem at school last fall. Me and her father feel sure her relationship with Abdul is going to be a real learning experience for her, one that helps her find maturity by discovering herself—" In her enthusiasm, AveMaría had revealed more than she'd intended to tell her friend at the outset. Confused, she broke off in mid-sentence, searching for a way to cover her tracks, and discovered it was already too late for that.

"His name is *Abdul*?"

91

"Well, yes. His family happen to be immigrants from Afghanistan, you see. Very hard working, doing the kind of jobs Americans won't—"

"They're *Muslims*, then?"

"Oh, Abdul's promised Contracep to convert! Everything's being arranged by Brother Billy Joe. It's going to be a nationwide story, Billy Joe says."

"AveMaría, are you and your husband *locos*? First, you abandon Holy Mother Church for a *gringo* circus tent, now you encourage your daughter to become involved with a follower of the Prince of Lies, a member of the Devil's Own Religion that teaches Our Lord is boiling alive in a pot of hot oil this very moment! Not to mention, she's only fourteen. Next thing I hear, you'll have found a girlfriend for Dubya. Listen to me, *querida*! Us *Mexicanas* up here in the *Estados Unidos* need to become *Norteñas* in our pocketbooks, not in our hearts and heads."

The conversation was not going at all the way AveMaría had imagined it. By turns surprised, aggrieved, and resentful, she felt finally abashed by her friend's reprimand, even slightly guilty. Of course Teresa, not being intimately familiar with either the peculiarities of the situation or the characters involved, couldn't help but view the entire business from a distance, as it were. Even so, her admonition against thinking too much like an American struck home. How often, AveMaría thought, had she herself, observing the same tendency in her husband, warned him against it? In his determination to become a real American, Héctor was far more obsessive than she. True, America was for Mexicans the Promised Land, but only for so long as they remained Mexican at heart. To that extent, she found herself in reluctant agreement with Teresa Aguilar. If Anglo parents, worshiping diversity as Americans did, were content to see their children marry Islamists, that was their business. Clearly, a Mexican mother could never consent to such a thing for her child. But Abdul Agha was going to become a Christian himself, first! As for the rest of it—regarding the propriety of Contracep's having a boyfriend at all—that was just Teresa's outdated, restrictive, and superstitious religion talking. It was too bad, AveMaría considered, that her best friend had to be what Brother Billy Joe called a Mackerel Snapper (and worse), but what was she to do about that? Only the week before, she'd considered discreetly inviting Teresa to join her for the prayer meeting that was meant to kick off the Crusade for Souls. Now, as a result of this conversation, it appeared to her prudent to postpone all evangelistic efforts until whenever Teresa Aguilar seemed more receptive to God's Call.

Therefore, all AveMaría said in answer to her friend's outburst was, "Well, in America, do as the *americanos* do, ha ha! Héctor and I want to throw a party for Abdul when he's saved, I'll call to let you know when we have a date, we hope you and Augustín will come—oh, and Castidad too, of course, if she wants to and has nothing better to do. Who knows; she might even meet *someone nice* there!"

That evening, Abdul, after dropping Contracepción at the gate, drove off at once without coming inside for cookies and milk. AveMaría, surprised and fearing a lovers' quarrel, asked why.

"Oh, *Mamá*, it's Friday and he has evening prayer service to go to. His father is the *Ihop*, so he can't skip church or be a minute late, even."

AveMaría, who had no idea what an *Ihop* might be, nodded sagely and said nothing. An hour later, after her husband had arrived home and the two of them were seated together in the den watching the six o'clock news, she asked him about it during the commercial break.

"An *Ihop*? No idea. Sounds like a pancake house to me."

"It's something to do with the mosque. Contracep says Abdul's father is the *Ihop* there."

Even had he not made it a matter of patriotic duty for the past five years to follow developments in the War on Terror conscientiously, the televised interview from Baghdad that had concluded just before the break would have supplied Héctor with the answer. He hit the MUTE button on the remote and set his dripping beer bottle down on the coffee table without bothering to place a coaster under it.

"*Imam!*" he exclaimed in a harsh whisper to his wife. "The word is *imam*, meaning an Islamist priest! This *tipo*'s father is the . . . uh . . . pastor of the Belen mosque, the head gazzink! Do you have any idea what this means, woman?"

AveMaría hesitated before giving an answer that seemed to her so obvious she had to imagine her husband's question was really a trick one.

"Why, I suppose he's just the same as Brother Billy Joe in our church," she said at last. "Just stick a coaster under that bottle—¡*por favor, querido!*"

Héctor regarded her momentarily with hopeless despair. Then he put his open hand to his forehead and ran it down his face as far as his chin. When he had done so, his despairing expression had been wiped away and replaced by a look of determined aggression.

"A so-called mosque is nothing but a terrorist cell," he began, "and the *imam* is the head terrorist. Do you see now what it is that you have done, AveMaría? Through your crazy desire to find Contracepción a *novio*, you have invited a dangerous viper into the bosom of the family!"

AveMaría at first was too shocked and ashamed to speak. Slowly, however, she became emboldened. Her conversation with Teresa Aguilar that afternoon seemed to have encouraged in her a strange and unaccustomed confidence.

"In that case," she said in a strong voice, rising from the sofa beside her husband, "we must see that Abdul is saved as soon as possible. *Gracias a Diós*, the Crusade for Souls begins just two weeks from tomorrow!"

Jihad on the Rio

O N A MORNING less than a week before the kickoff to Brother Billy Joe's Crusade for Souls, AveMaría, after she'd dropped Contracepción off at the mosque, was in the middle of a U-turn in the street when a car rounded the corner ahead on two wheels, heading directly for the Subaru. As there was nothing to do but sound the horn, AveMaría did so, striking the top of the steering column with the side of her right hand, in which she held an open can of Sprite. The jet of carbonated liquid blinded her momentarily, so she never saw the car leap the curb and run for a distance along the strip of concrete sidewalk. By the time her sight cleared, the vehicle had regained the street and crossed it and was pulling into the parking lot beside the mosque. Indignant, AveMaría put the Subaru in reverse and backed as fast as she dared into the road with the intention of giving the driver a piece of her mind through the window.

The car, an ancient Dodge Dart the sun-faded color of a spoiled tomato, looked familiar. (AveMaría was not given to noticing automobiles especially, unless it was something she thought she'd like to own.) So did the young man with dark, curly hair and wearing a white T-shirt and tan cargo pants climbing out on the driver's side. Why, she thought—*it's Abdul Agha!* But who was the turbaned man emerging from the passenger door wearing dark glasses and carrying a stick? Though she was too far away for a good look at his face, something about the *tipo* made AveMaría's skin crawl. Had not Héctor warned that every mosque was a snake pit of terrorists? Surely, this man looked the part. On second thought, AveMaría shifted the Subaru into drive and drew away from the mosque. She'd find a way to get the information she wanted out of Abdul when he delivered Contracepción home that afternoon.

But Abdul Agha did not bring Contracepción that day. Instead, the girl called around two o'clock to request that her mother come for her at three. Abdul, she explained, had to drive his father somewhere. Feeling slightly peeved—besides having planned an afternoon's uninterrupted work at the church helping prepare for the Crusade, she'd been looking forward to gratifying her curiosity regarding the spec-tacled man—AveMaría met her daughter as she'd requested at the mosque, where nothing much was happening except for an after-school religious class in progress. Neither Abdul nor his former pas-senger seemed to be about.

AveMaría, who'd prepared her strategy in advance, waited until they'd traveled a few blocks and were already ascending the access ramp to I-25 before remarking, in a jesting tone: "You know, Abdul almost ran smack into me after I dropped you at the mosque this morning. He must have been going at least thirty miles an hour around that corner—like a *maníaco*! If Gallegos, the cop, was to catch him doing such a thing, he'd have him deported all the way back to Afghanistan. I hope he doesn't drive that way when he's with you, *mia vida*! Did he take driver ed in Kabul, do you know?"

"*Mamá*, he was hurrying! His *papá* had an important meeting with some guy came all the way from Pakiland to visit him. He *had* to get him to the mosque on time!"

A sickly light, the color of a dying sun, rose at the back of Ave-María's mind. "Does his father wear glasses and carry a cane?"

"*¡Claro!*—he is blind! That's why poor Abdul has to drive him everywhere."

So that was the answer, AveMaría thought. Aloud, she added, "He drives his dad to the mosque every morning, then. Why doesn't he take you along, too, *querida*?"

"*O Mamá*, don't be silly. His father can't ever know about me! Abdul said he'd have, like, a heart attack if he knew his son was going with a *Nasrani*—a *kafir*."

"What's a *Nasrany café*?"

"It means *Christian, infidel*, in Arabic. Abdul explained it to me."

AveMaría was shocked at first, then angered. "An infidel? Who's an infidel? Me, or that blind towelhead in glasses? Is your father, then, an infidel too, *picarona*?"

"*Mamá*, don't get excited! It's like they keep telling us in school, all religions are really the same."

AveMaría saw clearly that it was not just Islamists who stood to benefit from Brother Billy Joe's Crusade for Souls, but her own fam-ily as well. (What was the good of Sunday school, she asked herself, when the public-education system spent five days a week undoing the lessons that nice Mrs. Bradford taught the kids?) She said as much to her husband that evening after supper, when Contracepción had retired to her room for what AveMaría presumed was her good-night phone conversation with Abdul.

"Won't it be wonderful," she added, "to see Abdul and Contracep feeling Our Lord's breath on their faces and receiving the Spirit from Him, hand in hand together?"

But Héctor only grunted as he took another Corona from the fridge on his way back to the den, where he'd taken to isolating himself of late. He was drinking more than was usual for him, AveMaría had noted in some consternation. Solitary drinking was unhealthy, she'd read, but the alternative for Héctor was the Taberna Aztlán where Jesús "Eddie" Juárez hung out every night. More and more, AveMaría was coming to suspect Jesús of being a bad—or, anyway, an unwholesome—influence on her husband.

The great problem AveMaría foresaw lay in enticing Abdul Agha into the revival meeting before he could recognize it as a Christian gathering. Fortunately, the Crusade was to be held in Tom Bradford's large equipment shed south of town. The decision had been made by Brother Billy Joe, who feared the shabby and decrepit-looking church roof might be off-putting to potential converts. And the organizing committee had scheduled an indoor barbecue before each meeting, which would give the first hour or so the atmosphere of the secular picnic Abdul would be expecting, rather than that of a religious gathering. Even so, AveMaría felt, it was going to be a touch-and-go situation, with much depending on Contracepción playing her part to the hilt. Having impressed upon the girl the magnitude of the stakes involved, she felt fairly confident of her daughter's success in pulling the thing off. Still, you never knew. The entire business was very much a calculated risk.

The great night arrived at last. Abdul, having arranged for his best friend Zamari to stand in for him at his job with the falafel shop on Sosima Pidaloa, left for "work" in his Dodge, as usual. He collected Contracepción at the Villa residence, and the two proceeded directly south on Route 314 to Bradford's machine shed, where AveMaría awaited them while Héctor sweated over a grill on which fat sausages browned. AveMaría, who'd been keeping her eye on the door, was impressed once again by what a fine-looking couple her daughter and the young Afghan made. She bustled over to them, took the boy's arm, and led the pair directly toward her husband and the sausages, which were already producing a savory odor. In the past, AveMaría had been conscious of some reservations regarding the Assemblies of God's teachings on the matter of alcohol. Tonight, its teetotalist theology seemed nothing short of a godsend—no beer kegs and makeshift bars standing around.

"Try one of these pork sausages," she urged Abdul. "They're almost as good as the ones we used to get in Mexico when I was a girl!" To her surprise, the boy preferred shish kebab prepared with mutton from one of the tough old sheep Bartolomé Naranjo raised on his ranch along the Rio Puerco.

AveMaría kept a fond eye on the loving twosome as they strolled through the crowd, a surprising number of whom, she saw, were young people, all of them wholesome and many of them—the girls especially—good looking. Observing her daughter's progress around the shed, she began to suspect herself of having underestimated Contracep's popularity as one young woman after another approached the girl in a friendly, giggling, and generally ingratiating manner. Then Brother Billy Joe ascended the platform, and everyone took a seat. Contracepción and Abdul sat toward the back of the building, AveMaría and Héctor up front. AveMaría held her breath in suspense as the preacher lifted his arms toward Heaven and began to pray: "O Father Godduh, have mercy on us miserable sinners as we gather here together—teetering on the smoky brink of Hell—in Your Holy Name!" Though she had to admit Billy Joe conducted a moving revival that evening, her appreciation was somewhat spoiled by her concern for its possible effect on Abdul Agha, who must surely realize by now he was in a vipers' pit of *Nasrany cafés*. However, the boy seemed cheerful enough afterward, AveMaría thought, chatting comfortably with Contracepción and a knock-out redhead of about sixteen she didn't recall having ever seen at church.

When the time came to leave Abdul shook hands gravely with Contracepción and drove off in his car, leaving the Villas standing in the parking area outside the machine shed.

"*Mi vida*, how did it go?" AveMaría demanded anxiously of her daughter. "Was he touched by the Spirit, do you think?"

The girl shrugged. "*¿Quién sabe?* I don't think he paid much attention during the meeting, he kept muttering something about a *lockbar*.

Later, when it was over and we were talking with Kathleen O'Malley, he seemed to be in, like, a better mood."

"Is she the redhead girl? I don't think I've seen her around before."

"Her and her family moved here last year from Ireland. They used to be Catholic before they joined our church. I see her at Sunday school every week."

AveMaría felt greatly relieved. "It sounds like it was a success after all—don't you agree, Panchito?" Héctor, who'd been scraping a semicircular clearing in the gravel with the side of his cowboy boot, looked glum and said nothing.

AveMaría was in a state of high anticipation the next week as she contemplated the second Crusade meeting on the following Saturday night. There were to be four meetings in all, and she had no doubt that, sooner or later, God would touch Abdul Agha's heart and bring him, weeping and staggering, up the center aisle to Christ. All that week, she kept an anxious eye on Contracepción, noting the girl's every mood and pestering her with questions regarding Abdul. From these AveMaría learned nothing of interest, save that the boy's father had inadvertently discovered his son's absence from the falafel shop the previous Saturday and that there had been hell to pay. How cruel and inhumane of these Islamists, she thought, working their children like slaves and for just a little extra money on the side! Meanwhile, Abdul continued to deliver Contracep to the house in his Dodge, where, after cookies and goat's milk, he bade her a formal farewell at the front gate.

That Saturday evening, the Villas again departed for the Crusade in two cars, Contracepción chauffeured by her handsome admirer and feeling like royalty. How envious Kathleen O'Malley would be when she realized that last week had not been a casual date and that she and Abdul Agha were actually in a serious relationship! At the barbecue, she made a point of seeking Kathleen out and hanging possessively on Abdul's arm while the three of them chatted. Then Brother Billy Joe clambered up to the podium, and it was time for everyone to take a seat and turn his thoughts from a pork rib Heaven to a world of sin and the agonies of Hell.

As they had the previous week, Héctor and AveMaría sat up front while the lovebirds seated themselves toward the back rows. Brother Billy Joe began once again by invoking Father God-duh and, in a short time, had the congregation warmed to a fervor that seemed to sweep through Brother Bradford's shiny new machine shed like a Pentecostal fire. Contracepción did her best to get in the mood, but in truth she had a care only for the curly-haired hunk beside her. He had never looked handsomer, she thought, his color high beneath his dusky complexion and his eyes flashing fire. Only what, she wondered, could he possibly mean by this word *lockbar*, repeated over and over again, in fervent tones, under his breath?

The ushers with their long-handled baskets had just started to take up the collection when a disturbance sounded from outside, beyond the wide steel doors of the shed. Contracepción heard rough voices raised in a roaring chant which, she realized dimly, somehow approximated the sounds Abdul Agha was still making from the bottom of his throat. "*Allahu Akbar! Allahu Akbar!*" There came next the sound of the doors being rolled back on metal tracks, followed by the riotous noise of trampling feet and the crash of the barbecue apparatus being overturned. A horde of dusky turbaned men laying about themselves with staves and crowbars swept down upon the Crusade for Souls, high in oath and praise of the One True God.

In the *mêlée* that followed, Héctor and AveMaría, frantically seeking their daughter, came upon her at last in tears of hysteria, barely in time to see Abdul Agha, hand in hand with Kathleen O'Malley, escaping through a small side door of the shed.

The Great Unrest

BROTHER BILLY JOE had been correct, Héctor reflected bitterly. Abdul Agha and the Crusade for Souls were a nationwide story all right, though everyone tried to pretend it was nothing more than a curious local phenomenon. From the start, the New Mexico media had sought the appropriate tone in reference to a "certain unrest" in Valencia County and their colleagues across the country had followed suit. As far as Héctor Villa was concerned, the business merely amounted to the Crusades all over again.

Once the machinery has been safely removed, a machine shed, unlike a cathedral, doesn't offer a great deal to damage. Bradford's barn remained largely intact after the attack, save for a few dents in the galvanized sheeting and the scorched places on the concrete floor where the barbecue grills had been overturned. Fortunately, the Muslims had been routed by the furious Christians before they could utilize the propane canisters as improvised suicide bombs, so no one was very much hurt beyond a few bruisings and some pulled hair. Still, the psychological trauma produced by the assault was enormous. The Moorish chieftains had been identified and arrested—including the blind cleric, Abdul's father, who had directed the attack from the safety of a new Hummer parked across the road. (The vehicle, loaded with firearms, had, according to police reports, been stolen from a driveway in Corrales a couple of weeks before.) Of the six or seven ringleaders, only two were found to be residents of Belen. The rest had been recruits from Santa Fe, Albuquerque, and El Paso. The revelations profoundly shocked the Rio Abajo communities, which had not suspected that the valley had become a corridor for international terrorism. AveMaría took to her bed for nearly twenty-four hours after the FBI office in Albuquerque announced that the senior Agha had been a member of the Taliban in his native land before the State Department granted his extended family refugee status and admitted them all to the United States within months of the commencement of hostilities by U.S. forces in Afghanistan late in 2001. Among the other masterminds of what a reactionary congressman from Colorado was

describing as "Jihad on the Rio," three had been granted visas to pro-
mote Islam as a "religion of peace" in America, one held an expired
student visa (Middle Eastern Studies at Michigan State), and a fifth
was a chemistry student from Pakistan on scholarship at the University of New Mexico. (Grave though the situation was, an un-Chris-
tian minority had been unable to refrain from gentle mockery of the
First Assembly of God Church and Brother Billy Joe.)

Despite attempts by politicians and the media to downplay the
religious confrontation, tension in Belen, as in other towns along the
river, was as palpable as the scent drifting from the feedlots at Antho-
ny. When, barely a week later, a car parked on an Albuquerque street
exploded at the curbside, the incident was widely rumored to have
been a car bombing, even though the city police attributed it to rivalry
between Mexican gangs. Police stations in the region were swamped
with reports of gratuitous insults offered to men wearing turbans and
women in burnooses, and Abdul's father's mosque was defaced by an
enormous drawing of a pig executed in pink spray-paint. Meanwhile,
Islamist sympathizers from around the United States weighed in with
their comments and imprecations. In the circumstances, the juvenile
court felt obliged to transfer Contracepción from the mosque to the
local chapter of the Darfur Relief Society International for the remainder
of her sentence, where even there no one was particularly polite to her.
(The *Albuquerque Journal*, in a lengthy investigative story, had recently
identified Muhammad-in-Alcohol as the effective cause of the "unrest,"
taking care to mention by name all those involved in the scandal.)

Héctor, while at pains to leave his own sentiments unexpressed,
could not help but feel vindicated by the events unfolding from his
wife's determination that their daughter should have a boyfriend
at whatever cost. AveMaría, for her part, seemed to have forgotten
entirely both her romantic hopes for Contracepción and Abdul Agha
and the role she'd played in fomenting jihad, in her relief at the Villas' narrow escape from terrorism and her fear that a terror campaign
was coming to New Mexico. "Panchito," she often implored her husband, "perhaps, after all, we should go home to Namiquipa! México
is a poor country, yes, but it is not an unlucky one, it is not *maldito*,
like El Norte! First the Trade Towers, now Bradford's machine shed!
O Panchito, if we remain here in Belen, we may all be martyred, every
one! Perhaps I should visit the *adivina* in Magdalena, and ask for her

advice?" (To this plea, Héctor always replied steadfastly that President Bush had a strategy for victory against terror, at home as well as in Afghanistan and Iraq where the terrorists were in their final throes, as he knew from watching Vice President Cheney on TV, and law-abiding Americans had nothing to fear.) As for Contracepción, her grief at losing Abdul was nothing compared with the humiliation she suffered on account of Kathleen O'Malley, who was frequently seen joyriding around town nowadays in Abdul's tomato-colored Dodge and whose outraged father was rumored to be preparing to apply the military skills he'd acquired during the Troubles in Northern Ireland to the coming Christian-Muslim wars in New Mexico.

Brother Billy Joe had rescheduled the remaining meetings of the Crusade for Souls, so Héctor was free in the days following the Battle of the Machine Shed to spend his evenings at the Taberna Aztlán in the company of Jesús "Eddie" Juárez, after AveMaría had taken an Ambien and retired early with Dubya asleep in Héctor's place beside her in the bed. Jesús "Eddie," Héctor had always suspected, was at best a nominal Christian who attended Mass only to maintain the peace at home and whose real interest was the bingo games on Saturday evenings and Sunday afternoons in the basement of Our Lady of Belen. Thus Héctor was quite unprepared to learn his friend's sentiments regarding Jihad on the Rio and astonished by the violence with which he expressed them.

"The goddamn Is-*lam*-ists," Jesús "Eddie" brooded over his sixth or seventh beer as they sat at "their" table watching the ten o'clock news. "They're heretics, *hombre*—say it was Mu-*ham*-mad that was crucified, not Jesus Christ at all! Not even the Anglo *Prot*-estants believe *that*."

Héctor did his best not to feel offended. "Not all Protestants are Anglos," he reminded Jesús "Eddie" mildly.

Jesús "Eddie" smiled tolerantly. He felt good that evening and was prepared to take an ecumenical view of things, being secretly pleased that Contracep had broken up with the raghead kid and was back on the meat market again.

"The worst thing about Protestants ain't they hate the Pope, it's that they're *mostly An*-glos," he conceded generously.

"*I* don't hate the Pope," Héctor told him. "President Bush and Laura flew all the way to John Paul the Great's funeral in Rome last year—remember?"

"That's because Bush wants the His-*pan*-ics all to vote for him. Some of them did, maybe—but not me, *hermano*. I'd rather die than vote for the goddamn Republicans! 'Cause, you know what? *They*'re all *An*-glos, too!"

Héctor saw that the conversation was going nowhere. "Well, the thing you have to admit about Protestants and Republicans is—at least they're not Islamists, anyway!"

"That's true, that's true . . . " Thoughtfully, Jesús "Eddie" aimed the neck of his beer bottle at his epiglottis. Then he set the empty bottle down with a bang on the table. "Wish one of them teetotalin sky-butts would walk in here to-*night*," he added. "I'd hold him down and feed him a coupla beers, just for the Hell of it!"

Jesús "Eddie" fell silent until the bartender had placed two frosty bottles before himself and his friend. When the man had got behind the bar again Jesús "Eddie" said in a conspiratorial voice, leaning close across the table, "*Com*-pa-*dre*—how about we start a crusade of our own, you hear what I'm sayin to you?"

Héctor's first thought was that his friend must be joking. "You think it would do any good?" he asked doubtfully.

"*Hombre*, how could we lose? We shoot at them, we kill a few, the rest blow themselves up—*boom-boom*!—just like in Iraq!"

Héctor understood that his friend, very far from jesting, was in dead earnest. "But that would be, like, war," he protested. "You can't just decide you want to kill people for whatever reason and then go out and start doing it—only the President of the United States can do that!"

"They started it!" Jesús "Eddie's" muddy eyes glowed with the light of religious enthusiasm. "Guy was tellin me the other day, said, this is the first time the Rio A-*ba*-jo's been invaded since the Civil *War*! Said he got it out of a book, somewheres—I don't know. These Islamists has got no rights in a democratic country. Hell, it'd be like shootin a pack of coyotes—*rabid* coyotes! I tell you, *compadrito*: Everbody—the cops, the FBI, the President of the United States—why, they'd all be lookin the other way while it was going on and give us a medal after it was over!"

Héctor was profoundly shocked. He felt deeply disappointed in Jesús "Eddie." "AveMaría wouldn't go along with any such thing," he said firmly, "and I don't think President Bush would, either. He believes in the civil rights of all Americans. And he thinks Islam is a religion of peace and tolerance. Anyway, this isn't Mexico, remember. Pancho Villa wouldn't have stood a chance, trying to get away with all that he did, up here."

"This is Nuevo México—not Mexico or America, neither one! In the Rio A-*ba*-jo, we do things *our* way, *hermano*—ever since Coronado and the Camino Real. What do you think he'd of done with a bunch of ragheads? Same thing he done with the f--kin Pueblos, that's what!"

Héctor understood that Jesús "Eddie," who ordinarily held his liquor fairly well, must have taken a few shots of rye with his beer earlier in the evening. Around the age of ten or twelve, he'd learned from dealing with his Uncle Rafael not to converse with drunks except when necessary, and never to try to reason with them. He determined to keep his mouth shut while nursing his own drink and awaiting the chance to make a diplomatic departure.

Héctor was preparing to ask the barman for his tab when a small, white, severely rectangular car of foreign make, like a breadbox on wheels, pulled off Route 47 into Taberna Aztlán's lot and parked directly before the window where he and Jesús "Eddie" sat watching. The front doors of the vehicle opened simultaneously and two men stepped out, one on either side. They were small, lean, dark-skinned men wearing trimmed black beards and turbans that glowed like ivory under the outdoor lights. With almost military precision, the two snatched the turbans from their heads, rolled them up, and stuffed them deep into the pockets of their long, dark coats. One of the men looked familiar, Héctor thought.

"Did you see that, *hombre*?" Jesús "Eddie" demanded. "Them towelheads are comin in *here*!"

They appeared in the doorway seconds later and paused there, looking carefully about as if casing the joint. Then they scuttled like rats to a shadowed corner of the room and seated themselves in darkness at a table for two.

"Can you be-*lieve* it?" Jesús "Eddie" hissed. "You think maybe they could be jack Muslims—walkin into a bar, just like that?"

The barman took their order and returned with the drinks. Héctor couldn't tell for certain what they were drinking: He guessed Tequila Sunrises. He was still trying to recall where he recognized the familiar-looking one from. There were so many Islamists on the Rio Grande these days.

Jesús "Eddie" swept his half-finished beer away with the side of his hand. "Come on, *compadrito*. The Crusade is about to begin—right here and now!"

The last time Héctor had been in a fistfight was in elementary school, when Adán Romero challenged him after he'd caught Lolita Sanchez giving him a kiss on the playground at lunchtime and he'd been forced to accept in order to save face before a woman.

"Suppose we just leave," he suggested nervously. "We make any trouble, the barman might not let us in here again." The familiar *tipo*, he'd realized in that instant, had been one of the jihadists attacking the machine barn.

"We *are* leavin,'" Jesús "Eddie" whispered. "Put your coat on now, and we'll pay up on the way out."

The light from the windows of the Taberna Aztlán fell just short of the front ends of the cars aligned in the parking area along the concrete stops. Moving stealthily and in a crouched position, Jesús "Eddie" approached the breadbox from behind and went round it, letting the air out of the tires one after the other. When he'd finished, he tucked a bar napkin under the wiper-blade on the driver's side. On the napkin, Jesús "Eddie" had written with a red felt-tip pen: CRUCIFY THE MUSLIM DOGS!!!

"There," he remarked in a satisfied voice. "Them f--kin camel jockeys will know we mean business, all right, when they come out later and get a load of *that*."

A Close Encounter With the Enemy

IN THE EARLY HOURS of the following morning, well after closing time, the Taberna Aztlán exploded in flames and burned to its concrete foundation in ninety minutes.

Héctor learned of the disaster shortly before 6 A.M. when Ave-María shook her husband awake to give him the tragic news. (Since the attack on the machine shed during the Crusade for Souls, she had made it a habit to take her radio to bed with the headphones clamped in place over her ears, in case of renewed hostilities.)

"I *knew* it was going to happen!" she shrieked. "The *jihadistas* have struck again! What other kind of *maníaco* would blow up a bar? O Panchito, you could have been blown up too—just minding your own business and drinking beer, harming no one!" In the horror and fear inspired by the catastrophe, it had not yet occurred to AveMaría that the destruction of the Taberna Aztlán might be something other than an unqualified disaster.

Héctor propped himself on his elbow, trying to escape from the dream that remained more real to him than the world into which he'd awakened. Like most dreams, it was neither a particularly pleasant one nor a nightmare. In this dream, he was having an earnest conversation with George W. Bush in a garish place, painted scarlet, purple, and gold, that looked like a throne room but must really have been the Oval Office, as he attempted to explain to the President how he'd managed to fail in becoming the first illegal immigrant ever elected to the U.S. Congress. When his wife woke him Héctor had been in the middle of suggesting, with all due respect, that the President might have had Tomasina Luna drafted into the Army and sent to Iraq just before Election Day. Now, as he reclined in a half-sitting position against the pillow, his mind proceeded to develop this scenario further.

"Give me the phone," he told AveMaría shortly, when he was fully awake at last. "I better call Jesús 'Eddie' this minute."

Mrs. Jesús "Eddie" answered the telephone. She and her husband had been awakened by a tremendous blast somewhere in the neighborhood at around four o'clock (she explained) and he'd left the house at the crack of dawn to investigate. From what Jesús had reported to her on his cell phone, the Taberna Aztlán was a total loss. Right now, she added, Jesús "Eddie" was at the police station giving the cops what he considered a valuable tip for their investigation. Héctor, who thought he could guess exactly the nature of that tip, had to question the wisdom of conveying it to the police department. With all his other troubles of late, he had no wish to be identified as the accomplice of the man who, otherwise single-handedly, had ignited World War III. Not wishing to alarm his friend's wife, however, he said nothing of this to Beatriz Juárez but asked her please to have Jesús "Eddie" call him after he left the cop shop.

"It is a miracle from God that he is still alive," AveMaría avowed as she took the phone from her husband and replaced it in its cradle, "as late as he sits up drinking beer, you know. Poor Jesús 'Eddie'! He could have been blown into a million pieces, Panchito! What did *he* ever do to hurt the Islamists? He hardly even goes to church, except to play bingo!"

When the telephone rang thirty-five minutes later, Héctor answered on the first ring. Jesús "Eddie" was on the line.

"Ah, *compadrito*, it is a terrible day for the Rio A-*ba*-jo! Vialpando, the police *chief*, said he couldn't comment before he'd talked to the media first, but I got it out of him, finally—we play bingo, me and Beatriz, with him and his *wife* ever Sunday at Our Lady. It was a Qassam rocket, they think—same as what the *A*-rabs in the Middle East use! Them sonsabitches don't have the guts to blow themselves up like they do in Iraq. But listen, *hombre*—we got the attention of them towelheads with that note I left on the windshield, yes?"

Héctor, carrying the cordless phone with him, walked outdoors into the backyard where AveMaría wouldn't hear his end of the conversation.

"I know, I know, that's the problem now. What did you tell Benjamín Vialpando, Jesús?"

"I said me and you was out last *night*, havin a coupla drinks together at the bar—no point in sayin how many; cops remember stuff like that—and the camel jockeys come in and set down, suspicious-like. Then on the way out we seen a white *car*, Korea make, with a sign KILL THE INFIDELS, written in red like blood, under the wiper blade. Vialpando wrote everthin down in a notebook and said he might want us to tell what-all it was we seen in court."

"But that isn't what we saw—I mean, the business about the note. And we'd be under oath, remember."

"Vialpando don't give a damn. He's a real Nuevo Méxi-*ca*-no— hates these folks as much as we do."

Héctor, seeing that argument with Jesús "Eddie" was unavailing as usual, held his peace. At least, his friend had had the good sense not to implicate the two of them. He felt relief at this but also a measure of guilt, though the false testimony had not been his and no oath to tell "the truth, the whole truth, and nothing but the truth" had been administered. (Héctor, who'd found it hard to get exercised over Bill Clinton's sexual escapades with Monica Lewinsky in the Oval Office, had been profoundly shocked by the President's subsequent perjury, which, in his view, more than justified impeachment.)

"I guess from now on we hang out at Paco's Place," Jesús "Eddie" concluded gloomily.

Listening on the truck radio between service calls, Héctor found the rocket attack on the Taberna Aztlán to be the nearly universal subject of discussion this morning, after Chief Vialpando held a press conference at ten to read a statement and answer questions from the media. The chief had mentioned that an unnamed witness had come forward to report two suspicious-looking males seen drinking at the Taberna hours before the attack—a fact corroborated independently by the barman—and that the police were on the lookout for a white vehicle of Korean manufacture with New Mexico plates. Excerpts from the statement regarding alleged witnesses were broadcast at regular intervals, causing Héctor to develop damp palms and a queasy stomach each time he heard them. Jesús "Eddie," he conceded, had done the patriotic thing in reporting the *jihadistas* to the authorities. Only, why had he been so dumb as to write the provocative note in the first place? When, finally, he couldn't bear to listen in anymore, Héctor struck the steering wheel with his fist and switched the radio off.

He arrived home at lunchtime to find the blinds dropped behind all the windows of his house and every door bolted shut. Within, Ave-María huddled with Dubya before the TV. In the next room, Contra-cepción lounged on her belly across the bed reading *Cosmopolitan*. Her mother had refused to drive her to the Darfur Relief office across town that morning.

"They have two suspects already!" AveMaría exclaimed as soon as she'd let her husband into the house. "Someone saw them having a drink at the Taberna Aztlán just minutes before the attack—bearded Islamists in turbans, cool as cucumbers, drinking beer just like anybody else! O Panchito, it really *could* have been you! I must call the *curandera* in Tome and ask her to make an *encanto* to protect us all!"

Héctor, who had little faith in *curanderos* and their powders, potions, and spells, nodded absently and went on to the kitchen to play back the voicemail that had accumulated that morning. The secretary to the principal at the high school, who'd continued as a private client of Pancho's Computer Service after her boss had forbidden her to hire the company on school business, had a problem with her router at home. A fourteen-year-old Anglo kid in the affluent Rio Communities across the river, who had his own account and was an *habitué* of some of the hardest porn sites on the internet, sounded beside himself with frustration after his system crashed. And a Mr. Cohen or Kahn (Héctor had trouble catching the name), calling from Belen's most disreputable neighborhood, was having difficulties with his wireless router. With any luck, he thought, he might be able to handle all three jobs in a single afternoon. As the days were short now, and the Cohen *tipo*'s district by the railroad tracks was one Héctor made a point never to visit after dark, he decided to make it his first stop after he'd eaten lunch and dropped Contracep at Darfur Relief to forestall her ending up in contempt of court.

His daughter, who'd looked forward to spending the entire day reading magazines and watching QVC and reruns of *The Bachelor*, was indignant at having to go to work, after all.

"O *Papaíto*," she protested from a mouth half full of the Twinkies she preferred for lunch, "there's no point my working just a half day— and anyway, *Mamá* already told them I was sick! Nobody wants to be around a person that's spreading germs everywhere! Besides, *Mamá* says the jihad's starting again! Suppose I was kidnapped, like those people in Iraq, and held for ransom, or shot in the back of the head and dumped in the river? Then you'd be sorry—but you don't care, *do* you? You don't really care!"

Héctor was about to reply that such atrocities can't happen in America—but didn't. America, after all, was changing very fast these days, thanks to all the immigration coming from God knows where—the Islamist countries that were threatening to set the world on fire, in particular. So he said only, "Don't be silly, Contracepción, and get yourself dressed for work—something decent, not one of those Britney Spears outfits your mother lets you buy. And shake a leg, *por favor*! I have an appointment downtown in half an hour."

By the time she came dragging out of her room with a sullen face and downcast eyes, wearing a getup that (Héctor thought) would make Paris Hilton blush, eight minutes remained before he was scheduled to meet Mr. Cohen (or Kahn) in east Belen. Neither of them spoke on the eleven-minute drive to Darfur Relief, where Contracepción slammed the car door hard and went trailing up the walk, dragging her woolen scarf behind her along the icy path. America is the best place in the world, isn't it? Why, then, Héctor wondered, do American children so often seem to be the worst?

East Belen, with its rows of shabby stucco bungalows stretching beside the switch yard, reminded him of Namiquipa. Here lay the breeding ground, he thought, of the juvenile delinquents who stabbed one another—and also innocent people—in the movie theater downtown and polluted the streets with the exhaust from their noisy low-riders. The Castillo Street address, within sight of the tracks, more than met his expectations. He got out of the van, locked the side doors, and went round to the rear panel ones, which he also locked securely after removing the tools he needed. The street smelled strongly of a mixture of coal and mesquite smoke. Number 11 looked deserted: no curtains hanging behind the wide front window shadowed by the overhanging porch roof but instead a blanket, tacked at an angle across it. No name on the mailbox, either, he noted, while four screw holes at the center of the heavy front door indicated where a nameplate had once been affixed. The button in the brass doorbell was loose, like an eyeball partially detached from its socket. Héctor punched it, waited thirty seconds, and punched the button again. On the third ring, the door swung inward slowly. In the dimness beyond, he could just make out a ghostly figure standing in the darkened hallway.

"Are you Mr. Cohen?" Héctor asked, squinting to see the figure more clearly. It struck him for the first time as odd that someone with a Jewish name should live in so poor a neighborhood.

"I am Mr. Kahn," a heavily accented voice corrected him, in an offended tone. "You are Mr. Pancho, the computer-service wallah?"

The face was swarthy, the beard black and thick, the clothes of a voluminous whiteness below what looked like a pure white cloud hovering above the head. A turban, Héctor recognized too late, when he was already past the threshold as the heavy door, vault-like, swung shut behind him.

Héctor, though not particularly adept at remembering faces (a grave failing in a would-be politician, as he'd discovered to his chagrin), could hardly fail to recall this one. To which of two men it belonged he could not have said, but of one thing he was absolutely certain: Its owner had been present at the ill-fated Taberna Aztlán, not twenty-four hours before.

Witness Un-Protection Program

MR. KAHN'S FACE had remained entirely expressionless throughout the forty-five minutes required to get the wireless router that
connected the three computers in the house back up and running, yet
Héctor felt as assured that he had been recognized by the other man
as he was in making his own identification.

He'd experienced an excruciating three-quarters of an hour, therefore, tinkering with the settings on each of the three machines, the
router, and the cable modem, while endeavoring never to turn his
back on Kahn while he worked, and keeping him in sight at all times.
Even so he was expecting, at any moment, an ornate dagger in the
chest, a jeweled scimitar across the throat. Who knew how many
terrorists were numbered in this cell and whether there might not
be others lurking in the rest of the house, around corners and in the
darkened hallway? The place resembled exactly the grim dens whose
images were broadcast by Al Jazeera after a kidnapping followed by a
threat of beheading: blankets pinned behind the windows, minimal
furniture, bare, grimed walls, a few thin bamboo mats scattered about
on the floor, and—away in the corners here and there—a hookah or
a cezve surrounded by cups and saucers. Had Héctor been familiar
with "Ali Baba and the Forty Thieves," the house might have reminded him of the brigands' cave in the forest, minus the heaps of treasure. As for Kahn, he seemed equally determined to keep the repair-
man under close surveillance, hovering so close at times that Héctor was able to catch the thin odor of water-strained tobacco in the
matted beard growing about the long, yellow teeth. Without doubt,
these computers harbored evidence of a multitude of satanic plots and
schemes aimed at destroying America and spreading Islam throughout the world. One careless move on his part—one accidental flick-
er of the screen exposing dark secrets never intended for his eyes,
or those of any other infidel—and the next instant his head would
be rolling among the coffee things on the floor. Still, he completed
his work without mishap, wrote out a bill for the job, accepted pay-
ment in cash from Kahn, and escaped the house with no misfortune

beyond the burning imprint of the *jihadista*'s dark, expressionless eyes upon his soul.

Immediately upon leaving No. 11 Callista Street, Héctor canceled his remaining afternoon appointments and drove directly to the police station, where he gave his story to the deputy chief—Vialpando was gone from the office that afternoon—and demanded that he and his family be placed immediately in the Witness Protection Program. The deputy, a pudgy Anglo named Corcoran with a thick roll of fat at the back of his neck and wearing a too-tight uniform, looked bored as he heard him out, seemingly unimpressed by his account. The request for protection he dismissed with what seemed to Héctor unnecessary contempt.

"WPP is for the really *big* fish," Deputy Chief Corcoran informed him. "We'll check your story out, buddy, and decide if you're one of them—or ain't." His small sneer and sarcastic tone suggested he himself had little doubt on that score.

Héctor, who'd expected his timely witness more than sufficient to prevent another catastrophic terrorist strike on the Rio Grande, was appalled by this laconic response.

"But it *had* to have been Kahn and his friend who fired the Qassam at the Taberna," he protested. "Those computers I worked on are probably connected with other terrorist cells—maybe even Al Qaeda itself! And what if me and my wife and kids get blown to bits by *another* rocket before you guys get around to checking out my story? What you need to do is round up a couple of men and go over there to Callista Street—*pronto*—and have a look for yourselves!"

Deputy Chief Corcoran's gaze was now definitely hostile.

"You ever hear of any such thing as a search warrant, *Señor* Villa? This ain't Mexico, you know. Cops can't just go around arresting illegal immigrants on our own. That's the federal government's job, even if they don't do nothing about it. What do you think the ACLU would say if we up and grabbed this guy on just anybody's say-so?"

On the way out of the station, though he took the paper at home, Héctor deposited a quarter in the box and extracted a copy of the *Valencia County News-Bulletin*. The photo above the fold showed the Taberna Aztlán as a smoldering ruin, and the lead story described plans to rebuild the place on location behind a defiant façade inset with 1,776 beer bottles cemented in rows. "Millions for tribute, not one cent for protection," he thought sardonically. It was a phrase he'd come across soon after crossing the border and remembered ever since. It had the genuine American ring to it, Héctor thought, like the Gettysburg Address or the Liberty Bell. He was highly disappointed in Deputy Chief Corcoran's thoroughly un-American response to his request.

His own first impulse in the crisis had been to do whatever was in his power to do to protect his country. Having fulfilled that duty, Héctor felt that his immediate responsibility now was for the preservation of his family—apparently, without the aid and cooperation of the law. For the moment, he hadn't the slightest idea how this task was to be accomplished, since whatever plan he decided on was certain to meet with the hysterical reaction of his wife when she learned that the Villas were now in actual, rather than just potential, danger. As it was necessary to inform Jesús "Eddie" at once of the run-in with Ali Kahn and his unsympathetic reception by the deputy chief, Héctor thought he would use the occasion to seek his friend's advice in the crisis. Possibly Jesús "Eddie" would feel some alarm on his own behalf, but Héctor doubted it. Nor did he find such alarm justified, since, the more Kahn tried to recall what Héctor's companion at the Taberna Aztlán had looked like, the more likely he was to see Héctor—and only Héctor—seated there among shadows in the half-dark. He tried Jesús "Eddie" on his cellphone and found him in Paco's Place downtown.

"Ah, *compadrito*," Jesús "Eddie" exclaimed, "the murderin sonsa-*bit*-ches that destroyed our Taberna and forced us to drink in a dump like this one deserve to be caught as soon as *pos*-sible and have their *cojones* fed to the pigs! Come on down here, *compinche*, and drink a coupla beers with me. The Corona's the same, anyways, and plenty cheaper than what that *ladrón* at the Taberna used to charge."

Paco's Place, on West Reinken Avenue, was a quarter or less the size of the Taberna Aztlán, with room only for a single widescreen TV. Héctor discovered Jesús "Eddie" seated at a table before it, with his feet up on a chair and a basket of popcorn beside him on the table. Jesús "Eddie's" basketball team was way behind, and already the carpet surrounding the screen lay under a thick covering of corn.

"You, a soccer fan, are lucky, *hombre*, to care nothing for these American games. Livin in Am-*er*-ica, you do not have to watch your team lose time after *time*, week after week—*hijos de puta*!" Jesús "Eddie" interrupted himself to launch a spray of popcorn at the struggling players.

Héctor, always sensitive to his shameful inability to appreciate the sports so dear to his fellow Americans, said nothing. Instead, he drew back a chair beside Jesús "Eddie," out of the line of fire, and took a handful of popcorn himself.

"S'up, *hermano*?" Jesús "Eddie" inquired. "You look like you just got fingered to run for office a-*gain*."

As he had never credited Jesús "Eddie" with being the sensitive or observant type, Héctor had to conclude that a compound of misery and fear must be smeared across his features like a facial. So be it, he told himself: He was not, in any event, the kind of *hombre* to beat around the bush.

"I met one of the terrorists from the Taberna Aztlán this afternoon," Héctor explained. "Actually, I spent almost an hour with him at his house, working on his computers. The name is Ali Kahn. I recognized him the moment I walked in the door. I know he recognized me, too."

Jesús "Eddie" grunted angrily, half-rose from his seat, and shook his fist at the favored team. Then he sat down again and gave a long, astonished whistle.

"No shit! The crazy raghead might have killed you! It is a very, very unlucky thing for you you were *re*-cognized, *compadrito*. Now, the terrorists know who to go after when they want to make a hit on some-*body*."

This was hardly in the spirit of sympathetic concern and helpfulness Héctor had been expecting.

"They know how to find you, too," he responded sharply. "For all we know, Kahn followed me this evening, on my way over here."

Jesús "Eddie" swallowed his beer the wrong way and sat for a moment, choking and spitting into his cocktail napkin. When he'd recovered, he put the bottle down and took a long, careful look around Paco's Place. Among the Stetsons and gimme caps were a cyclist's helmet and even a Bavarian alpine hat with a feather stuck in the band, but no turbans that either he or Héctor could see.

"We need to get us some pro-*tec*-tion from the cops," Jesús "Eddie" said at last.

"I asked about that when I made out my report at the station. The deputy chief said no way. Their Witness Protection is for VIPs only."

"You're a VIP. You ran for Congress."

"Yeah I did. And had to quit." Nothing, Héctor had learned to his regret, is so American as celebrity—except the abysmal obscurity that inevitably follows celebrity's loss.

Jesús "Eddie" sat in silence for several minutes, ignoring both the TV screen and the popcorn bowl.

"This is serious business, *hombre*," he concluded.

"Yeah, tell me about it."

"Looks to me like the Juárezes and the Villas better migrate for a spell, until the cops can pick up these two guys."

"I had the same idea. Only—where do we migrate to?"

"That's the question, that's the question . . . "

Jesús "Eddie" sat back and closed his eyes. Héctor himself was in need of a double shot of tequila, but the service at Paco's Place left something to be desired, and he found it impossible to get the barman's attention. While he was attempting to do this, Jesús "Eddie" opened his eyes suddenly. "I got it!" he said.

"Got what?"

"My family owns part of an old ranch out on the desert halfway between Deming and Columbus, just a house and a few out-*build*-ins. The ragheads won't never find us there. We'll go south and hang out for a while until they catch the *hijos de su madre* and send them away for a long paid vacation at Guan-*tán*-amo, courtesy of Uncle Sam."

Héctor considered. He was familiar with the general locale: an expanse of sotol and mesquite desert, flat as a drilling pad, sunstricken in summer and swept by cutting winds and sandstorms in winter, whose principal inhabitants were antelope, coyotes, rattlesnakes, and tarantulas. AveMaría, after more than twenty years in the United States, barely tolerated a roadside picnic. And he had a tough time imagining her and the family living under the same roof with the Juárezes. Beatriz had never troubled to disguise her good-natured contempt for Mexicans, illegal ones especially, while AveMaría was deeply disapproving of Jesús "Eddie's" extravagant drinking and of the influence she supposed him to have on her husband.

"How big is this place?" he asked reluctantly.

"Plenty big, plenty big! Why, at one time, my grand-*par*-ents, aunt and uncle, cousin Elena and their families were all livin there to-*geth*-

er! Lots of room for everbody, *compadrito!*"

Héctor sighed inaudibly. It seemed an offer he couldn't refuse. And it would likely not be long—not more than a week or ten days, he expected—before the Belen police, acting on his tip and Jesús "Eddie's." caught up with Abdul Kahn and his accomplice and put them safely behind bars.

"OK," he agreed resignedly, "when do we leave?"

"I don't know about the Villas," Jesús "Eddie" told him, "but the Juárezes are out of here early tomorrow *morn*-in—before the next Qassam hits."

The prospect of informing his wife and children that they would be evacuating their house overnight and going off to live indefinitely in the desert, like the Lebanese refugees on TV, seemed to Héctor more daunting even than a tour in Iraq. For courage, therefore, he ordered a final beer, fortified by a shot of rye. Had not President Bush called upon all Americans to sacrifice for the cause of freedom?

IV

Mexico Way

THOUGH HÉCTOR HAD LIVED all his life in a desert climate, he was a town kid whose closest experience of the desert itself had been to drive across it at 50 or 60 miles per hour. Now that he was actually living there, he found the reality of the experience daunting, even frightening. For Héctor, the Chihuahuan Desert was an expansive boredom relieved occasionally by some small but acute unpleasantness, like discovering a coiled rattlesnake beneath your chair after sitting down to a cup of coffee in the pale morning sun, in the intervals between onsets of winter wind and driving dust storms out of the west. As far as one could see, the Juárez ranch was surrounded by the sotol and creosotebush desert, its nearly absolute flatness relieved only by the relatively negligible Tres Hermanas Mountains to the south and the much more impressive Florida Mountains, a massive barrier of pink and rust-colored rock rising between the ranch and the pleasures and excitements of Las Cruces and El Paso fifty miles to the east as the crow flies. Between Columbus to the south and Deming, north on Highway 11, the ranch was a fifteen-mile drive from either—a long way, it seemed to Héctor, to go for "a coupla" drinks, and an even longer way home.

He'd entertained himself at first at the Pancho Villa State Park between Columbus and the international border, but its exhibits were limited (easily surpassed by the Hijos de Pancho Villa collection in Namiquipa), most of what the park had to show him was old hat, and he lost interest after only a couple of weeks. AveMaría and Contracepción resented having to drive a hundred and thirty miles round trip to shop at the Neiman Marcus in Cruces, and Contracep, who missed her friends in Belen, professed to be dying of boredom as well. Even Dubya, who'd insisted on bringing his collection of two dozen or more stuffed lions with him, was restless and fussy. Why, he demanded, several times a day, couldn't he visit the *leones* at the Lion Habitat? They were living in the desert, weren't they? Wasn't the desert where the *leones* lived? So why wouldn't Papá take him to the Habitat *now*? The worst of it, Héctor suspected, was that, for the next five years at least, he'd be unable to enjoy Las Vegas the way he'd once been able to do.

The Juárezes did better, at first. For one thing, there were only two of them. For another, Beatriz, not being a party girl, was content to spend her days doing volunteer work at Holy Family Catholic Church in Deming and her evenings watching reruns of *Seinfeld* and other syndicated sitcoms on TV. Then Jesús "Eddie" got a DUI on one of his solo trips to the bars, was lodged in the Deming jail overnight, and forfeited his driver's license for 90 days. Since Héctor spent many hours in his van each day, driving from one distant repair job to the next, he was not enthusiastic about chauffeuring his friend to the watering holes of Columbus after hours. (The Columbus taverns were fewer and less agreeable than those in Deming, by comparison almost a big city, but Jesús "Eddie" had placed the town under economic sanctions and declared it subject to a general boycott until his license had been returned to him.) Since both men had now to do their drinking at home, the house was unpleasantly crowded most evenings, everyone fighting over the TV while Jesús "Eddie" threw popcorn at the screen, a practice Beatriz seemed not to object to but which AveMaría (who disliked her husband's friend more with every passing day) deplored. (And she definitely didn't care for the way he had now of eyeing Contracepción.)

In spite of Jesús "Eddie's" assurances that the ranch house was "plenty, plenty big" with "lots of room for everybody," it was in fact very small and cramped, hardly more than a large cabin—unpainted and weathered to a grayish black streaked with brown, built of cottonwood planks hauled from the mountains, and consisting of four square rooms with drop ceilings and small windows cut into the walls. The place was heated by a coal stove that doubled as a cooking one, water had to be hauled from the well where it was raised in scanty amounts by an ancient creaking windmill, and a four-seater outhouse fifty yards away beyond the satellite dish struck the girls especially as an inadequate substitute for indoor plumbing. Each morning, Héctor awoke with the sinking feeling that he was back in Mexico, and he went to bed every evening wondering if he'd be able to return to his comfortable American home anytime within the next six months. From what he could tell by watching the Albuquerque news, the authorities had had no success so far in apprehending Ali Kahn and his associate. Héctor could not shake the uneasy suspicion that they were not even trying.

Still, living off in the desert as they were doing, away from crowds of foreigners drawn from all over the world to the flourishing communities along the Rio Grande, he felt relatively safe on the old Juárez ranch. There was some, but not much, traffic along Route 11, and the house was set back from the highway a good half-mile, at the end of a rough, unpaved drive. Apart from the antelope, hawks, eagles, and rabbits, a profusion of rattlesnakes that seemed always underfoot on warmer days, and a few stray cattle, the only life he perceived among the brush and cactus were occasional groups of dark figures far out on the desert against the sheltering Florida Mountains, trekking purposefully northward at a sustained pace. From his twenty years' experience of the United States, Héctor guessed they were hikers. Americans are prone, he'd discovered long ago, to a mania for backpacking, rock climbing, and similar strenuous and otherwise unimaginable pursuits. President Bush himself rode a mountain bike, which seemed to Héctor as crazy, almost, as snowboarding or kayaking. Well, it was all harmless enough, except for his doctor urging him to take up some equally energetic sport as a means of losing weight and keeping his blood pressure at acceptable levels without medication. Even so, Héctor marveled at these people's temerity. The Floridas were said to be infested with mountain lions, one of whom had recently killed an unwary rancher after he'd dismounted from his horse to search on foot for a lost calf up a brushy side canyon.

Living so close to the border and Las Palomas, itself not more than 150 miles from Namiquipa by relatively good roads, Héctor had a creeping sense of guilt for not taking advantage of this opportunity to visit his family in Chihuahua. He tried to alleviate his unease by promising himself to kill two birds with one stone by attending the meeting of the Hijos de Pancho Villa next June—although he had to assume, if only for his own peace of mind, that he and the family would have been able to return safely to Belen long before then. Meanwhile, for the first several weeks of his stay at the ranch, Héctor made it a point to stay out of Mexico, including Las Palomas where computer repairmen were, indeed, in great demand but where also the fees commanded by experts like himself were unconscionably low.

This was before he and Jesús "Eddie" discovered the Pink Store, an enterprising establishment combining under one roof a restaurant, crafts shop, and general store, only a few hundred yards from the border in Las Palomas and readily distinguishable by its garish exterior and the prominent ELKS sign out front. Though the Pink Store's prices reflected its popularity with the gringo tourists, a bottle of beer, in U.S. dollars, was still a bargain. Better yet, from Jesús "Eddie's" point of view, was the apparent disinclination on the part of the local *policía* to enforce whatever driving-and-drinking laws, if any, were on the books. Consequently the Pink Store was an immediate hit with the friends, a home away from their crowded abode where the pressures of two-family life were growing increasingly irksome.

It was Jesús "Eddie" who suggested that a quick once-over of somebody's computer in Las Palomas would more than cover all the beers he and Héctor could possibly consume in one evening. After that, the visits to the Pink Store became more frequent. Héctor would drive his van through the international crossing, drop Jesús "Eddie" at the store, and make a professional call or two before rejoining Jesús at the restaurant, his pockets bulging with folded-over pesos. The single drawback was the lack of a TV set—which was no disadvantage at all for Héctor, who strongly suspected that Jacinta Ruiz, the manager of the restaurant, would take a dim view of feet on the table and popcorn tossing. Jacinta was an attractive woman of about thirty-five, whose dark skin, slender figure, and lean, sinewy forearms reminded Héctor of Pancho Villa's *soldaderas* as they appeared in photographs from the Mexican Civil War.

By seven in the evening the tourists, having retreated across the border to the safety of the U.S.A. for the night, were mostly gone, and the restaurant was quiet, frequented mainly by a few elderly men seeking a peaceful alternative to the raucous and violent *tabernas* where the young hotheads looking for a girl and a fight hung out. As Héctor was the designated driver until Jesus "Eddie's" ninety-day probation was up, he limited himself to four beers a night while watching his friend drink twice as many, or more. Jesús "Eddie," who could carry his liquor like a gentleman when he wished to do so, was on his best behavior, and often Jacinta Ruiz would join them after she was through cleaning up in the kitchen and setting up for breakfast the next morning. Héctor found the dining room most elegant with its vigaed ceiling and handsome chandeliers, scarlet painted walls hung with framed paintings and milagro crosses, and life-sized statuary, beautifully handcarved from some wood he did not recognize.

124

Through the open door at the end of the restaurant, from the table at which he and Jesús "Eddie" habitually sat, a set of five carved figures about three feet tall were visible, ranged along an oaken sideboard. The figures, draped in women's clothing and wearing garden-party hats from a long-ago era, in fact were skeletons, the bony cheeks splashed with rouge, the unfleshed chests hideously exposed above the décolletage of their elaborately trimmed gowns. These statues fascinated Héctor. They reminded him of the Nuestra Señora de la Muerte in Mexico City, whose picture he'd seen in a magazine recently. The caption beneath the photo had explained that Nuestra Señora, who held a cigarette between her gumless teeth and a bottle of whiskey in one fleshless claw, was the patron saint of sinners, to whom evildoers addressed their prayers as one who understood them and their wicked ways. Trust the Catholic Church, Héctor had thought, to dream up something like that!

One evening when he had finished his quota of beers and Jesús "Eddie" continued to slake his thirst at table while conversing with Jacinta Ruiz, Héctor, drawn by the gruesome figures to explore the shop adjoining the restaurant, came upon an entirely different piece of statuary. About a foot in height, wrought in plastic and painted in lifelike colors, it was a representation of a sombreroed Centaur, mounted on a high-stepping horse and carrying a scabbarded rifle under the off saddle skirt. Héctor recognized the image at once. It was modeled from his favorite Pancho Villa photo, a copy of which hung above his desk in his study at home in Belen. It was an obvious work of art— for him, a must-have item. He picked up the statue and turned it over, thinking to find a price tag stuck on the base. Seeing nothing, he carried the figure along with him to the restaurant.

"*¿Cuánto cuesta?*" he asked Jacinta Ruiz.

She glanced at the statue contemptuously.

"Fifteen pesos, if you think it worth so much. For me, it is the ugliest thing I ever saw."

Héctor was shocked. "But it is from one of the most famous photos of Pancho ever taken!"

Jacinta Ruiz stood her ground. "It is ugly because the man himself was ugly, *un monstruo*," she insisted. "My family has lived in Palomas almost one hundred years. May Pancho Villa rot in Hell for what he did at Columbus!"

"But—you yourself are *mexicana*!"

"Yes I am *mexicana*, and proudly so." Jacinta drew the sleeves of her silk blouse over her wrists and patted the silver brooch at her throat. "But my great-grandmother, Mathilde Saenz, had many American friends, among them Maude Wright and her husband. You know who was Maude Wright, *Señor*?"

Héctor was not a paid-up Life Member of Hijos de Pancho Villa for nothing.

"Wasn't she the wife of the gringo rancher in México Pancho murd—I mean, killed on his way to attack Camp Furlong?" he ventured. "He kept her with his army until after the attack, then let her go."

"*Exacto.* Also, Maude was my grandmother's closest friend. The Saenzes and the Wrights owned neighboring ranches. Mathilde never forgave Villa for what he did to Maude and her husband—shooting him in cold blood on the steps of his own house! She always said a savage like Pancho Villa ought to have been shot in the back by his own soldiers."

Jacinta Ruiz snapped a red-painted forenail against the plastic figure. "Only the gringo tourists are interested in Pancho Villa," she concluded. "We sell thousands and thousands of dollars' worth of Villa stuff every year. It is like a sickness with them, as far as I'm concerned."

Héctor Agonistes

FOR MORE THAN A WEEK after his encounter with Jacinta Ruiz, Héctor avoided the Pink Store, finding excuses to drive Jesús "Eddie" to Geronimo's Bar & Grill in Deming—which Jesús much preferred, sanctions or no, anyway—instead. During this time the Centaur's statue stood on the top shelf of his computer hutch, where he had to make the effort to raise his eyes in order to behold the thing. Handsome as it was, the statue gave him no pleasure now but rather a sense of distress, arising from his moral confusion. In truth, Héctor found he could no longer admire it without suspecting that he really was a bit of a traitor.

He was an American, after all—not yet a citizen, granted, but citizenship would surely follow in time, once the late unpleasantness arising from his failed political candidacy was resolved. Whereas the Ruiz woman, a bona fide *mexicana* for whom Pancho Villa had fought and died, reprobated Villa and all he stood for because he'd been a relentless enemy of the gringos, certain of whom her great-grandparents had befriended. Héctor himself had few American friends besides Brother Billie Joe and Jesús "Eddie," and he wasn't sure Jesús "Eddie" counted as an American. Never before had it occurred to him that his pride in being a descendant (though a collateral one) of the Centaur might be at odds with his fervent commitment to his adoptive land, including a 100-percent adherence to the American Creed. Jacinta Ruiz had exposed the contradiction for him, and Héctor was discovering to his immense chagrin that it was not a matter he could conscientiously ignore. Nor, unhappily, was it one he felt comfortable discussing with AveMaría, who disliked Villa as a notorious polygamist and philanderer and resented both the society dues her husband sent annually to Namiquipa and the time he spent away from home each summer— "partying," as she called it, with the Hijos.

It was a good ten days before it occurred to Héctor that help was right under his nose—more precisely, just across the border in the Pink Store itself. Despite her hatred of Pancho Villa, Jacinta Ruiz was certainly *simpática*—and obviously well disposed toward his namesake, whose arm she was given to squeezing affectionately each evening on his arrival at the store and again as he left the bar, following Jesús "Eddie" out to the van. He wished he might talk with Jacinta alone, without his friend around. And when—Héctor wondered—would *that* ever happen? The possibility was unimaginable, short of Chihuahua becoming a dry state.

His chance, by some miracle, arrived soon enough, within a matter of a few days. Jesús "Eddie," stir-crazy already from living off in the boondocks and hungry for the bright lights and dark dives of the Rio Abajo, was also concerned about the state of his several rental properties in Belen, ancient 'dobes crumbling into weedy yards he'd inherited from an uncle and that he leased short-term to winos, vagabonds, and kids from the local community college. As hiding out on the border precluded working his job as a handyman around town, the income from these properties was Jesús "Eddie's" nearly sole source of support during his sojourn at the ranch, supplemented only by Beatriz's monthly disability check from Santa Fe in compensation for her late-developing color blindness that had forced her to quit her job as a beautician when she became incapable of distinguishing one tint of hair dye from another. Consequently, Jesús "Eddie" determined that he must return to Belen to make sure of his houses and collect the rent payments that had somehow failed to find their way to Rancho Juárez in his absence. Beatriz was going along as chauffeur, and both she and her husband planned on disguising themselves to escape recognition by the Muslim community in Belen. In spite of his eagerness to see them off, Héctor could not resist the desire to witness the Juárezes in whatever garb they might choose to get up in for the trip north. Ave-María had no interest in whatever sort of spectacle Beatriz and Jesús "Eddie" made when they went. She just wanted them to go.

After arguing the question back and forth, loudly, for days, the pair decided on assuming the identity of a military couple on leave from Fort Bliss, a role they reasoned should be sufficient to deter any bloody-minded would-be jihadist assassin from a violent assault on their persons. (No one, Héctor had to agree, underestimates the U.S. military.) At an Army Navy store in El Paso that advertised itself as the place where the Minutemen shopped, they purchased fatigues, combat boots, and stiff-brimmed camouflage military caps, which they wore home in the car afterward in order to acquire a feel for their new clothes. Héctor's instant reaction to the sight of the Juárezes in uniform standing outside on the turnaround was that the Immigration Office had come to arrest him at last, but the next moment he was laughing so uncontrollably he'd had to run to the outhouse and remain there a good five minutes to avoid offending his friends.

Jesús "Eddie" and Beatriz departed next morning for Belen, carrying with them an extensive shopping list made up by AveMaría, after an impassioned and tearful plea by Contracepción that she be allowed to go along to visit her friends upriver. When the Juárezes were gone at last and his daughter lay sulking face down across the bed, Héctor retired to the parlor where he had his computer hutch and put in an hour and a half on billing work, while AveMaría and Dubya went shopping in Deming. Distracted and restless, he worked without enthusiasm and knocked off finally around noon, when he wandered into the kitchen in search of lunch. Héctor was wholly unaccustomed, after twenty-one years of married life, to preparing his own meals. Now, in his wife's absence, he took four slices of bologna from the ancient icebox, placed them between two slices of white bread he found in the rusty breadbox decorated with faded hand-painted flowers, and made himself a sandwich. He wrapped the sandwich in wax paper and buttoned it into the pocket of his woolen shirt. Then he yelled at Contracep that he'd be home in an hour, lifted his parka from the peg behind the door, and walked out into the pale glare of a cold winter day. For the first time, perhaps, in his adult life, Héctor Villa was taking a walk.

Prompted by an impulse of which he was barely conscious, he wandered down the drive and across the asphalt strip of highway, crawled painfully on his belly beneath the four-strand fence, and proceeded into open desert in the direction of the mountains. The mountains resembled those with which he'd been familiar as a child in Namiquipa, but that did not explain the allure they had for him this brilliant winter afternoon. Héctor perceived these carved massifs as the faded, nearly indistinguishable background of early twentieth-century photographs in which armed troops, wrecked trains, and—in particular—a proud sombreroed figure, mounted horseback and carrying a rifle under his saddleskirt, occupied the foreground, surrounded by the immediate caliche and sotol desert. But here was a background without a subject, nothing but the empty desert across which he seemed to wade heavily, as if through a foot of sand. Héctor halted to get his breath, then moved doggedly forward again. The mountains seemed to retreat ahead of him, deeper into the empty photograph in which he moved. They were a great deal farther off than he'd imagined, viewing them from the ranch. Stopping for the fifth or sixth time, he looked behind himself and was surprised—shocked even—to see how far he'd come, though the mountains themselves appeared no nearer. It occurred to Héctor he should fortify himself for the long walk back. He looked about and spied a manzanita tree growing at the edge of an arroyo thirty yards away. Now almost completely winded, he staggered on and collapsed against its blackened trunk, beneath the web of leafless branches. Héctor worked the trunk between his shoulder blades and pulled the sandwich from his shirt, wishing he'd thought to bring a bottle of water with him. Fortunately it was winter or he might have died of thirst on the desert like the immigrants he'd seen on TV. However, the sandwich tasted good to him, though he'd spread Contracep's tasteless brand of mustard on the bread instead of the spicy brand he preferred.

Héctor had finished the sandwich and was regretting having used mustard at all on account of his now acute thirst when he heard the measured crunch of shoes on gravel and looked up to see seven people, four men and three women, approaching along the bottom of the arroyo. All were Hispanic, dark-skinned, wearing jeans, torn parkas over snap-button Western shirts, and sneakers, and carrying packs on their backs. The men wore their hair almost as long as the women's, but it didn't appear to have been washed as recently. The lead man stopped and stiffened like a pointer dog when he caught sight of Héctor beneath the tree. Then he appeared to relax and moved forward again with confidence, baring a double-row of square white teeth in a wide grin beneath his black mustache.

"¡*Buenas tardes, compadre! ¿Adónde va usted?*"

Héctor gave him a wary look. In Belen, strangers never spoke to each other, whether on the street or at the mall.

"*A ninguna parte.*"

"*¿Y de dónde viene?*"

Héctor shrugged. "From around here." He'd noticed the leader carried a plastic bottle slung across his shoulder on a nylon cord. "Can you spare a swallow of water? I forgot to bring any with me."

He assumed these hikers were from Douglas, which these days had a large Hispanic population. Héctor was impressed. He couldn't imagine assimilating to the point of taking up a kick-ass Anglo sport like backpacking, himself.

The leader squinted, leaning forward on the palo verde pole he'd cut and trimmed for a walking stick.

"How is it you come across with no water, no food, *hermano*?" he asked sternly. "Have you not read the survival guide the government hands out to everyone? Our people are dying like flies in the desert every day. Now I must risk dying of thirst, too, because you did not trouble yourself to come prepared."

Héctor, perceiving the truth at last, felt like a fool. With great dignity, he stood from under the tree and confronted the interlopers.

"You have made a mistake," he told the alien. "I am an American" (he had almost added "citizen") "living in New Mexico. My home is over there" (he pointed toward the ranch that appeared as a speck in the endless desert stretching west to the Arizona border). "I have lived in this country for twenty years and I'm used to having all the water and food I want, whenever I want it. I don't have to carry it around on my back, like a *tortuga*."

All six illegal aliens, grouped close together now as if for self-protection, eyed him with hostility.

"*Claro*," their leader said, coldly. "Are you then a *hermano* or a *gringo*? It is Eulalio Guzmán who asks."

It occurred to Héctor for the first time that these people might be armed and dangerous.

"I'm both," he said at last, trying to hold his voice steady. "Don't worry," he added quickly, perceiving a yellow glint in Guzmán's eye. "I'm not going to report you to the *migra*."

The alien smiled sardonically. "Then you are a *hermano*," he concluded, "and it is a lucky thing for you, too. Do you remember how Pancho Villa once served the *gringos*, many years ago but not so many miles from where we stand now?"

Héctor wanted to tell him he'd forgotten more about Pancho Villa than the other man would learn in a lifetime, but he held his tongue instead.

"And now," the alien continued, "you may have a swallow of water—if you still want it, *por supuesto*. Do you?"

Héctor didn't.

Attempting a dignified pace, he waded off into the desert in the direction of the ranch that seemed impossibly far away. A sense of pride forbade him to look back over his shoulder until he'd gone a couple of hundred yards, and by then the invaders had vanished among the mesquite and sotol. More than an hour later, dry-mouthed, with aching lungs and sore hip sockets, Héctor arrived home where he was greeted by his tearful wife, who in panic at his disappearance had reported him missing to the Luna County Search and Rescue a half-hour before.

He carried the cellphone outdoors where the reception was better, dialed Search and Rescue, and canceled the alarm. (It occurred to him to report the invading aliens while he was at it, but he thought better of this.) Then he climbed into his van and drove south on highway 11, toward Columbus and the Pink Store. It was too early in the day to begin drinking, but Héctor was not in search of alcohol this afternoon. He needed to have a talk with Jacinta Ruiz, and he couldn't wait until the sun had crossed over the yardarm to do it.

Villa Blanco, Villa Negro

REVEALED IN THE HEADLIGHTS of the van, Las Palomas had never looked so depressing to Héctor as it did in the twilight of the late winter afternoon. Indeed it appeared to him as positively sinister, a ghost town in which the few flesh-and-blood inhabitants were the apparitions, and the thronging specters from the past the true living beings. He considered, in that instant, taking a U-turn in the potholed street and making a run back across the border for home. Instead he drove on to the Pink Store and parked directly beneath the Elks sign on the north side of the building. Jacinta Ruiz, after all, was no one to be afraid of. And Héctor felt himself, suddenly, in greater need of a drink than he remembered ever feeling. Thank the Lord, he thought, Jesús "Eddie" wasn't along this time to share it with him.

Héctor locked the van, having taken care to leave nothing of value in view on the front seat, and entered the bar, brushing past the Tarahumara woman who waited just behind the door with her hand extended, palm up. He passed round the end of the service counter that had once served as the bar and went on to the dining room, where eight or ten *campesinos* in tight jeans, new cowboy boots, and filthy quilted vests drank beer and smoked unfiltered cigarettes as they faced the wide-screen TV. There was no sign of Jacinta Ruiz. Héctor sat at a table as far away from the Mexicans as he could get and pretended to devote his attention to the TV, where a soccer game was being broadcast from Venezuela. Héctor, though an *aficionado*, violently disapproved of Venezuela's president, who only recently had denounced President Bush as the Devil from the rostrum of the U.N. General Assembly in New York. Therefore he did his best to ignore the game, sitting with a vacant expression as he waited for Jacinta to show herself. Through the door on the far side of the room he could look into the store, with its arrangement of gaudy pottery and the ceramic bowl sinks that were so popular these days (AveMaría was keen to have one installed in the house in Belen), where he'd bought the Pancho Villa statue. Héctor wished now he'd brought the image along with him in order to return it, assuming Jacinta Ruiz would agree to take the thing back.

"*¡Buenas noches*, Héctor! *¿Cómo estas?*"

He turned from the TV where the Venezuelan team had just scored a goal on the Mexican one and saw Jacinta, holding a tray laden with a half-dozen dripping longneck bottles and smiling at him.

"Can you not watch the game at home on American TV?" Jacinta asked. "And where is your *compañero* this evening? Without Jesús, I almost did not recognize you—sitting alone like this!"

She passed behind him to the *campesinos'* tables and placed the bottles, one by one, before the disgruntled men. "*¡Que se chinguen los venezolanos!*" one of them urged vehemently through his drooping mustaches. Héctor observed they were not placing bets, no doubt because nobody was willing to make a wager against the Mexican team. He noted also that Jacinta took care to collect all the money owed her on the latest round.

"And what can I get for you tonight, *mi querido*?" she asked, setting a pink cocktail napkin down before him on the table.

Her low, solicitous voice was soothing to Héctor—better even than drink, it seemed to him. However, he'd driven all this way, and it didn't seem polite not to order anything.

"I'll have a Corona," Héctor said, "and a cup of menudo." He hadn't intended to order food. Perhaps it was the homey, almost intimate, atmosphere of the Pink Store that provoked his hunger.

His cellphone went off while he was waiting for the soup to come out from the kitchen.

"*Oye! Oye!* Héctor, it is your wife calling! Please tell your son he must take his bath, otherwise you will give him a good licking when you get home!"

"What's he doing now?"

"Watching Animal Planet. There's a two-hour special about lions in Africa. It isn't suitable for a kid Dubya's age, anyway—how the lions eat their cubs so the lionesses can go into heat right away and get pregnant again. Also the natives are all Islamists, apparently."

"Tell him to turn the TV off and get in the tub—*pronto*."

"I turned it off already, can't you hear? That's what all the yelling going on in the background's about."

Jacinta Ruiz placed the soup cup before him and withdrew tactfully.

"Well, put the kid on and I'll give him what-for."

When he'd delivered the virtual thrashing over the phone, Héctor discovered he was in need of another beer. Jacinta brought it and sat down across the table, from where she had a view both of the *campesinos* and of the entrance door at the far end of the room. At this time of year tourists were few, while the drinking population of Las Palomas seemed to have settled in early at one or another of the several watering holes in town. The time, it seemed to Héctor, was ripe for the conversation he'd come for, if only he could find a means of initiating it. He hadn't felt so tongue-tied and awkward since the occasion of his first date with a girl named María-Brígida, more years ago than he cared to think of, in Namiquipa.

"So what did your wife have to say when you came home with that hideous statue the other day?" Jacinta wanted to know.

Héctor, in his delighted astonishment, wanted to kiss the girl. (It had not gone this way with María-Brígida, who, so far from cooperating with his conversational—and other—plans, had begun the evening by mentioning she'd never kissed a boy without going to Confession afterward.) Speechless with gratitude, he was unable to answer immediately, except to utter a few babbling disconnected syllables.

"She—she hasn't seen it yet," he confessed at last. "I hid it away in my office in order to . . . think about it for a little while."

"Oh?" Jacinta Ruiz sounded puzzled.

"Yes . . . You see, I have always regarded Pancho Villa as a great—a very great—man. He is my hero, from whom indeed I am descended. You should know, I am a member of Los Hijos de Pancho Villa in Namiquipa," he added proudly.

"*¿Verdad?*" Jacinta sounded more amused than otherwise.

"*¡Sí!* In fact, I am Keeper of the Doors. All my life, I have heard nothing but good spoken of General Villa—except from Americans, of course. But the other day, I heard from you a different story."

Jacinta Ruiz frowned and stared at the tabletop.

"It is true, I do not admire the man—in fact, I hate and despise him!"

"But why? You are, after all, *mexicana!*"

"And you," she said, smiling, "are *americano*—are you not? It seems to me we have had this conversation before."

Héctor, in his confusion, did not answer her at once.

"I—I am *mexicanoamericano*, of course." Or was it *americano-*

mexicano? It had seemed all that was settled in his mind, once and forever, twenty years ago. Now he realized he did not know what to think.

"Whether you are Mexican or American," Jacinta told him, "the bandit Villa fought and killed your people—Mexicans and Americans both—on either side of the border. He was a thief and a murderer, not a revolutionary or a soldier at all. I suppose you have read about Villa at Juárez, Villa at Celaya, Villa at Parral, Villa in Mexico City—Villa at Columbus. I mentioned to you, not long ago, the business of Maude Wright and her husband. But are you acquainted with the story of Villa and the McKinney Ranch—this side of the border, only a few miles from here?"

Héctor was. Unfortunately, the event was less pretty even than the incident involving the Wrights, which indeed had taken place only the day before. Villa and his army of 399 soldiers were encamped within striking distance of Columbus, which they attacked the following night. That morning Villa sat cross-legged beside his campfire drinking coffee when three horsebackers appeared on a rise several hundred yards away. One of the riders waved in recognition, and then all three put their horses forward at a trot toward the camp. They were Arthur McKinney of the Palomas Land and Cattle Company, an old acquaintance, and two of his ranch hands. While the cowboys sat their horses to watch from a distance, McKinney approached the fire and inquired of the General how the revolution was going. Villa assured him it went very well and ordered one of his men to serve Señor McKinney a cup of coffee. The two men chatted casually together for several minutes. At last, Villa remarked in a friendly manner, "You know, Arturo, I'm making war against the gringos, too, and I guess I'll just start right here with you." Quick as lightning, a Villista threw a loop of barbwire around McKinney's neck. The rancher, ready to take a joke, was in the middle of an appreciative laugh when his eyes bulged out suddenly and his tongue protruded. A second Villista tossed the other end of the wire over a cottonwood branch and jerked the rancher off the ground, above the tin cup rolling in the dust. Seeing their boss suspended in midair, the cowboys took a deep seat and spurred their horses to a run. Before they'd covered a hundred yards, Villa's men roped them from their saddles and dragged them to death behind their own horses. While the incident was hardly among the most lurid episodes in the great man's career—compared, for instance, with his shooting of ninety Carrancista "bitches" at Torreón in November 1916—Héctor found it distinctly embarrassing in the context of his conversation with Jacinta Ruiz.

"Yes," he agreed in a constrained voice, "I know about . . . all that."

"To read of such things in books is not the same as hearing about them from one's own family. Mathilde Saenz—my grandmother—was a friend of the McKinneys, as well as the Wrights. Everyone was friends with everyone in the border country in those days, *mexicanos* and *americanos* alike—even the Indians, some of them. *¿Y por qué no?* We were all neighbors, living in a hostile land, reliant upon one another for help and cooperation. But where is the monument to that, I want to know? Instead, there is Pancho Villa State Park—demanded by Mexicans in Palomas and Columbus, paid for by the Americans in Santa Fe! *¡Santa María!* Whenever I drive by that *maldito letrero,* I want to get out of the car and chop it down!"

Jacinta Ruiz's black eyes sparked, her scarlet upper lip curled as she spoke, and her shapely body went rigid with contempt and defiance. She looked very proud—and also, Héctor could not help noticing, very beautiful. He tried assuring himself he'd never recognized her beauty before—and shrank in shame from this attempt at such gross self-deception.

"I must see to my tables," Jacinta said abruptly, rising from her chair and smoothing her skirt behind her. "Do you, too, desire more beer?"

"No thanks," Héctor said quickly. "I need to be getting on home now for supper, before my wife becomes worried for me."

Her knowing, wholly sympathetic, smile confounded him.

"When Jesús returns from Belen," Jacinta Ruiz assured him, "she will not be so worried, and then you can sit late with me again. *Buenas noches,* Héctor."

Twenty-five miles up the highway, in another country, AveMaría, FOX News, a good meal, and bed awaited him. Héctor paid his tab, put a generous tip down beside it, and went out into the shadowed streets of Las Palomas. It seemed to him he could hear, after 90 years, the echo of battle just across the border, where one half of the still undreamed-of Héctor had fought the other half with rifle, sword, and case knife, in the predawn darkness splashed by the gutter and smoke of blazing pitchpine torches brandished aloft.

The Enemy in Plain View

FOLLOWING HIS CONVERSATION with Jacinta Ruiz, Héctor took down from the shelf the statue of the Centaur that had been gathering a coat of the fine yellow dust blown in from the Chihuahuan Desert through chinks in the ranch-house walls and put it away in the closet, and he did not visit the Pink Store again until after Jesús "Eddie" returned from Belen more than a week later. Even then he found excuses to hang out at Geronimo's in Deming instead, until Jesús "Eddie" protested. "Listen, *hombre*, it is safer drinkin in Mexico, away from the interstate where the terrorists are. Did you know that Indians—those black ones from India, not the Apache—own two motels in Deming? Not all Indians are Buddhists, *compadrito*. Millions and millions of them are Islamists, wantin to come here to this country to answer the phones for us! You can smell the curry from one end of the town to the *o*-ther! Who knows if Ali Kahn has friends there to watch us, Héctor! Besides—the beer is cheaper at the Pink Store, while that Jacinta Ruiz—she *likes* us, *compadrito*!" Jesús "Eddie" finished with a lecherous smirk at his friend, accompanied by a dig in the ribs with his elbow. He'd missed the presence of both Contracepción and Jacinta during his sojourn upriver.

So Héctor consented, with acute misgivings, to pay the Pink Store another visit. He was in a grudging mood to start with, a reflection in part of his family's simmering resentment at the Juárezes' return to the ranch house. Héctor was too honest a man to overlook the fact that the place was, after all, the property of his friend—or anyway of the Juárez family—and that Jesús "Eddie" and Beatriz had shown the Villas an act of great kindness and generosity in allowing them to hide out here in a time of peril. Only—life had been so comfortable, relatively speaking, in their absence! Contracepción had appropriated to herself the second bedroom and carried the single TV in there, against AveMaría's and Dubya's vociferous protests. (In this dispute, Héctor had taken his daughter's part, inviting his wife's sympathy on behalf of a teen-age girl marooned on a frigid desert in winter and deprived of friends, school, and shopping, and promising Dubya access to Animal Planet for one full hour before bedtime.) It had not helped that the Juárezes had arrived without warning from Belen to find most of Contracep's wardrobe, including a voluminous assortment of girlish underthings, mixed with piles of CDs and magazines, spread across the bed and around the room. Though Jesús "Eddie" had been gratifyingly nonchalant about the mess, Beatriz had seemed somewhat miffed. And now the holiday season was coming, with the dismal prospect of the two families having to endure Christmas together under a single (and rather narrow, as well as leaky) roof. Jesús "Eddie" had reported that Belen continued to be amok with rampaging A-rabs, so the chances of their returning home for the holidays appeared less than nothing.

"OK," Héctor agreed, "but only for a couple of beers. I need to be up early to drive to Silver City in the morning. Anyway, AveMaría doesn't like it when I stay out partying until eleven or eleven-thirty at night."

"Beatriz didn't use to, neither," Jesús "Eddie" told him. "Said she expected her husband to stay home nights and *talk* to her. I said, 'When did I ever do anythin when I'm home cep drink beer and watch TV?' And what do you think was her answer to that, *hombre*? Said, 'You know, you're right. This way, I get to watch *Seinfeld*, stead of havin to watch you watch *spor*-ts programs!'"

Because Héctor's van had just enough gas to take them as far as Deming in the morning and gasoline was at nearly $3.50 per gallon in Columbus, they took Jesús "Eddie's" pickup. Héctor got behind the wheel, as Jesús's license was suspended for weeks yet. He drove slowly—so slowly that Jesús "Eddie" protested.

"*Compadrito*, you drive like an old *An*-glo woman with blue hair! This is a Dodge diesel, not a Buick Park *Av*-enue. I have a thirst, *hombre*! At this speed, we arrive at midnight and have to sleep *o*-ver!"

Héctor, goaded by the thought of such a catastrophe, goosed the engine to 70 mph and less than a quarter of an hour later the truck rattled across the final cattle guard and was waved through at the border crossing by the sleepy Mexican officer seated before a flickering portable TV set.

"He knows us by now," Jesús "Eddie" boasted. "We could bring a load of guns through here, no *trou*-ble—start our own Mexican Revolution! *That* would get the Anglos' at-*ten*-tion, *hombre*!"

At the Pink Store, Jacinta Ruiz seemed happy to see them again.

"*¡Ah, Señor Jesús!*" she greeted Jesús "Eddie." "I am so glad you are back with us! And now Héctor's wife will not worry when he stays out late at night!"

There were fewer drinkers than usual in the restaurant, and Jacinta—to Héctor's painful discomfort—had plenty of time to sit with him and Jesús "Eddie." While she was pleasant to both of them, her manner with Héctor seemed to him special, combining coyness with a feline concentration Jesús "Eddie" failed to observe but that flattered and excited Héctor, in spite of himself. He had never known a woman like Jacinta Ruiz, he thought—at least, such a woman had not shown such interest in him in a long, long time; not, so far as he could remember, since before his marriage. Reminded in this way of his marital vows, Héctor felt very guilty indeed.

To rid himself of the bad feeling, he drank more beer than he ought to have done and made no protest as Jesús "Eddie" ordered one round after the other. They sat later than usual at the Pink Store. It was a quarter to midnight when the two men told Jacinta good night and wandered out into the frozen desert in search of the pickup. Héctor offered to drive, but Jesús "Eddie" said it was OK—he felt sober as the Pope and knew a back road detour through the desert that would take them home safely without risking an encounter with State Patrolman Rudy Cabeza de Vaca along Highway 11. "We can't afford to both of us lose our licenses," he added. Héctor, who was seeing double, felt content to let his friend have his way. The truck swerved unintentionally as it passed through the border crossing, but the guards on both sides of the international line appeared to notice nothing amiss and allowed the Dodge to vanish into the darkness beyond the pooled light of the arc lamps. When Jesús "Eddie" had driven only a couple of miles toward Columbus, he hit the brakes hard and brought the truck to a stop, cursing. Twisted round in the seat to stare behind himself through the rear window of the cab, he backed rapidly past two blizzard posts to a Powder River gate set into the barbwire fence at the head of a two-track dirt road.

"Here we are, *hombre*," Jesús "Eddie" said. "Hey, I almost missed the goddamn *turn*. The gate ain't locked. Just lift the catch and swing it wide enough to let the truck through. We'll be home in forty, forty-five minutes, and f--k Cabeza de Vaca. He's the one had my license pulled in the first *place*."

The road, which was narrow and badly rutted, cut west into the desert across a nearly unbroken expanse of creosote bush and mesquite thickets that closed up in places, scraping the side panels of the pickup and snagging the tow mirrors. The ruts shunted the truck back and forth in the track and canted it steeply over, on one side first and then the other, as the headlights heaved up toward the night sky, then plunged to illuminate the bottom of a dry wash or hollow ahead. Jackrabbits bounded across the pale ribbon of frozen clay, and once the white belly and underwings of an owl swooped low across the windshield and merged with the shadows where, less than an instant before, a rabbit had vanished. Jesús "Eddie" drove very fast, prompting Héctor to take a tight grip on the handle mounted above the door. A thousand galaxies of stars, brilliant in the black sky above the light path cut by the headlights, wheeled overhead as the pickup, locked into the deeply rutted caliche, followed the turning, twisting road. Here and there a solitary ranch light burned far out on the desert, riding the darkness like a distant ship on a nocturnal sea.

Other roads, some hardly more than parallel scratches between the sotol cacti that stood like suddenly alerted men in the twin light beams, the rest barely distinguishable from the track they were following, diverged at intervals to the right and left, so that Héctor worried Jesús "Eddie" would lose his way among them, if in fact he hadn't lost it already, and that the two of them would freeze to death overnight in the desert wilderness. But Jesús seemed confident in his sense of direction and presently they came to a sizable dry wash, fifty feet across and ten or fifteen deep, coursing between vertical banks of clay overhung by brush. Here the track, descending by a steep ramp of dirt and loose gravel, joined the wash and commenced to run along its sandy bottom, following in the wide meanders. Héctor did not at all like the look of this wash, inescapable from within its sheer earthen walls, but he had no choice except to hold his peace and trust in God—and Jesús "Eddie." He was wishing that it were God who was driving, and Jesús looking down benignly from behind the starry firmament above, when the truck rounded a bend and the lights, reaching two hundred yards up the narrow canyon, revealed a dozen or so figures ahead entering the next bend in the wash. Héctor's immediate thought, that these people must be bandits, was corrected on the instant by the realization that this was not Mexico and that, in any case, bandits do not hunt their victims in the bottoms of dried-up creek beds in the midst of unpeopled deserts. As he watched, the figures, acting perturbed, turned to glance behind themselves before disappearing around the bend at a redoubled pace.

"Illegal aliens," Jesús "Eddie" said tersely, stepping on the accelerator. "We'll be on them in no time—ain't no way they can climb out of this wash. It may be we'll just have to run them *down*—eh, *hombre*?"

From past the bend, they saw the aliens ahead of them once more, much closer now and already running, spread out across the bottom.

"What if they're armed?" Héctor asked nervously. Many years ago, as a young man, he'd been compelled to accept the fact that, in spite of being a descendant of General Villa, he was not, by nature, a brave man.

"I got a pistol under the seat," Jesús "Eddie" assured him—as if, Héctor thought resentfully, that was a satisfactory answer to his question.

They were less than a hundred yards from the group when it broke suddenly, scattering across the creek bed to take cover behind boulders, pieces of driftwood, and clumps of brush. Some of the figures moved with the lithe, muscular athleticism of men, others with a woman's slower, wide-hipped gait. These also appeared to be dressed more warmly against the cold, the heads well covered with what looked to be dark woolen hats.

"They're *A-rabs*!" Jesús "Eddie" shouted. "Islamists! Terrorists! Not *mexicanos* at all! The guys have beards, and the women are wearin burgers over their faces, just like on TV! *Hombre*—it is a trap Ali Kahn has set for us! Of course, they are heavily *arm*-ed. Now is no time for stupid bravery, *compadre*! We must escape with our lives and warn the Border Patrol in Deming."

He gunned the engine and the truck surged forward in the sandy track, fishtailing, its tires spinning and whining in the sand. Héctor sat stunned, watching the canyon widen gradually ahead. He'd had no idea coming across the border was so simple, so easy a thing— for Mexicans, *claro*, but not for Islamists. Should he alert the White House, where he still had name recognition? By this time tomorrow, the gang could be in Albuquerque—or on their way cross-country to

Washington, D.C. Fortunately, Jesús "Eddie" had recognized the terrorists at once for what they were. To Héctor, they'd appeared similar to the group he'd encountered near the ranch house not long before—except for these women wearing their hair tied up in dark kerchiefs.

"What can the Border Patrol do?" Héctor asked doubtfully. "Illegals come through here all the time. I met a group myself when you were in Belen.

"Of course," he added quickly, "those ones were Mexicans, not Mohammedans."

Jesús did not answer straightaway. At last he declaimed, in theatrical tones: "*Compadrito*—it is time for Jesús 'Eddie' and his friend, Héctor *Vi*-lla, to take *ac*-tion! Together, we will defend our beloved *coun*-try—the Rio Ab-*a*-jo!—against the foreign enemy."

But Héctor was not really listening. How (he wondered) had Pancho Villa managed to make it across the border to attack Columbus? There had been a Border Patrol in 1916, hadn't there? He couldn't recall having ever read anything about it.

Cupid's Thunderbolt

IN THE WEEKS following the encounter with the Islamist aliens in
the *arroyo*, Jesús "Eddie" and Héctor were men possessed by a single idea, though not the same one. Jesús thought only of joining up
with the recently formed Critter Company, a militia group based in El
Paso but with a chapter in Deming, and dedicated to fighting Islamists
at the border. As for Héctor, his sole, overwhelming thought was to
get home to Belen with his family, far from the bewitching siren at the
Pink Store in Las Palomas.

Never in twenty-something years of married life had he been
tempted by another woman—until now. Héctor struggled to assure
himself that his desire for Jacinta Ruiz was completely natural, therefore entirely normal. Adultery is as American as apple pie, and just as
healthy. Indeed, it is positively pro-American, as anyone who watch-
es TV and reads *People* at the barbershop or on the checkout line at
the supermarket knows. And yet, for some reason he couldn't fath-
om, he was unable to acknowledge that yielding to his male instincts
by cheating on AveMaría was acceptable behavior. In what he clearly recognized to be a failure of imagination and nerve, Héctor blamed
only himself. Had he come to the United States as a child, perhaps he
might be more completely acculturated to modern, progressive American ways. Instead, the notion of infidelity stuck in his craw like a beer-
can tab in a magpie's gullet—except when he sat drinking with Jesús
"Eddie" in the Pink Store bar, waiting for his friend to visit the toilet
and leave him and Jacinta alone together for three precious minutes.
It was why, every time, he attempted to talk Jesús "Eddie" into driving
to Deming instead. In these efforts he regularly failed, and this failure Héctor also blamed on himself. Obviously, he wasn't being very
persuasive, and he knew all too well the reason for this. When the
time came for "a coupla" of drinks after dinner, Héctor wished to be
nowhere in the world but in the mesmerizing presence of Jacinta Ruiz.

In vain he worked at firing Jesús "Eddie's" enthusiasm for the
Critter Company to still greater heat, as a distraction from the cheap
beer and attractive company at the Pink Store. (Jesús, though not

as smitten with the girl as Héctor was, had ceased digging him in the ribs and offering lewd encouragement to extramarital pleasures. Having given up on Contracepción—for now, anyway—after living under the same roof with her for weeks without eliciting the slightest sign of interest from the girl, Jesús had recently become distinctly rivalrous in the presence of Jacinta and Héctor.) At this formative stage in their organization, the Critters met only twice a week, once at the chapter leader's home in Deming on Sunday and again the following Saturday morning for military training at the border adjacent to Pancho Villa State Park. The Critter Company had been founded to compete with the Minutemen, whom it considered unsound on the immigration issue on account of their unwillingness to raid across the international line onto Mexican soil. Its name was borrowed from Gen. Nathan Bedford Forrest's celebrated Confederate cavalry, of which the Critter's leader—a German-born American named Wolfgang Mitternacht from the Air Force base at Alamogordo—had learned from reading Shelby Foote's three-volume history of the Civil War. As none of the Critters, including Mitternacht, could ride a horse, the men were obliged to train on foot, dressed in appropriately critterish garb in which they resembled Rendezvous reenactors on the upper Green River. The Company's relaxed schedule left Jesús "Eddie" plenty of time for beer drinking at the Pink Store, giving Héctor little room for maneuver but allowing him the consoling thought that, at least, he never permitted himself the company of Jacinta Ruiz without the presence of a chaperone. In the end, encouraged by Jesús's enthusiasm for the pleasures of hiking around in the wintertime desert with a heavy pack on his back and a pistol on his hip, Héctor himself enlisted in the Critter Company, more to divert his mind from Jacinta than from the conviction that anybody, short of the 150,000 troops in Iraq, could do anything to control illegal immigration across the southwestern border. (Not even President Bush believed that.)

Héctor had always counted as one of the many advantages of early expatriation his avoidance of military service in either one of his countries of residence. Now in his forties, with a slight paunch and not what one would call "in shape," he'd been apprehensive of the discipline militia training entailed. His first morning in the field, attempting to stand upright under the weight of the Jansport daypack on the hardpan desert floor with an icy wind slashing through his buckskin suit and whipping the leather fringes along his legs and arms while Wolfgang Mitternacht strode up and down bawling orders from under his pulled-down coonskin cap, Héctor already regretted having signed up with the Critters. Why was it necessary to learn to salute, to make an about-face, to sound off, to assume formation, to march in step? This wasn't the Charge of the Light Brigade, was it? The Minutemen's routine amounted to sitting out in lawn chairs under umbrellas, drinking beer and panning the scrub across the border through binoculars—he'd seen it with his own eyes during that unfortunate incident over in Arizona. By lunchtime, he understood he'd made one of the bigger mistakes of his life. His throat was parched by the dry air, his lungs ached with the cold, and the pressing weight of the pack seemed to be telescoping his spine like a portable fishing rod. Beside him, Jesús "Eddie" was blue in the face and looked to be on the verge of heart attack. The twenty-five or thirty other Critters, too, were obviously done in.

At twelve noon precisely General Mitternacht ordered them to fall out, and the exhausted men had already commenced to stagger toward their pickup trucks when an unfamiliar voice issued a countermanding order. "Hold it right there, dudes!" Héctor raised his head exhaustedly and perceived, through reddened, wind-teared eyes, a group of tourists from Pancho Villa State Park aiming a battery of video cameras at the Critter Company. Numbly, insensibly, he stumbled ahead on a zigzag course toward Jesús "Eddie's" Dodge.

"Anyone up for beer at the Pink Store?" one of the Critters called in a weak, breathless howl like the cry of a gutshot coyote.

The Pink Store! The words rang in Héctor's ears like alien sounds from another dimension in space. He hadn't had a single thought of Jacinta Ruiz, not one, in the three hours since training exercises had begun at 9 A.M. Now, he found, he couldn't think of anything else—except beer and a warming shot of whiskey.

The Critters, crowding through into the bar in full regalia, caused a considerable stir at the Pink Store where the male half of Las Palomas's leisure class sat over drinks, enjoying a peaceful Saturday afternoon. Héctor had a glimpse of Jacinta's startled face before the onslaught, and then of her nubile figure bending and swaying gracefully from the waist as she hastily pulled tables together. Wolfgang

Mitternacht took a seat at the head of the company and sat with his hands on his knees, staring truculently about as if he would challenge someone to a sword duel. Héctor tried to catch Jacinta's eye, but she went off behind the bar for cocktail napkins, apparently without having recognized him.

Jacinta was called to the kitchen before she could return with the napkins and was away for some time. Mitternacht was instantly impatient. He scowled, and drummed loudly with his fingers on the table. Then he reached around, seized a drained beer mug from the table behind him, and commenced banging the wood with it while he shouted for beer in a field-marshal voice. At the second vociferation the Mexicans set down their bottles and stared, as conversation in the bar ceased. Héctor shrank into his seat, wishing he were less conspicuously dressed.

To his huge relief, Jacinta Ruiz returned at that moment from the kitchen with an order pad and pencil in hand.

"*¿Alguien me llamó?*" she asked politely.

Wolfgang Mitternacht gazed upon her with contempt.

"Speak English," he ordered abruptly.

But Héctor was fed up with the *tipo*, whether he was his military superior or not. "She doesn't have to speak English," he interrupted in a firm voice. "She's in her own country over here. This is Mexico, remember."

Mitternacht started as if he'd been shot, and glared at him.

"But all this"—he gestured inclusively with his hand—"all this belonged to America once!"

"No, it didn't," Héctor corrected. "It's the other way around." Apparently, the German educational system was as poor as the American one, he thought.

"*¡Héctor!*" It was Jacinta who spoke to him. "I didn't recognize you in that Indian getup! Are you all supposed to be Apache? You must be shooting a movie or something!"

"We're the Critter Company!" Jesús "Eddie," sitting farther down the table, sounded insulted. "Guardin the border to keep the Is-*lam*-ists out of the Rio Ab-*a*-jo!"

"And Jesús too! I have to tell you guys, I haven't seen any Muslims come through here lately."

"*We* did!" Jesús "Eddie" informed her. "Just a week ago, at *night*, drivin home from here! Wearing them black burgers over their faces, and everthin!"

"*Me acuerdo de eso.*" Jacinta's face was poker straight. "I was worried for you that evening. I have not forgotten a man who left here one night after many drinks and drove off the road into the *arroyo* to avoid hitting what he said was a *fantasma.*"

General Mitternacht, recovered from his shock at Héctor's insubordination, recalled the more important thing.

"Beer!" he shouted, waving the empty mug in her face.

"You are *alemán*?" Jacinta inquired. "We see many of your people here, from Alamogordo and Fort Bliss. It seems they use El Norte as a crossing point to come across the border into México. But we *mexicanos* do not mind—so long as not too many come here, of course."

Héctor caught up with her just outside the bar, on her way to the kitchen to pick up an order.

"Jacinta," he said earnestly, "I am very sorry. That ma—that *patán*—who insulted you just now, he is not my friend. I owe you my deepest apologies. Please believe me when I say that I did not bring him or these others here—in fact, it was them who brought Jesús 'Eddie' and me!"

She was smiling at him now. Héctor felt immeasurably relieved.

"I know. I have seen some of them, including the German, drinking here before. Only not dressed up, the way they are today."

Héctor found that he was shaking with emotion.

"I should have hit him for talking to you that way," he stammered.

Her kiss came as fast as a striking snake—but honeyed, and full on the mouth. His arms were around her, and he had the confused impression that she, not he, had placed them there. They held together for what felt to Héctor a measureless interval beyond time, before Jacinta released him suddenly and took a step backward.

"I must go now," she said in a low voice, "and take drinks out to your . . . friends. I will see you again very soon, Héctor?"

Héctor did not return to the bar right away. Instead he went on to the room marked CABALLEROS, where he washed his hands thoroughly with soap and water. Then he brushed his hair carefully with a pocket comb, tilting his head first at one angle and then another. He did this even though he hardly recognized the face staring back at him from the small mirror set into a gaudy gilt frame, hand-painted and hand-carved from wood. Indeed, he scarcely saw the face at all. Héctor Villa was in a state of shock.

He sat dazed while the Critters boasted to one another of their training exploits and discussed the gear they needed for deployment. Having drunk the first beer almost at a swallow, he lingered over the second until the frost vanished from the outside of the bottle and the bubbles subsided within it. Héctor could not tell whether he had just experienced a resounding triumph or suffered a terrible defeat. Like Zerlina confronted by the amorous Don, he wanted, and yet he didn't want.

What he particularly failed to understand was why it was all such a big deal in the first place. Why, Héctor wondered, were men like this? Why couldn't they be content with just one woman? Why was it that kissing another woman, or a thousand women, seemed irresistibly desirable, when kissing her was no different, after all, from kissing your wife? It wasn't important, was it? Then why did he feel, in this earth-moving instance, that it was infinitely so?

Had the Critter Company been meeting at the Taberna Aztlán in Belen, Héctor might have been tempted to stop by Our Lady afterward for Saturday-afternoon Confession. He escaped the Pink Store under cover of twenty-five jostling Critters, without Jacinta Ruiz seeing him leave.

In the Looking Glass

THE HOLIDAYS were fast approaching, and for the first time in his life Héctor could find no joy in the prospect of the Christmas season. Homesick, guilt-ridden, pinched in his wallet by his irregular business schedule, and worn down by the rigors of patrol with the Critter Company, he felt physically and mentally exhausted. The lack of privacy at the ranch house rubbed his nerves raw, and so did his wife's nagging and his daughter's incessant vocalizing. AveMaría had insisted the family begin attending services at the Assemblies of God church in Lordsburg, which meant a 160-mile round trip every Sunday. (She persisted even after he'd explained to her, patiently, that his Sunday church obligations conflicted with his sworn duties as an active Critter in good standing.) And Contracepción, bored to distraction on the ranch, had recently conceived a burning ambition to become the new Britney Spears. ("I mean," Héctor overheard her explaining to her mother, "she's like, you know, so fat and pregnant and divorced and everything—it's time for her to move her lard butt over and let someone else have a turn, for a change!") In pursuit of the dream, she'd ordered all the Spears CDs from *Amazon.com* and begun singing along with Britney for three or four hours a day. Though he was too kind a father to say so, her voice sounded to Héctor—who was the first to admit that, with the exception of Mexican Civil War *corridos*, he knew nothing about music—like a cat strangling on a hair ball. The sound had much the same effect on Beatriz Juárez, only more so. When Contracep suggested to him that the Pink Store might be interested in having her stage a concert there some evening, Héctor understood that the sins of the father were being visited, in spades and squarely, upon the father.

As little as he understood himself, Héctor understood Jacinta Ruiz even less. How could a nice girl like her chase after a man with a wife and two children? And what, really, did she want from him? Perhaps Jacinta was what was called a skivvy (a word he'd heard in a movie set in England in the days of Queen Elizabeth I). Or perhaps she was one of those women who couldn't control herself, like AveMaría's younger sister Carlotta, a hot number if he'd ever met one. (Luckily for him, Héctor reflected, AveMaría had got there first.) It could also be that she was simply an outrageous flirt. Then again—he had to be fair about this—Jacinta might simply be in love! For Héctor, a soft-hearted man when it came to the opposite sex in particular, this thought was particularly distressing. As a young buck back in Mexico, he'd always hated having to disappoint a woman.

He would never, never (Héctor assured himself) have crossed the threshold of the Pink Store again after that devastating event in the shadows around the corner from the bar, had the Critter Company not adopted the place as its unofficial watering hole. Every Saturday now after exercises, the Critters gathered at the Pink Store for beer and war stories, under the bemused gaze of the local clientele. Emboldened by training and the confidence inspired in its individual members through General Mitternacht's drilling, the Company had formed squads of three and four men each, any five of which were on posted duty twenty-four hours a day along the border between the Cedar and Potrillo Mountains. Already, Héctor had served two graveyard shifts with Jesús "Eddie," after slipping miserably out from under the warm covers at a little before midnight. ("If you ever wanted to fool around on me, *mi amor*," AveMaría murmured sleepily on the second of these occasions, "this would be, like, the perfect excuse.") The valley north of Columbus and west of the Florida Mountains had in the past two years become a major corridor for northward migration and the Critter units always saw plenty of action, at all times of the day. Because they were not permitted to shoot anyone, and the Border Patrol unfairly devoted its investigative resources to sightings by Minutemen on duty in the same sector, there was little the Critters could do but shake their fists, make faces, and yell at the wire jumpers, though this at least gave them a feeling of accomplishing something.

For Héctor, visits to the Pink Store were occasions of ecstatic agony—or agonized ecstasy, he couldn't have said which. Weighed down by guilt, he felt simultaneously lighter than air, at once older than the hills and younger than a new-birthed star. Over and again, he asked himself whence came this passion he had conceived for Jacinta Ruiz and when, without discovering an answer. It seemed rather to have taken hold of him by degrees and imperceptibly, in response to . . . Héctor wondered what. Had she sent the first, perhaps unconscious, signals to which he'd responded, or was it the other way round? Or had they met each other halfway? Héctor inclined toward the third proposition, perhaps because, by allowing him to regard himself as something less than a callous adulterer and Jacinta rather a fallen star than a designing woman, it was the most reassuring of the three. At any rate, what mattered now was that this secret relationship that had developed somehow between a woman named Jacinta Ruiz and a man called Héctor Villa was both real and infinitely gratifying to his heart—also, that the thing must not be permitted to proceed beyond a certain point. Jacinta, Héctor perceived—or thought he did—seemed pained, as well as puzzled, by his occasionally distant manner. And she doubtless wondered why he never paid a visit to the Pink Store alone. His greatest worry, though, was that Jesús "Eddie" might get the wind up and confide his suspicions to Beatriz. While Héctor had implicit confidence in his friend, he could not have said the same for his friend's wife—or anyone's wife, for that matter, including his own. And yet, so far, he was guilty of nothing, absolutely nothing! (Excepting, of course, that single kiss round the corner in the twilight.)

Oppressed in almost equal measure by guilt, the demands of the holiday season, and Contracepción's relentless "rehearsals," as she called them, Héctor sought distraction in his responsibilities as a foot soldier in the Critter Company. Conscientious by nature, he took these duties seriously, even when it meant rising at midnight and spending hours out in the desert scrub, bundled in heavy clothes against the terrible cold to hold the line against the relentless invasion from the south. Many if not most Americans (Héctor had noticed over the years) spoke of what they referred to as "isolationists" in a manner that suggested they classified these reprobates in the same category with neo-Confederates and people who belonged to country clubs. This hostility was perplexing to him, in part because he had begun over the past year to consider himself an isolationist of a sort—though, naturally, he knew better than to say so outside the privacy of his own home. America, so far as Héctor Villa was concerned, was, quite simply, not just the one best place on earth but the only good place in a violent, immoral, and undemocratic world. What kind of American would not wish to build a wall around America the Beautiful, to keep that outside world from getting inside? Only those (he'd concluded) who, if not actually evil, were at the very least unpatriotic Americans. It was a matter for him of the utmost confusion and distress that President Bush himself, in every other way a paragon of the American nationalistic spirit, should be among those scoffers at isolationism, and a critic of the proposed Seven Hundred Mile Wall along the Southwest border. Was it possible the President was simply out of touch with Mexico and the Mexican people? Perhaps he suffered from the delusion that the average Mexican had all the heroic and patriotic qualities of Pancho Villa himself. If only (Héctor lamented inwardly) the thing were really so!

All that was necessary to make these globaloney internationalists and unpatriots see the light, he was convinced, was to send them to work a single twenty-four-hour shift on the southwest border, where they could experience sordid reality for themselves. God only knew, that reality was all-encompassing and inescapable down here. Hordes of immigrants from literally everywhere stampeding north amid clouds of dust among the cholla and sotol; armed coyotes brandishing handguns; Mexican army soldiers showing their heads from around every other mesquite bush; Minutemen blowing whistles and shouting GPS locations into their two-way radios; drug mules scampering past like kangaroos; *agents provocateurs* of the Nation of Aztlán thrusting pamphlets advocating *Reconquista* and an end to White America into the hands of the hastening illegals; turbaned men and veiled women flitting like genies and phantoms through the night, pursued by shrieking Ku Kluxers in their white robes and pointy white hats that reminded one uncomfortably of the Washington Monument; the Ku Kluxers themselves chased by gaggles of American hippies holding signs that read WELCOME TO AMERIKA, AMIGOS! CHE LIVES!—Héctor, in his wildest imagination, had never anticipated such chaos, such a zoo. And the detritus left by the invasion was equally unbelievable: acre upon acre, square mile after square mile of thrown-away backpacks, strewn underwear, empty baby bottles, used diapers and condoms (how did anyone manage successfully to deploy a condom in circumstances like these?), half-eaten tortillas and rounds of Indian fry bread, the remains of shish kebabs still on their metal skewers, small brass hookahs and abandoned Middle Eastern and oriental rugs, plastic Buddhas and Confucius dolls, here and there a witch doctor's rattle surrounded by a fringe of what might have been human hair, and Indonesian masks carved in what might equally have been the image of primitive devils or orangutans—all these things, taken together, representing an intergalactic rainbow of aggressively importunate human cultures.

After a week of this madness, Jesús "Eddie," overwhelmed by depression and defeatism, sought time out in a shabby *taberna* in Columbus, leaving Héctor—to his modest pride—to fight on. Christmas was upon him like the Hound of Hell. In his gravely depleted financial state, the invasion battlefield offered an almost infinite array of free gifts, all of them his for the taking. In a period of a few days, Héctor gathered a winnowing of the spoils of war and bore them home in triumph to his wife. AveMaría, for the most part gratified and impressed, acquiesced in all of these trophies, the sole exception being a pair of smallish oblong rugs, beautifully woven of the most brilliant colors and fringed at both ends, that Héctor had particularly admired. "Islamic prayer rugs," she insisted, "the work of the Assist of Evil—El Diablo himself! I won't have them in the house— what would Brother Billy Joe have to say? *¡O Jesús María y José!* You can throw them on top of that fallen-down barn out back, where the snakes come to warm themselves on nice days."

Jesús "Eddie," after a few days hanging out at the bar and having his Rio Abajo diction mercilessly mocked by the Mexican-Americans of Columbus, made an heroic decision to return to the front. Working together as a team late one mild December afternoon two days before Christmas, he and Héctor set out from the Juárez ranch in Jesús's Dodge truck, on the way south to the border. At Columbus, Jesús "Eddie" made a right turn onto Route 9 heading west in parallel with the international line toward the New Mexican boot heel. There was little traffic along the road (most of the vigilantes had returned to their homes for the holidays) and one trail of exotic litter after another showed where alien bands had recently crossed, taking advantage of the temporary withdrawal of the patriot forces.

"Why do the *cabrones* want to live in the Rio Ab-*a*-jo anyway, seein as we talk so goddamn funny?" Jesús "Eddie" demanded. "How about we follow that two-track over there on the left—see if we can jump some *mojados* comin up the *arroyo* from the border."

The truck made slow progress in the wash and twilight was gathering when Jesús proposed going the rest of the way on foot, carrying with them long-handled nickel flashlights of the type that was standard issue to border-patrol agents and the backpacks containing their survival gear. They had walked no more than two hundred yards when Jesús "Eddie" gestured violently at Héctor to get down, dropped to his hands and knees, and began crawling forward on the gravelly bottom. Héctor, surmising that he'd caught sight of something ahead, did the same.

The clay felt unpleasantly chill and clammy under his bare hands, but there was no time to search out the gloves in his pack. Shoulder to shoulder with Jesús "Eddie," Héctor crawled on up the wash, which, having narrowed considerably, commenced now to meander, first to the left, then to the right, making a sequence of blind turns.

"Not *mojados*," Jesús "Eddie" hissed, "—*Islamists!* You can tell by the curry *smell*. We're almost on them now. Get ready for a fight, *hombre!*"

He was still speaking when, from around the next curve in the bank, two faces, side by side in the wash, appeared abruptly, not ten feet ahead. They were Mexican faces, adorned by drooping mustaches and surmounted by black baseball caps. The faces' owners, also on hands and knees, similarly carried light packs on their shoulders. On seeing Héctor and Jesús "Eddie," they started, then reared back in astonishment.

"*¡Hermanos!*" one of the men exclaimed. "What is it you think you are doing? You are headed in the wrong direction!"

"*¡No!*" his partner exclaimed. "They are right! El Norte must be *that* way"—he jerked his thumb behind himself. "Our coyote—he has lost his way in the dark and is leading us back into México! *¡Maldito sea!*"

Jesús "Eddie" stared at him, confounded. "If you guys really *are* Mexican," he asked in a surly voice, "how come you smell like Is-*lam*-ists?"

For Better and For Worse

THAT **C**HRISTMAS **WAS**, in every respect, the horror Héctor had feared it would be.

Homesick, broke, unchurched (AveMaría, after the second round-trip drive to the Assemblies of God church in Lordsburg, had decided to hold a Sunday prayer service at home instead), cooped together like rats in a cage, the Villas, with the Juárezes, endured a holiday season that (Héctor reflected bitterly) was about as merry and joyous as Ramadan. On Christmas Eve AveMaría, who'd decided she couldn't bear the prospect of celebrating the birthday of Christ without giving, made a last-ditch shopping trip to El Paso where she ran up $1,500 worth of credit-card charges at the malls. ("I know," she protested when Héctor reminded her it was money they didn't have. "But it's less than half what we *usually* spend for Christmas, Panchito!") Even Christmas dinner was spoiled for him when Beatriz, who wanted a honey ham, and AveMaría, who insisted on turkey, failed to agree and the families compromised by taking themselves out to the Denny's in Deming where Héctor overheard Contracepción, on the way to the ladies' room, giving the pimply young waiter her e-mail address, which she immediately accessed on the new laptop her parents had given her for Christmas. ("He says they have karaoke in Deming, *papaíto!*") The worst came that afternoon when Beatriz, after listening to Contracep rehearse her Britney routine for three-and-a-half hours straight, had an hysterical fit that ended when she flung a plastic champagne glass against the wall and threw the CD player onto the dirt turnaround in front of the house. AveMaría rushed to defend her firstborn and the two women grappled together, snarling deep within their chests like lionesses and yanking at each other's hair and jewelry. When at last each retired in tears to her room and a semblance of peace had been restored, Jesús "Eddie" winked broadly at Héctor. "Looks like everyone's goin to live till mornin. What say we run down to the Pink Store for a coupla *drinks, compadrito?*"

For most of the week between Christmas and the New Year, the two women were hardly on speaking terms. Their silence left a sound vacuum Contracepción was more than eager to fill. To cope with the uproar of rehearsal AveMaría resorted to earplugs, while Beatriz raised the volume on the TV to earsplitting levels. The ensuing pandemonium drove Héctor and Jesús "Eddie" out of the house and down to the border, where they divided their time about equally between the line of invasion and the Pink Store. As most of the Critter Company remained on holiday in the bosom of their families, the friends had the bar mainly to themselves, the local clientele, and Jacinta Ruiz, who seemed never to take a vacation, or even a day off from work. From one day to the next she was there to greet them: a slim but shapely figure in a bright print Indian dress that left her brown stockingless calves and ankles bare above leather sandals, the strength of her handsome face heightened by the severely pulled-back hair that exposed the delicate, perfectly formed ears decorated by pendants of silver, coral, and turquoise and emphasized the large liquid eyes in which Héctor imagined he perceived uncomprehending reproach. Her pertinacity in the face of rejection astonished him, and so did her discretion. Any other woman, similarly scorned and losing all hope at last, would have accused him of improper behavior before his friend—perhaps even the assembled house. But Jacinta, he told himself, was not just any woman. And so his heart went out to her, even as his mind drew back. He would have taken her in his arms at any moment, had his wrists not felt bound together at the small of his back. *Vorrei, e non vorrei.* The poor girl wanted so very badly from him something that he simply couldn't bring himself to give her.

More than his absence from home and from his attenuated business—more even than the future of his besieged country—Jacinta Ruiz weighed on Héctor's mind, and on his conscience. And then Fate interposed itself once again, and he found he had yet another worry to contend with.

Beginning a day or so after her mother's row with Beatriz Juárez, Contracepción had kept increasingly to herself, huddled over her new computer when she was not engaged with the CD player. Héctor noticed how secretive she seemed—even with Dubya, who pestered her a dozen times a day with requests to look up lion websites on the internet. His favorite was *www.FatherOfLions.org*, devoted to George Adamson and the many lions (Elsa the lioness among them) he had adopted and acculturated to the Kenyan wild, with its elaborate index and numerous color photographs. To save time, Contracep had book-marked the site for ready retrieval. In practice, retrieval proved over-simple when Dubya, after observing his sister at the keyboard for 20 minutes, succeeded in logging on and going directly to the site as eas-ily as she did, in this way proving himself to be his father's son. After that, Contracep guarded the laptop as girls in Héctor's day used to pro-tect their virginity. She was so fierce about it that her parents, exchang-ing anxious glances, began to fear their daughter might be exploring sites inappropriate to an innocent girl of fourteen. It never occurred to either of them that Microsoft Outlook Express, not Internet Explor-er, might be the proximate threat to Contracepción's morals.

At around eight in the morning at midweek, Héctor arrived home with Jesús "Eddie," frozen and exhausted after a night on the line, to dis-cover his wife standing, grim-faced and rigid, in the primitive kitchen.

"Why do you look at me that way, María?" he asked her. "If break-fast isn't ready yet, that's OK, that's OK. I'll take coffee first, while I check my e-mail."

"Go to your daughter," AveMaría said in a graveyard voice, indi-cating their bedroom with her chin.

"*¿Pero porqué?*"

"Ask her," AveMaría told him.

For the first time in what seemed to him months, absolute silence lay behind the bedroom door. Héctor, still with his cap on, went and knocked on it. When Contracepción did not respond, he opened the door and looked in. She lay sprawled across the bed, her face hidden in her arms.

"What's the matter with you?" Héctor asked, sounding more harsh than he'd intended. He had to ask twice before receiving a muffled answer.

"Mamá won't let me go to Deming with Bo."

"Who the hell is Bo, *por el amor de Diós*?"

"Just . . . some guy. You met him. He works, like, at Denny's."

Héctor remembered.

"You gave him your e-mail address. So he's been writing you?"

"We've been e-mailing each other all week," the girl pleaded. "He wants to take me to Deming tonight for—you know, for karaoke at the community center. O *papaíto*, puh-*leeze*—I sing all the songs better than Britney ever did herself!"

It did not seem to Héctor that he could bear another crisis in his life.

"And how old is this *tipo*, I am asking?"

"He's twenty-four."

"Contracepción—you won't be fifteen till this spring!"

"But I'm old for my age—Jesús 'Eddie' says so! And I'm experienced, too! I was with Abdul, for, like, *weeks*!" Had he not taken this as a taunt, Héctor could not perhaps have summoned the nerve to put his foot down as firmly as he did.

"*Hija*, you are not going any place with this man!" It was in that instant that inspiration struck. "But if you truly wish to sing karaoke, then I—your father—will take you myself!" Jesús "Eddie" could go alone to the Pink Store tonight, if it meant so much to him. Probably, he'd take advantage of Héctor's absence to put the moves on Jacinta Ruiz. Well, so be it, and good luck to him! After weeks, Héctor had arrived at his decision without realizing he'd made it. Every normal, healthy American adult had an extramarital affair at least once in his life. Therefore, not to have an affair was un-American. Very well, then: He, Héctor Villa, chose to be guilty of un-Americanism. He would not cheat on his wife! He felt unworthy and ashamed, though he understood very well it could not be otherwise. He had accepted the ultimate challenge to his identity as a One Hundred Percent American—and failed miserably.

That evening Héctor scarcely noticed the uproar of the karaoke concert, including the prominent part his daughter played in the affair. He had conceived a plan that would formalize his decision of twelve hours ago by making it an irreversible one. In his preoccupied state, Héctor was able almost to ignore Contracepción's lack of modesty in performance and the ardor of the budding male vocal stars pressing round her.

AveMaría and Beatriz responded enthusiastically to Héctor's proposal that the two couples should attend the New Year's Eve party at the Pink Store together, Jesús "Eddie" notably less so. Indeed, in their eagerness to solicit sartorial advice from each other and to compare the effects, the two women nearly forgot their quarrel of a few days before.

The four of them traveled in Jesús "Eddie's" crew-cab truck. Héctor had volunteered as designated driver. A winter storm with hard winds driving a dry snow that lay upon the highway like a dusting of winter pollen reduced visibility and caused Héctor to proceed with caution, to Jesús "Eddie's" huge impatience. The Pink Store, lit up like a Polish church, glowed in a ruddy nimbus of snow. *"¡Qué linda es!"* AveMaría and Beatriz exclaimed together.

The place was surrounded by parked vehicles, and Héctor had to leave the Dodge at the opposite curb. He and Jesús "Eddie" handed the girls down and helped them, teetering on spike heels, across the frozen street between the potholes. Héctor was struck again, as he had been when AveMaría showed herself to him an hour before in her party dress, how lovely his wife looked that evening. Indeed, it seemed to him he'd never been so proud of her. Comparing AveMaría with Beatriz, he could not help feeling a little sorry for Jesús "Eddie," even though he was one of those men who appeared never to notice his wife at all.

Spilling out from the vestibule, a huddle of Mexican males was gathered by the door in front of the Pink Store, drinking beer and taking shots of tequila from bottles they handed round. Indifferently, they made way for the American party who, once inside the building, were compelled to elbow their way with repeated exclamations of *"¡Disculpe! ¡Disculpe!"* toward the restaurant.

The restaurant and bar had been cleared for dancing, the tables and chairs pushed against the walls as far as the end of the dining area, where a six-piece mariachi band on a raised platform played enthusiastically for a dozen or so couples on the dance floor. Silver and gold bunting hung from the pink and scarlet walls, and from the polished vigas overhead. A carved wooden figure of a monk (or was it Saint Peter?) wearing a key suspended from his belt, eight feet tall and slightly sinister in aspect, wore a *ristra* round his neck. Héctor's heart banged and the butterflies in his stomach beat with strong, bat-like wings. A sweeping glance around the room took in the absence of the presence he was searching for. Instead a wiry young man unknown to him, with greased, back-combed hair and dressed in tight black pants and a white nylon shirt, came toward them from the bar to inquire if Héctor and his party wished to be seated. He placed them immediately in front of Saint Peter, around the corner from a small alcove filled with bric-a-brac.

While their wives sat inventorying the merchandise, trying to decide what to buy for souvenirs, Héctor and Jesús "Eddie" ordered drinks—bourbon on the rocks for themselves, sparkling wine for the girls. Jesús wondered aloud if any of the Critter Company would show up, but Héctor hardly heard him. It couldn't possibly be that Jacinta Ruiz wasn't here tonight. Her absence would weaken his resolve, and ruin his best-laid plans.

The band's loud playing deterred conversation but it was an inspiration to the girls, who proposed that their husbands should offer them a dance. Exchanging pained looks, the men assented—Jesús "Eddie" carried his drink onto the floor with him—and, for the next ten or fifteen minutes, they "danced," Héctor more lead-footed than usual as he searched the crowd for the face and form of Jacinta. At last, feeling the call of nature, he excused himself and went to the men's room where he nearly collided in the doorway with a youngish man of extreme good looks who reminded Héctor absently of Rodolfo Fierro, General Villa's dashing executioner.

Half an hour later, when AveMaría wished to dance again, Héctor was aware of having overindulged somewhat in bourbon. Jacinta Ruiz, he felt certain by now, was not going to make an appearance tonight at the Pink Store. However, to please his wife, he assented. The dance was an old-fashioned one—some sort of polka—he hadn't danced since his days as a young blade in Namiquipa.

Héctor had mostly forgotten the steps, he discovered, and the bourbon he had drunk was an aid neither to his memory nor to his coordination. Trying to hold tight to AveMaría while keeping his feet free of hers, he reached out for balance with his right foot and trod hard on a shoe belonging to the couple dancing past them. The shoe was jerked away, and Héctor, glancing over to apologize, found himself speechless. Jacinta Ruiz was beautiful tonight—her bare arms and shoulders brown and molded, her dark mane coiffed, her profile straight as a statue's—in the arms of Rodolfo Fierro. She gave him, as she passed, one long, serene, utterly disinterested look before being swept on by Fierro, who scowled at Héctor over her shoulder and uttered some incomprehensible, presumably rude, remark.

"I think you just stepped on that poor girl's foot," AveMaría told her husband. "Panchito, you should practice dancing with me more—and drinking with Jesús 'Eddie' less! Anyway, no more bourbon for you. Don't forget—you're the designated driver tonight."

"¡Mi Casa Es Su Casa!"

HÉCTOR **WOKE** on New Year's morning with a reverberating headache that made his wife's remonstrations (in the circumstances, AveMaría had been appointed emergency designated driver to take the party home safely the night before) the more painful to bear. He felt thoroughly ashamed of himself—first for getting drunk, and second for . . . the other thing.

Héctor could not decide whether his plan had been a success, or not. Had Jacinta Ruiz really got the message he'd intended to send her last evening? Or had she been hoping to appeal to his jealous instincts in the arms of the handsome Rodolfo? Perhaps even—the thought penetrated like a manzanita thorn—she had never felt anything for him, and, falling victim to his own vanity, he'd simply imagined it all and made a fool of himself for nothing. He had no idea where to begin sorting the thing out, and a hangover was no aid in the matter.

In another part of the house, someone was practicing vocal scales—Contracepción beginning her warm-up for another rehearsal. (Hadn't the girl had all New Year's Eve to practice while she babysat Dubya?) Perhaps the Juárezes would flee to Las Cruces for the rest of the day, to take advantage of the post-holiday sales.

Héctor's New Year's resolution had been to return home by the first of February. How, he asked himself, could his family be in greater danger in Belen than on the Juárez Ranch, directly athwart the path of countless jihadists swarming across the border each night? (More to the point, who was he—Héctor Villa, a collateral descendant of The Centaur—to be intimidated by a couple of immigrant Islamists hiding out like rats in a decaying tenement house?) As a corollary to this resolution, Héctor had determined on making a bold reconnaissance of Belen for the purpose of seeing for himself what the strategic situation there really was.

When she learned that her husband intended a visit home, Ave-María announced that she and the family were coming, too—a proposition Héctor promptly vetoed as being too dangerous. Until he could ascertain the threat level posed by Ali Kahn and his associates, he insisted, his wife and children would stay put on the Juárez Ranch—no ifs, ands, or buts. His intransigency sent Dubya into a tantrum and put AveMaría into a pained sulk. Only Contracepción, in her preoccupation with her laptop and her singing career, acted indifferent to the paternal decision. Héctor, who'd fully expected Jesús "Eddie" would wish to join him on the trip, was greatly relieved when his friend declared himself content to stick to his post at the border—"defending the Rio Ab-*a*-jo down here on the front line," he said. Jesús, though often useful in an emergency, was rather too conspicuous (Héctor felt) for a delicate reconnaissance mission such as this one, as likely as not to turn up in a trench coat, dark glasses, and a cowboy hat. Furthermore, his proclivity for the bottle made him a potential liability around the local watering holes, where (as an earlier generation of embattled Americans used to say) "Loose lips sink ships."

Like a fighter pilot departing on a volunteer mission, Héctor accepted the tearful farewells of his womenfolk and left the Juárez Ranch on the Ides of January in AveMaría's Subaru, which, besides getting twice as many miles to the gallon as his van did, had the added advantage of failing to identify its owner in large red letters along the side panels.

The day was cool, cloudless, and windless, the pale winter sky a mild blue sealant annealing the ragged circular horizon with the folded, scoriated, tawny-pink desert dotted with sotol, yucca, and creosote bush. To save miles and avoid Las Cruces, Héctor took the slower cutoff from Deming northeast to Rincón on the Rio Grande, south of Truth or Consequences. It was fine, after so many weeks of constraint, to be away from the ranch, and even (he had to admit) from his family. Since he'd had the time to take AveMaría's car for an oil change every 3,000 miles, the Subaru had been running beautifully and Héctor felt oddly lighthearted as he drove north on I-25 at 80 mph. North of Elephant Butte, the valley of the Rio opened out on both sides of the highway and then it really was as if he could see forever, from the low-lying, rather sinister Black Range to the west, across the Jornada del Muerto and the San Andres Mountains to the high peaks, gleaming with snow, of the White Mountains far away in the east. Though no outdoorsman, Héctor found that this vast wide-open country, a land of expansive valleys transected by mountain ranges and punctured by solitary bergs like mangled iron, appealed to and soothed his spirit. And why should it not, it occurred to him suddenly—it was all a part of the northerly extension of Viejo México!

His spirits fell after he took the first exit off the interstate and followed South Main Street into Belen. Héctor had never before thought of the town as seedy looking, yet that was how it struck him this shining, perfect afternoon. The outlying houses were small, hardly more than adobe shacks, many of them in a state of partial collapse and surrounded by litter and junked cars. The scene overall was familiar in a way that was strangely disturbing. He puzzled briefly and discovered the answer. The place reminded him of the Third World—in fact, of TV footage he'd seen of those dusty, underdeveloped Iraqi towns in the desert away from Baghdad. All that was required to complete the effect, Héctor thought, were a few gowned and turbaned figures walking about. When he reached the downtown district and saw what looked like a couple of swamis leaving Geraldo's Mexican-Chinese Café as he sat waiting at a stoplight, Héctor understood that Jesús "Eddie's" gloomy report the previous month had been only too accurate. Belen was being taken over by the Enemy.

In his flush days, Héctor would have put up at the Holiday Inn Express at 2111 Camino del Llano. Today, he checked into the Super 8 at 428 South Main. He ate a late lunch at TJ's Mexican Restaurant—a favorite of his and Jesús "Eddie's," and a place one would not expect to be patronized by Moors—and stopped afterward at Dominguín's Sporting Goods, where he purchased two boxes of .44 Magnum shells for the handgun he'd transferred that morning from the van to the Subaru. Héctor toyed with the idea of stopping by Paco's Place for a shot or two of liquid courage, but decided he really didn't need it—yet. So far, no one had appeared even to recognize, let alone challenge, him. And he would begin a serious reconnoiter of the town only after dark, when the Enemy could be expected to show his face. Now, he meant to check on his own house to see that all was well and that the pipes hadn't burst, or the furnace exploded, in his absence.

To Héctor's astonishment, a vehicle sat on the concrete apron outside the garage—an ancient Chevrolet Suburban painted as many colors as Joseph's coat and obviously pieced together from parts selected from a smorgasbord of junkyards in two countries.

The white fence surrounding the house, stained a rusty pink from the blowing winter dust, had pickets missing here and there, leaving gaps through which Héctor caught glimpses of patchy dead grass and a scattering of children's toys. The shades and blinds were dropped behind all the windows, save for the one fronting the master bedroom from which the glass had been partly knocked out and a Zapotec blanket hung behind the frame. Héctor's first thought was that, in his somewhat abstracted state of mind, he had come to the wrong house. But it was not so. The number above the front door was his, and so was the name on the mailbox resting atop the red-white-and-blue post. Héctor parked against the opposite curb, climbed out of the car, and started across the street. After a few steps he turned, walked back to the Subaru, and took the .44 from under the driver's seat. He held the gun in his hand for a few seconds, then put it back beneath the seat and retraced his steps empty-handed. Héctor strode through the once-intact gate that hung now on one hinge and up the walk to the front door. He lifted the knocker and with it struck three ringing blows. Finally he took a step back from the door and waited. He was about to strike again when the door opened slowly inward against a short stout mestizo wearing his hair combed forward over the upper half of his face, too-tight blue jeans, and a black muscle shirt that exposed the elaborate tattoos along his thick arms.

"*¿Quién es?*" he demanded in a truculent voice.

Héctor was too astounded to resent this. "*¿Quién ES?*" he replied. His tone conveyed no retort but a natural, uncomplicated desire for an answer.

"I am Zapata—Hipólito Zapata. Who wishes to know?"

"My name is Héctor Villa. I am the owner of this house. And just what is your explanation for being here?"

A woman appeared behind Señor Zapata, as short as he but much fatter. As Héctor's eyes adjusted to the semidarkness beyond, he became aware of the whites of what seemed dozens of pairs of eyes, all of them fixed on him.

At the name of Villa, Zapata's suspicious, haughty face—the face of a proud householder—expanded in a wide, toothy expression of welcoming delight.

"¡Ah, Señor Villa! *¡Buenas tardes!, ¿cómo está?* It is so good to meet you! Josefa, just look! It is 'Pancho' Villa, of whom we have heard so much!" Zapata stepped back and held the door wider, describing a sweeping downward motion with his arm, a wide gesture of hospitality. "*¡Señor—pase, pase por favor! ¡Mi casa es su casa!*"

Like a man in a dream, Héctor complied. Hipólito Zapata shook both his hands at once, and Josefa too stepped forward and gave him her small, limp, fat one. Behind her the eyes had withdrawn among piles and heaps of strewn debris, random as salients in a natural landscape. The house smelled of burnt lard and maize, and the kitchen was full of smoke. Héctor could not believe his eyes. He didn't recognize his own home.

"I do not understand," he told Zapata in his strongest, no-beating-about-the-bush voice. "Please explain. How it is you know about me. And what you are doing in my home."

Zapata shut the door firmly and locked it. Then he grandly gestured Héctor toward what remained of AveMaría's favorite sofa.

"*¡Josefa—trae dos cervezas ahora mismo!*"

He seated himself beside his guest on the sofa, sat back, and folded his arms comfortably over his stomach.

"*Compadre*—is it possible you have not been told? That you do not know who is Hipólito Zapata? That I do not believe!"

"Know you? Of course, I don't know you! Why in the name of the Devil should I?"

"But I am the second cousin of Eufemio Villa, three times removed! You have been too long away from your own people, *hermano*—a real *jefe* living up there in Washington, D.C. In the *Casa Blanca*, so I am told!"

"I haven't been living in Washington. I've been in New Mexico, on the border—" Héctor started to correct him, before he caught himself. Loose lips sink ships, including his own little boat.

Zapata looked bewildered.

"Our Eufemio—he told me you got yourself elected something-or-other and moved the family to Washington. He said, 'There's plenty room in Pancho's house for you to live while you're looking for work in Albuquerque. He won't mind—a *jefe* like him living like Porfirio Díaz in the *Casa Blanca* with Jorge Bush.' That's when he gave me the key, so I wouldn't have to break in like a *ladrón*—an *escalador*!"

Josefa brought two bottles of beer and a bowl of fried pork skins, and went away to the kitchen again. From every corner of the house, the eyes were reappearing, advancing like those of feral creatures emerging from the jungle shadows. It seemed to Héctor the Zapatas must have at least a dozen children, or even more.

"*¡Salud, primo!*" Hipólito raised his bottle for a toast. "*No te inquietes*: We'll be out of here in a month—two, at the most—when I find the job I am looking for in Albuquerque. *Comprendes*—more than the minimum wage, benefits, a month's vacation paid. This is El Norte, *hermano*! Hipólito Zapata knows how to make the most of it."

An object buried deep in Héctor's pocket vibrated suddenly like a serpent's rattle. He rolled sideways to free the pocket and drew his cellphone out.

"*Oye! Oye! ¿HÉCTOR?*"

"*!Sí, sí—díme!*"

It was AveMaría, sounding hysterical.

"*Oye!*"

"Yes, yes, I'm here, *¡díme!* What is it, AveMaría?"

"Contracepción!"

"Well, what about her?"

"She's run off to Vegas with some singer! While Dubya and I were away at the Wal-Mart in Deming! She left a note on the kitchen table. Beatriz found it and showed it to me when I got home! We thought she'd been kidnapped for ransom, at first!"

Five minutes later Héctor closed up the phone and returned it to his pocket. Then he stood from the sofa with great dignity.

"If you and your family are not gone from my house in one week," he told Hipólito Zapata, "I'm calling the Homeland Security Department to carry you out. *¿Comprendes, amigo? ¡Escúchame bien!*"

Reprise in Vegas

THE LONG DRIVE from Belen to Rancho Juárez was for Héctor an endless agony. He found the place in the greatest confusion. AveMaría vacillated between grim determination and hysterics as she packed a suitcase and Jesús "Eddie" tramped back and forth in the sitting room, shaking his fist and vowing to track down Contracepción's fiendish paramour, tear his head from his body, and break his spine in five places. Amid the uproar only Beatriz Juárez seemed calm and unperturbed while Dubya, having caught over and again the word *Vegas* in the otherwise unfathomable back-and-forth, raced from one end of the house to the other on all fours, emitting leonine roars between earsplitting shouts of "¡*Leones! ¡Leones! ¡Quiero visitar más leones—muchos, MUCHOS leones!*" For an instant, the relief Héctor found in the thought that he and his family would shortly be leaving this terrible establishment was compensation (almost) for the dread he felt at the prospect of visiting Las Vegas again.

While his wife was putting up a box supper to bring with them on the overnight drive to Nevada she gave her husband the facts of the case as she knew it, which turned out to be little enough. Contracepción had spent the hours immediately following her father's departure for Belen in the bedroom listening to Britney Spears and reading and writing e-mails on her laptop. At around eleven-thirty, AveMaría had put her head through the door to ask if she wished to accompany Dubya and herself to the Wal-Mart in Deming and afterward for lunch at Tacos Mirasol. The restaurant was a favorite of Contracep's, so her mother was surprised when the girl declined the invitation, explaining—in rather mysterious tones, AveMaría recalled—that she had important mail needing to be answered immediately. AveMaría, who thought this a reasonable explanation at the time, had left at once for Deming with Dubya. They had spent nearly two hours at the store (forty-five minutes buying groceries and household necessities, an hour and fifteen minutes while AveMaría shopped the women's clothing department for winter discounts) and gone on to enjoy a leisurely lunch lasting an hour and a half at Tacos Mirasol. Finally, the drive home had taken twenty minutes. At the house they'd been met by Beatriz, who'd just got home herself from the Pink Store where she'd met Jesús "Eddie" for lunch on his noontime break at the border to discover Contracep's handwritten note on the kitchen table, weighted by an exhausted bottle of Paul Mitchell hair spray. The women's first thought had been that Contracepción had been kidnapped and forced by the kidnapper to write a runaway note. But AveMaría pointed out that most criminals, who suffered from low IQ, were too unintelligent to think of so clever a ruse. The note, unambiguously in Contracep's hand, explained that she had gone to Vegas with a famous talent scout who'd promised to make her a singing star. Not to worry, it added: Siggy had assured her Britney was washed up in Vegas, and she'd grab off all her bookings in a couple of months. Once she was a star, Contracepción promised, she'd buy her parents a big home in Vegas and a new Lexus each. Fortunately, AveMaría had phoned her husband in Belen before calling the police—an act, Héctor reminded her, whose surefire result would be their daughter's arrest on a charge of having violated her probation in Belen.

The Villas got started for Las Vegas shortly before 11 P.M. Héctor began by trying to talk Jesús "Eddie" out of coming with them. But when persuasion failed he put his foot down with a firmness and decision that shocked and astounded his friend, causing him to back off like a hyena confronted by a lion. Héctor had calculated the distance by road to be 624 miles, for an estimated ten-and-a-half or eleven hours' driving time. It would have been helpful to have a clue as to where, in a city of 600,000 people, his daughter and Siggy might be found, but Héctor thought he had a pretty fair idea. Before getting in the car, he'd typed the words "Britney Spears" and "Las Vegas" into Google and discovered that Britney had performed her "Dream Within a Dream" World Tour at the MGM Grand Hotel in 2002. It was a start, at least, though easily the most unpleasant one imaginable. It had occurred to him that in an undercover operation around the MGM he'd be unrecognizable to anyone, Juanito Villalobos included, in disguise as a keeper at the Lion Habitat.

Why (Héctor beseeched God) had his beloved Contracep inflicted this terrible ordeal upon him? He drove as far as Tucson, where AveMaría took the wheel while Héctor tried to get some sleep and Dubya snored wetly on the back seat. In Phoenix they stopped for gas at a convenience store and the boy, awakened, bought a stuffed lion that took up most of the seat and obscured Hector's view through the rear window. From Phoenix he drove the remaining 287 miles on to Vegas, keeping awake with strong coffee and the radio set low. He turned the radio off finally near Williams, Arizona, when the D.J. put a Britney song, "I'm Not a Girl, Not Yet a Woman," on the air. At a little before noon they arrived in Las Vegas, where Héctor steered directly for the MGM Grand and was nearly crushed by a chartered Greyhound bus on the way to the hotel. "*¡Leones! ¡O-o-o mis leones!*" Dubya began shouting as soon as he recognized the place.

Héctor had decided, on the dull desert drive from Phoenix, to book a room at the MGM even though, as his bank account stood these days, he could hardly afford it. (What else was plastic for? he reminded himself.) The hotel was familiar territory, as well as a prime attraction for Britney wannabes. While Dubya was dozing the last fifty miles into town, his father and AveMaría had agreed that she and the boy would establish an observation post in the hotel lobby at a convenient distance from the Lion Habitat, while Héctor checked out the musical entertainment being offered that week. A sense of the most extreme urgency impelled both parents. Nothing less than their daughter's virginity was at stake, while even now they might be too late, the sacred cause already lost—and forever!

After searching for a half-hour on one of the house computers Héctor felt satisfied that, if Britney Spears really were in town this week, she wasn't booked to sing anyplace. Sir Elton John and Céline Dion were playing at Caesars Palace and Barry Manilow was at The Hilton with "Manilow: Music and Passion." Thunder From Down Under, the male revue from Australia, was performing at The Excalibur and The Mirage offered The Beatles' "LOVE." The Chippendales had been booked at the Rio and the MGM itself offered "La Femme," imported direct from the Crazy Horse in Paris. Where Contracep and Siggy might possibly fit into any of this, Héctor had no idea. He could (he realized in despair) hang out for months on end at these shows— to the tune of $59.95 to several hundred bucks a pop—without ever catching sight either of his daughter or her showbiz boyfriend, whom he wouldn't recognize from a zoo keeper with a pooper-scooper over his shoulder. If he was going to find Contracepción, and in time (the act was hardly a lengthy one, especially with a young male), Héctor could not afford to wander blind around downtown Las Vegas. He needed to think like Philip Marlowe in *The Big Sleep*, played by Humphrey Bogart, accustomed to tracking seedy people in seedy places like L.A. (a town Héctor had always deplored as hopelessly Mexicanized in a sordid low-class way, an American Juárez on steroids).

The name Marlowe suggested alcohol and tobacco and thoughts of both put Héctor in mind of a drink, considered by some health experts he'd read to be conducive to mental concentration when indulged in with restraint. Therefore, having ascertained that AveMaría and Dubya, fortified by colas and a bag of fried pork rinds, were at their post in the lobby he ducked into Zuri, a martini bar open 24 hours a day where, on the recommendation of the barman, he ordered a gin gimlet with Rose's Lime Juice, straight up.

The gimlet, of which he'd been initially skeptical, was exotic but delicious. Further to concentrate his mind by distracting it from the gorgeous, near-naked females who came and went in the bar, Héctor requested a cigar from Zuri's signature humidor and sat with it above crossed arms, thinking. When he felt the gin infusing his brain so far as to induce thought, he ordered a second gimlet and went on thinking. But the harder he tried to think, the more petrified his brain seemed to become. And the more he drank to soften it up, the more squashily recalcitrant it grew. Héctor consulted his watch and read the time: five-thirty. Already half a day had been wasted, and he was getting there himself. What kind of a father would sit all afternoon at a bimbo bar while his own daughter was being deflowered? Héctor called for the check and was numbly trying to calculate a fair tip when two girls flounced in and perched themselves on the two tall seats to his right. Rather, they would have flounced had they been wearing skirts instead of a slightly more modest version of thong panties below and pasties above. The girls looked to him to be very young—hardly older, if at all, than Contracepción, Héctor thought. Both of them acted over-excited, tossing their hairdos from side to side and talking even more expressively with their manicured hands than with their gaping painted mouths. To his astonishment, the barman accepted their orders of two infused vodkas without requesting IDs. While he was away mixing and shaking the drinks, both girls took wallets from their pocketbooks and drew out what looked like identical business cards to admire, turning them over and over in their hands and giggling hysterically. Héctor glanced sideways at the nearer girl. Her card read:

USA WORLD SHOWCASE
3960 HOWARD HUGHES PKWY #500
LAS VEGAS, NEVADA 89109
CORPORATE OFFICE: (702) 400-6315

He returned to his study of the check and decided to leave twenty percent, as it was easier to calculate than fifteen. He had just signed the credit card receipt when he overheard one of the girls squealing, "Oh, Danele, I just, like, *know* we've got it made with Justin! He's hot for me—I could, like, feel the body heat, y'know? He's all set to book us at The Mirage right now, without even waiting for the World Showcase, soon as I—you know"—she giggled again, and gave her friend a knowing dig with her elbow—"give him a little of what it is he's really after!"

Héctor's instincts, working above the gin, responded in the instant. On impulse, he turned in his seat to address the girl directly.

"Can I please have a look at that card for a second?" he asked her.

The two of them stared at each other in astonishment, then burst into laughter.

"So, like, what are you auditioning for?" the first girl demanded, and covered her mouth with her hand.

"I just want to write that address down, if you don't mind," Héctor told her.

Over the next three days, he and AveMaría combed the city of Las Vegas, traipsing from one booking agency to the next in search of anyone who might have been approached by Siggy and Contracepción while Dubya passed the time at the Lion Habitat, supervised by a nanny who charged twenty-five dollars an hour in her job. Héctor had not realized Las Vegas was so big, nor that it embraced talent enough to keep so many scouts and booking agents in business. It was no doubt on account of business pressures that so many of them were dismissively impatient and rude, except on those occasions when they mistook him for an ethnic character actor looking for work of the "*¡Ay Chihuahua!*" variety. Typically short, bald-headed, and sweating, with circular waistlines tented in loud shirts, they lurked like moray eels in cramped, smelly offices amid steel filing cabinets, guarded by professional-looking secretaries (professional as in the oldest profession, Héctor thought). For three full days, from nine in the morning until five at night, they approached these dragons, patiently and somewhat apologetically. No, no one by the name of Siggy or Contracepción ("Is that name for real?") had stopped by the office. ("I'd remember that one, buddy, believe me!" "What do you think I am, a lousy private dick?") At the end of the first day, he and AveMaría were close to tears. By the conclusion of the second they had nearly given up hope, less of finding Contracep in the end than of rescuing her innocence on which they were aware the meter was ticking, as on their mounting hotel bill. By the evening of day three both parents were in despair, and Héctor talked of calling the police as a measure of last resort.

Nervously as well as physically exhausted, they dragged themselves back to the MGM Grand, where Dubya and the nanny awaited them near the front desk. The little boy spied them first and raced forward across the lobby, knocking the knees of gathered couples who stared after him disapprovingly.

"¡Mamá! ¡Papá! I found Contracep—I saw her, I did! She's over there with the *leones* at the *Lion Habitat!*"

V

The Hobbyist

THE JOYOUS RETURN to Rancho Juárez was dampened, but in no way spoiled, by a certified letter from the Belen Municipal Court that awaited Mr. and Mrs. Héctor Villa on their arrival there, threatening their daughter with immediate juvenile detention if she did not return within ten days' time to complete her court-ordered work with Darfur Relief. Héctor thought afterward that Judge Ulibarri, had he known how much relief of an entirely different sort his letter would produce in the bosoms of the miscreant family, probably wouldn't have written it. Terrorists or no terrorists, the Villas were going home! Héctor could not remember being so happy since he arrived in the U.S.A. twenty years before.

Meanwhile, the family gave thanks to God for the recovery of Contracepción, who seemed none the worse for her experience in Las Vegas save for a bruised artistic ego. Siggy (she'd realized after twenty-four hours) had no musical connections whatever in town but plenty of romantic ones, amounting to a kind of harem. When she refused to cooperate with his plans for her on their second night together he'd become abusive, until Contracepción had fled the apartment and spent the night in a chair at the bus station downtown. Unshaken in her ambition to support herself in her quest for artistic celebrity, she'd applied the next day for a job at the MGM and been referred to the Lion Habitat, where the position of poop-scooper was available after the previous incumbent, on a methamphetamine high and under the delusion that he was a lion himself, had entered the big cats' exhibit one afternoon an hour before the pride was scheduled to be removed to the ranch, out on the desert away from town where the animals were quartered for the night. On Contracep's second day at work, Dubya, during a visit to the Habitat, had recognized his sister on the opposite side of the plate-glass window and pestered the nanny until he had her attention. Héctor, after he'd calmed down, had wanted to set the police on Siggy and was dissuaded only when Contracep insisted the *tipo* had never told her his last name and that the apartment she'd escaped from was in fact a girlfriend's, not his own pad. It had also occurred to Héctor that the girl should be examined by a gynecologist, but AveMaría refused absolutely to sanction the idea. Their daughter, she declared firmly, needed to know that her parents had implicit trust in her. So Héctor, reluctantly, had backed down. He had enough to ponder as it was, he thought. In spite of his elation at getting Contracep back, he felt a deep sorrow, springing from doubts and disillusion, in his heart. What kind of society (Héctor could not help but ask himself) made possible an ordeal such as the Villa family had suffered the past five days?

When the Juárezes learned of Héctor's decision to return his family to Belen, Jesús "Eddie" and Beatriz announced their decision to return home, too. "Them goddamn *A*-rabs don't scare *me* none," Jesús "Eddie" had declared, striking what he intended as a belligerent pose. "I'm goin to start a Critter Company myself, soon's I get home—drive all the f--kin ragheads out of the Rio A-*ba*-jo." (He'd delivered this speech largely for the benefit of Contracepción, who was within hearing distance at the time. Jesús "Eddie" didn't buy her parents' story that their daughter had escaped her adventure with her virginity intact, and he felt certain that, having once yielded to Siggy, she was softened up for further advances from anyone lucky enough to have a chance with her.) Indeed the couple left nearly a week earlier than the Villas, who found themselves pinched between the judge's ten-day deadline and the time it took the *migra* to clear the Hipólito Zapatas from their house. (What happened to his relatives after that, Héctor never learned, nor cared to know.)

When AveMaría walked through the door and saw the condition her house was in, she fell across the stained and torn upholstery of the sitting-room sofa with such deadweight force that her husband feared she had suffered a heart attack. It would take weeks and weeks, she sobbed upon regaining consciousness, to clean up the mess and put things to order again, though she never expected to rid the house of the smell of those *puercos* entirely. Seeking to console and reassure his wife, Héctor promised the family that, until the place had been restored to its habitual pristine condition, the Villas would eat out downtown every evening to spare AveMaría the added burden of cooking. The immediate, wholly unforeseen result of his announcement was a violent argument between Contracepción, who favored Taco Bell and Kentucky Fried Chicken, and Dubya, who preferred

Frankie's Grill & Ice Cream Parlor and McDonald's. Héctor settled the issue for the time being by driving everyone to the Golden Corral on South Main Street, a steak and barbecue house that was far too expensive as a regular thing but made a nice treat on the occasion of the Villas' first night at home. The family retired early, resting uneasily on stripped beds beneath rough Mexican blankets after AveMaría declared the bed linen was spotted with bedbugs and smelt of burnt lard, like everything else in the house.

Contracepción returned to work at Darfur Relief the next day, and by week's end Héctor was servicing several of his old accounts. And AveMaría's cleaning estimate proved to have been overly pessimistic when, with help from Theresa Aguilar, she made the Villa house livable once more within a fortnight. Outwardly, at least, the family had been restored to normalcy. And yet . . . Héctor could not throw off the feeling that, beneath the surface, everything had changed—perhaps forever.

Somewhat to his surprise, and much to his dismay, a brief ten weeks' absence from Belen entailed a loss to his business that was not to be made up overnight. Héctor found himself with a greatly diminished income, but also an unprecedented number of leisure hours on his hands. Some of this time he spent in the company of Jesús "Eddie," hanging out at the new Taberna Aztlán which had arisen like the phoenix from its ashy pyre between Highway 47 and the Rio Grande. But Héctor could not drink all day, even had AveMaría permitted him to do so, and winter temperatures made decorative projects in the yard unpleasant. In search of a new hobby that could be practiced indoors, he scanned the *Valencia County News-Bulletin* for club meetings and other community activities unrelated to the great game of politics. The service clubs, such as the Lions and Rotary, failed to interest him and anyway were involved in games of footsie—or actually in bed with—certain state and local politicians, including Tomasina Luna.

Apart from Pancho Villa, Héctor had never been much interested in history. Several weeks after the Villas' return to Belen, he read in the *News-Bulletin* a column contributed by the Valencia County Historical Society concerning an incident that had occurred in the mid-1600's along the Camino Real, some miles south of the present-day hamlet of Contreras on the Rio Grande. A party of Apache warriors had attacked a Spanish caravan and made off with the contents of a treasure wagon, which according to legend they had floated across the river and buried high on the slopes of Ladrón Peak. Héctor was less interested in the legend itself than he was to learn that there was such a thing as the Valencia County Historical Society. In his enforced leisure, he had spent many hours already surfing the web for tidbits concerning The Centaur. A Pancho Villa State Park already existed, apparently in answer to a dire public need. Why not (Héctor wondered) a Pancho Villa Historical Society, affiliated perhaps—at least in the beginning—with the county one? Villa had been a celebrity of sorts in the El Paso of his day and there had to be many Villa enthusiasts still in the Rio Abajo, some of them descended, it could well be, from the General's girlfriends in El Norte. And it would be a great feather in his cap, in respect of the Hijos de Pancho Villa, should he succeed in founding a kind of American chapter in New Mexico. The more Héctor considered the idea, the more certain he became that here was a dream that could not fail. It would be of great help, of course, if he could prove that Pancho Villa had ever visited Valencia County—better yet, that he'd slept there, however unlikely the thing sounded—but Héctor did not consider this an insuperable problem. Nothing was easier in America, he'd observed, than to launch and keep afloat another compelling urban legend.

In his excitement, Héctor confided his plan to Jesús "Eddie" that evening at the Taberna Aztlán. Jesús, who had never evinced any particular interest in The Centaur, was wildly enthusiastic—not about the Pancho Villa Historical Society but rather the treasure story.

"*Compadrito*, this is a-*ma*-zin, in-*cred*-ible! I have known of this legend since my Grandfather Luis told me of it when I was a *muchachito*, this high!" With his hand Jesús "Eddie" indicated a level about three feet above the bar wood, and one above his head. "I have believed in it ever after, and the fact that you, *amigo*, have read about this in the *pa*-per proves to me that it is true after all!"

Héctor was skeptical, but the warmth of Jesús "Eddie's" response was contagious.

"If there really is treasure buried up there on Ladrón Peak, why hasn't it been found in four hundred years?" he wanted to know.

Jesús "Eddie" gave him a pitying look. "Because people haven't looked for it in the right *place*—that's why, *amigo*."

In the end, Héctor wasn't hard to convince. The romance of a quest for hidden treasure appealed to him at a time in which the romance of so much of his life in America was fading, and he found the prospect of a new dream to replace the one he had lost, or was losing, inspiring. He could not help but be further impressed by Jesús's apparent readiness to drop his plans to found a Rio Abajo Critter Company—the more so as the alien, in particular the Muslim, problem in Belen was now very bad and getting worse. Turbans, headscarves, *niqabs*, and burqas were a common sight all over town these days. (On the positive side, neither Ali Kahn nor his accomplice had showed his face since the return from Rancho Juárez.) Perhaps, Héctor concluded, a treasure hunt was just the hobby he'd been looking for as a distraction from his worries and a source of relaxation from a lifetime's hard work.

"So when do we start?" he asked.

Using his thumb and forefinger, Jesús "Eddie" snapped a kernel of unpopped corn at President Bush's image on the widescreen TV. Héctor winced, but he did not protest as once he would have done. He was beginning to wonder, very privately, whether Dubya was really all FOX News made him out to be. The President, on his way back to the White House after facing off with the Senate Foreign Relations Committee on the issue of the Iraq war, was grinning broadly, his smile wide as the Cheshire Cat's—wide enough (Héctor thought) to swallow the world.

"Soon's we both have another round," Jesús "Eddie" said.

"I'm buying," Héctor told him. He was beginning to feel like a multimillionaire already.

Curandera

BECAUSE HÉCTOR had experience as an historical researcher looking up books on the subject of Pancho Villa at the public library, it
was agreed that he should be the one responsible for ascertaining the
location of the treasure, and that Jesús "Eddie's" job would be to out-
fit the expedition to Ladrón Peak when the time arrived to set forth
upon their quest.

To his chagrin, Héctor discovered that historical detective work
required a good deal more knowledge and expertise than checking out
books from the library did. At a loss where to begin, he settled finally on the *Valencia County News-Bulletin*. Having printed the story,
Héctor reasoned, the paper's editor must be well versed in the events
it described. In fact the editor was too busy to see him, and the recep-
tionist referred Héctor to an editorial assistant who said she worked
part-time for the newspaper while taking classes at the University of
New Mexico Valencia Campus. The treasure story, she explained, had
appeared in what was known to the trade as a "canned" article, meaning that no one at the *News-Bulletin* knew anything whatsoever about
the subject matter. If Héctor needed further information, she suggested he visit the Harvey House Museum at 712 Dalies Street and ask to
speak with the column's author.

Héctor had heard of the museum, but only as the custodian of a
miniature-train collection. He drove there at once and was told by a
docent that the address of the Historical Society was 104 North First.
Irked, he got back in the van and drove on to First Street. Historical
research, Héctor saw, was a lot more tedious than he'd realized. Perhaps, after all, he should have started with the internet, which meant
a saving in physical effort at least, as well as in gas. When he found
the Society closed and no one about to answer the bell, he decided
it was the last straw and returned home straightaway. Computers
were his business and if he couldn't find what he was looking for on
the web, chances were the thing didn't exist, or never had in the first
place. In the easeful privacy of his office, Héctor seated himself before
the glowing screen and typed CAMINO REAL APACHE RAID STOLEN

TREASURE LADRON PEAK into the search engine and hit SEARCH. He was still at it three hours later when AveMaría got home from the supermarket after picking up Contracepción at Darfur Relief. Nothing. Zilch. Nada.

That evening at the Taberna Aztlán, Héctor recounted the events—or nonevents—of his discouraging day to Jesús "Eddie." His friend was sympathetic, but not particularly helpful otherwise. History was bullshit, he asserted. His Grandfather Luis would have been able to tell Héctor everything he needed to know about the Camino Real legend. Unfortunately, Grandfather Luis was dead. Hence there was nothing Héctor could do but consult a *curandera* if they were to lay hands on the Spanish treasure.

"I thought *curanderas* healed people," Héctor told him, doubtfully.

"*Hombre,* they do, they do. But they are also a kind of *bruja.* The best ones can see *e-*verthin, they can foretell the future—and the past! There are not many left a-*round* here any-*more*—most of them are in Mexico. But Beatriz knows one, right here in town. She is very *old,* compadre—maybe a hundred years or more! Also she is a *patrona* at Our Lady of Bel-*en.* Only, the priest does not know of this. He would excommuni-*cate* her if he found out about it, Beatriz says. She's got mad and threatened to tell him—many *times*—but in the end she has always chickened *out.*"

The thought of consulting such a woman, or even being in the same room with her, gave Héctor the creeps. His own mother had visited *curanderas* regularly in Namiquipa and the surrounding villages, and no good had ever come of it—rather the opposite. Also he did not believe such dire measures to be necessary, at least not yet.

"I am an experienced historian," he reminded Jesús "Eddie." "If I can discover new things about Pancho Villa, things that have never been known to anyone before, maybe I can learn where it is we should dig for the treasure. I will give myself a month to do this. If I fail, then I will consult with Beatriz's *curandera.*"

"In order to concentrate properly you will need to drink a lot of *beer,* amigo," Jesús "Eddie" assured him. "We must meet here ever *night,* and talk over everthin you have found out that day."

Héctor compressed his lips in a thin line. He could not help feeling somewhat annoyed. Jesús "Eddie" was effectively unemployed, and living off his wife.

"Don't forget I have a business to run, as well as search for treasure," he reminded his friend tartly.

"Buried treasure" was inseparable in his mind from "map," and so it occurred to Héctor to resume his search by scrutinizing every map of the area he could lay hands on. A shop in Los Lunas had for a year or more kept in its display window a hand-drawn map of territorial New Mexico—perhaps two-and-a-half by three feet in size—which he had admired for nearly as long. In addition to cities, towns, wagon roads, railroads, and trails, the map had marked upon it historical incidents summarized in a crabbed hand at the sites where they had occurred. Recognizing that this map might well be useful to his enterprise, as well as valuable in itself, Héctor resolved to purchase it, assuming the price were small enough to escape notice by AveMaría. As yet, he'd said nothing to his wife regarding the treasure quest, for fear she'd tell him to quit wasting his time and devote his energy to drumming up new service contracts instead of pursuing wild-goose chases in the desert.

Héctor, who'd half expected to learn the map had been sold, was greatly relieved to find it still on display in the window. He parked out front and entered the store. It was a frame and print shop, rather more elegant than anything he was accustomed to patronize. Though somewhat intimidated Héctor walked boldly enough to the rear of the place, where an Anglo who appeared to be in his early thirties was seated on a stool behind a tall desk, at work with a straight rule, an elbow rule, and a pencil. At Héctor's approach, he looked up from the desk and smiled with polite reserve. The young man had on chinos and a blue golf shirt with a golden sheep stitched over the right breast. His owlish glasses were horn-rimmed, and a wing of smooth flaxen hair fell almost over one lens. Héctor wasn't certain he cared for the type.

"May I help you?" the young man asked pleasantly. Héctor turned round halfway and gestured toward the front of the store with his thumb. "That map of New Mexico in the window," he said. "I'd like to have a look at it, please."

"Of course."

The shop owner slipped from his stool, crossed to a wide desk, pulled out a drawer, and drew a large sheet of paper from it. He placed the sheet on his desk over the one on which he'd been working and smoothed it with his hand.

"There you are," he said. "Hand-drawn territorial map of New Mexico, from the late 19th century."

"I want the one in the window," Héctor told him.

"Why, they're all the same—facsimiles, you know. I believe the original is in the State House in Santa Fe."

"You mean, it's a copy—there's a lot of them out there?" Héctor didn't trouble to hide his crushing disappointment.

"Oh, yes. They're run off all the time—very popular with newcomers to the state. Only twenty-five dollars apiece."

So much for secrecy, Héctor thought. On the map he located the boundary notch just west of El Paso and traced with his finger the northwesterly course of the Rio Grande. The drawings and lettering were crowded, dense, and scratchy, hard to read. "Does it show an Apache raid on a Spanish caravan on the Camino Real in the middle 1600's?" he asked, after searching in vain for almost a minute.

"I don't know, let's see." The young man turned the map to face him and bent close above it. "Rather difficult to read, but no, I should say not," he concluded, raising his head. "Of course, such attacks were frequent. Nearly regular occurrences, for decades."

"Then who would know?" Héctor asked in dismay.

The shop owner, noting his desperation, looked surprised. Then he smiled. "Someone at the university, perhaps? You might try there."

Héctor understood that, his type or not, this was a good young man after all. "Can you recommend anyone in particular?" he asked gratefully.

"Well . . . You could try Dr. Salvador—Salazar Salvador—on the Valencia campus. Comes in here all the time, looking for stuff to do with the Southwest border area and so forth. He's said to be an expert on the subject."

Chiefly from gratitude Héctor went ahead with the purchase, counting out twenty-five dollars from his wallet while the young man rolled the map tightly and inserted it into a cardboard tube. It took him three days to run Dr. Salvador to earth in his faculty office between classes. The Professor was a small, thin, weak-chested man in his thirties, with a sallow complexion and wild hair shot prematurely with gray, dressed in work boots and jeans and wearing rimless glasses jammed back into his eye sockets. Héctor disliked him on sight. University hippies and radical types had never been his favorite sort of people, ever since his own days at school.

"I'm sorry to be a nuisance," he began, "but the man from the print shop suggested I talk with you."

Dr. Salvador heard him condescendingly. The walls of the cramped, disorderly office were covered with Nation of Aztlán and faded César Chávez posters and a number of framed historical prints.

"Jeremy Spode," he agreed. "He is an OK person, for an Anglo."

"He said you're an expert on border stuff."

The Professor smiled humorlessly. "I am an *activist* on the border, not an expert," he corrected.

"Anyway, you know a lot about it—right?"

Dr. Salvador looked smug and ran his fingers through his hair.

"I'm looking for information about an Apache raid on a Spanish caravan on the Camino Real in the mid-1600's, I think it was. The Indians are supposed to have stolen a lot of treasure from it and buried it in the mountains somewhere around here." Since the Professor did not at all look like a treasure hunter himself, Héctor considered it safe to mention the hidden plunder.

Dr. Salvador stared at him as if he were a bug. "First, I should not have to tell you, a Chicano, that it is incorrect to speak of 'Indians'; they are 'indigenous peoples.' Second, the indigenous people you speak of did not 'steal' anything. They simply took what was rightfully theirs. Third, I do not acknowledge the Spanish criminals and their genocidal empire. They do not exist for me. I would never teach my students about the history of those people. I would not teach them about the history of El Norte either, except they need to know about it if they are to destroy it, and recover their land and their heritage—to recreate the historical Nation of Aztlán!"

Héctor perceived that his first impression of this man had been an accurate one. "How can you wish to destroy America?" he demanded in a voice unsteady with emotion. "America has given us everything we have—freedom, equality, human rights, equal opportunity, a good job. If you hate it so much, why don't you go back to Mexico and leave us Americans in peace?"

Dr. Salvador's stare of murderous hatred would have done credit to Rodolfo Fierro. "You are a Twinkie," he hissed; "—brown on the outside, white on the inside. Get out of my office! I have students waiting to see me."

So Héctor got. He noticed that the students lined up outside the door looked exactly like Dr. Salazar Salvador, only younger.

It was apparent to him now that he must consult with the *curandera*—the *bruja*—despite his misgivings, indeed his fear. (If even a Catholic priest disapproved of such a person, what would Brother Billy Joe think?) Héctor dreaded the prospect of confronting her amidst an array of vials, potions, and witch's brews. He felt like a character out of *The Exorcist*. But there was no other way he could see to locate the treasure. So that evening at the Taberna Aztlán (what traitor, Héctor thought indignantly, had given it that name?), he reluctantly informed Jesús "Eddie" of his decision.

Beatriz Juárez arranged for the consultation. The *curandera's* real name was Alicia Montano, but she was known professionally as Carmen Cortez. Though she and her husband lived in a handsome house in a new subdivision north of town, her office or studio or whatever you called it was in a crumbling, small adobe house a block from the railroad tracks downtown where the better sort of Catholic was unlikely to observe her coming or going from work. As she insisted on meeting her clients at night, Héctor had to face his ordeal nearly cold sober, after a double shot of whiskey at the Taberna. He considered packing a gun under his coat when he met his appointment, but decided in the end against it.

Treasure Mountain

IN THE ELATION and excitement produced by Héctor's interview with the *curandera*, he and Jesús "Eddie" could barely resist the impulse to start at once for Ladrón Peak. A late-winter storm of unusual force for central New Mexico restored them to their senses, blanketing the peak and the mountains to the southwest and east in wet snow and immobilizing the city of Belen for thirty-six hours. Each time Héctor's eyes were drawn—as happened at least a dozen times a day now—to the whited silhouette of Ladrón, he thanked the Lord Jesus that he and Jesús "Eddie" had not been caught out on its craggy and precipitous slopes, with nothing to protect them from the elements but Jesús's pickup truck and a nylon tent. After consulting the *Farmer's Almanac* they set a tentative date for sometime in late April, when the threat of serious cold would have passed and before the summer heat set in, for the launch of the expedition.

Hermana Carmen Cortez (as the business card taped beside the doorbell read) had fulfilled Héctor's worst misgivings. Whether or not she was actually aged a hundred, as Jesús "Eddie" had claimed, she was, without doubt, the ugliest human being Héctor had ever beheld. As a small child, he'd been taken to visit a museum in Mexico where the family had been shown an exhibit of mummified babies in a glass case. Carmen Cortez looked like that but bigger, with a fall of hair dyed a hideous purplish color with highlights added to it. The darkened room was lined with hanging sheaves of dried herbs and shelves on which bottles, vials, and canisters were arranged in rows. A fire of pinyon pine logs burned in the fireplace, perfuming the close atmosphere, and a ponderous table built of age-darkened wood occupied the center space. On the walls, portraits of Catholic saints hung between the shelves. Behind the table Carmen Cortez herself sat in a high-backed chair, mercifully difficult to distinguish at first glance in the dim light thrown by a dozen votive candles and the dropped rattan blinds at the windows. Héctor was speechless, but the *curandera* lost no time getting to the point.

"Beatriz tells me you are not here to be cured, that you wish for something else from me. What is it that you want, then? You don't look very healthy to me." The voice, coming from so fragile a figure, was astonishingly strong.

Spotting a vague shape in the gloom that had the general aspect of a chair, Héctor lowered himself upon it and found that he had surmised correctly.

"I am told you have the power of sight, Señora Cortez," he began. "I am looking for something terribly important."

"*Hermana* Carmen . . . And just what is it that you seek? Beatriz Juárez assured me you are not a Catholic."

"No, Hermana. First Assembly of God."

Héctor recounted for her the legend of the buried treasure, aware for the first time in the telling how improbable, even silly, the entire business sounded. Hermana Carmen, however, appeared to take him seriously.

"We shall see what we shall see," she said. "You have brought a map of the treasure mountain with you?"

Héctor drew the folded 7.5-minute quadrangle map, prepared by the National Geological Survey and including Ladrón Peak and vicinity, from his coat pocket and passed it across the table to the *curandera*, offering as he did so silent thanks to Jesús "Eddie" for his foresightedness. Héctor himself would not have thought to bring a topographic map, with Ladrón Peak conveniently marked by an X, along with him to the appointment.

The *curandera* took the map and studied it. In the half-dark, Héctor was unable to observe her expression as she did this.

"Ladrón Peak is a place of very bad magic," she said at last. "Many evil spirits are about there. They are certain to be guarding the treasure."

"Yes, but—where exactly *is* the treasure?" Héctor asked her impatiently.

Hermana Carmen refolded the map carefully on the table. She drew a rosary from the bosom of her dress and placed her hands on top of the map, clasping the string of shocking-pink plastic beads. She closed her eyes and sat that way, moving her lips silently as she told her beads, for what seemed to Héctor a very long time, until he was certain she had dozed off and was talking now in her sleep. He was on the point of rapping the edge of the desk to waken her when suddenly she set the rosary aside, unfolded the map again, and spread it wide on the desktop. Finally the *curandera* jabbed the map violently with her right forefinger and opened her eyes wide. Héctor watched this performance in dismay. His mother had employed the same trick, using her Bible, whenever she had an important decision to make. But this was supposed to be magic!

Carmen Cortez removed her finger from the map and marked the spot with a red crayon. Then she pushed the map toward Héctor for his inspection. However, as he had no experience in reading topographic maps, the indicated site told him nothing.

"There you will find the treasure," the *curandera* asserted, "hidden long ago by the Apache. You must search for a boulder split in two by a bolt of lightning and smelling of sulphur, and dig ten feet beneath it on the downhill side. Two hundred and fifty dollars, please."

"But—Beatriz said it would be more like twenty-five! And my wife has the checkbook."

"I take the card," Hermana Carmen assured him.

On his way out, Héctor brushed against a man going past him into the adobe house. In the darkness of the unlit street he failed to see the face clearly, but even so he didn't like the little he saw. The *tipo* looked like a treasure hunter to him.

The winter, which had been an exceptionally cold one, hung on a good deal later than usual that year. It was already the second week in May when the treasure hunters, encouraged at first by a burst of warm weather and finally overjoyed when it appeared that summer had arrived to stay, determined on the weekend following to begin their assault upon Ladrón Peak. According to Jesús "Eddie," the *curandera's* X mark was placed high on the mountain at the head of a dry canyon running southeast for many miles into the desert, and Héctor was willing to take his word for it. As a younger man, in his teens and twenties when he was still in shape, Jesús "Eddie" had spent much time exploring the peak, circumnavigating its extensive base by four-wheel-drive and climbing on foot as high on its nearly vertical cliffs as he and his *compinches* had dared to go. The treasure location, Jesús had assured his friend, was indeed a perilous one, ensuring an attempt fraught with many dangers, including sheer drops of hundreds of feet, gravel and talus slides, falling boulders, bad footing, rotten rock, and lightning strikes. Though Jesús "Eddie" was cavalier about these dangers, they gave Héctor pause. However, partly from pride, but mainly from treasure-lust, he tried not to show his discomfiture and determined to stick his courage in the screwing-place, as he'd heard somewhere of someone having once done. In fact, the prospect of his impending encounter with Ladrón Peak was considerably less daunting than that of informing AveMaría of the planned adventure. If only (Héctor reflected) God had blessed women with more imagination!

Although he had already met his responsibilities by discovering the precise location of the treasure, Héctor was more than willing to aid Jesús "Eddie" in acquiring the gear they needed for the expedition. Jesús had made a list back in March, but, as new items of an indispensable nature continued to occur to the two of them, that list was now an extensive one. Beginning with Jesús "Eddie's" Dodge pickup and his igloo tent, it included one set of tire chains and a sheepherder jack, one pickaxe, two shovels and a handsaw, one hatchet, a Leatherman multi-tool, one kerosene and one electric lantern, 500 feet of nylon rope, two sets of rain gear, two sleeping bags, blankets, one 10x16 canvas tarp and two pillows, two hunting knives, a .44 Magnum and a .45-caliber revolver, a .270-caliber hunting rifle equipped with an adjustable 2x9-power scope, a Dutch oven, two cigarette lighters for starting fires and a box of Blue Diamond wooden matches, two picnic coolers, four cases of beer, and three bottles of blended Scotch. At Héctor's suggestion, Jesús "Eddie" added two antivenin kits, though he insisted that rattlesnakes did not venture to such high elevations as the two of them would be exploring.

Ten days before the expedition was scheduled to depart, Héctor did whatever it is one is supposed to do with one's courage and informed AveMaría of the treasure quest. He chose for the occasion an intimate steak dinner at the Golden Corral, his wife's favorite restaurant, after the two of them had left Contracepción and Dubya at home to fend for themselves with a box of microwaveable beef burritos and a quart of chocolate ice cream. Owing to wifely gratitude or to the romantic atmosphere, AveMaría, greatly to Héctor's surprise, offered no objection whatever to his adventure, which seemed rather to appeal to her imagination. As a fervent admirer of *The Treasure of the Sierra Madre*, she had no difficulty imagining her husband as Humphrey Bogart, "lusting for the treasure that cursed them all the more he yearned for a woman's arms" (as AveMaría remembered the posters had read). So far from considering the affair a wild-goose chase, she appeared even more confident than he both of the existence of the treasure and the likelihood that Héctor and Jesús "Eddie" would discover it in the end after many dangers and adventures. People, she insisted, don't believe for hundreds and hundreds of years in something that never existed in the first place. Moreover, she had heard of this Carmen Cortez, who was said to be a very powerful *curandera* who had healed many people of cancer and was supposed to have special powers in curing erectile dysfunction. If the *curandera* confirmed that the Spanish treasure was indeed buried on Ladrón Peak and foretold the location where it would be dug up, then these things must be so. And wasn't Héctor glad now to have lost his race for Congress two years ago? If he was a politician today and living in Washington, he'd never have the time to go on a treasure hunt. The Villas could use the money, and now they'd be able to buy Brother Billy Joe the church roof he wanted and never feel the pinch themselves. Anyhow, it was better to be rich than famous or powerful, AveMaría concluded. Finally, where was a person more likely to stumble on a fabulous legendary treasure trove, after all, than in El Norte, Land of Opportunity?

The expedition to Ladrón Peak set out early in the morning on a soft spring day late in April, before the young clouds had begun to form above the wilderness of the upper Gila River country west of the Rio Grande and the Manzano Mountains lying east of the great river. The party was seen off from the Villa residence, where Beatriz Juárez had joined AveMaría and the children beneath a banner depicting Nuestra Señora de Guadalupe. In the interests of mission security, neither Dubya nor Contracepción had been entrusted with the secret of their father's quest. Instead, they'd been told that he and Jesús "Eddie" were making a camping trip to the Gila River to fish for trout. At almost the last moment, Dubya cried out that they'd forgot their fishing rods, and disaster was averted only by Jesús, who quick-wittedly assured the kid that their rods were the collapsible kind and packed securely in the bed of the pickup beneath the rest of the gear. As the Dodge drew away down the street, Héctor, watching in the tow mirror as his family diminished behind the brilliant folds of Our Lady's own banner, felt his eyes grow wet and his throat close up. Perhaps he would be bitten by a rattlesnake and die in the desert without ever seeing them again!

Though Ladrón Peak rose twenty miles southwest of Belen by line of sight, the journey to the broad, roughly circular base of the mountain was much farther, by winding and tortuous four-wheel-drive track across deep canyons and steep *arroyos* in which the Dodge toiled, rolling, pitching, and careening, for nearly five hours. Now the mountain reared nearly above them, a massif of warped, twisted, and decaying volcanic rock blazing out against a high blue sky beneath the white noonday sun, and still the treasure seekers had not begun the steep ascent to the top of the wide pedestal where they'd planned to make base camp that evening.

In spite of the bright sharp light, the vivid colors of the rocks overhead, and the relieving touch of a light spring wind, Héctor gazed upon the mountain with apprehension amounting to dread. Had not the *curandera* mentioned that Ladrón Peak was a place of bad magic, alive with evil spirits? He'd forgotten her warning, until now. And now was too late to turn back. AveMaría would never believe that her husband was anything but a craven worm, a *cobarde*.

"*¿Otra cerveza, compadre?*" he asked Jesús "Eddie," in what he hoped was a steady and lighthearted voice.

A Night on Bald Mountain

HÉCTOR, who had never camped out in his life before, was entirely unprepared for the nighttime cold of the high desert in late spring. And he had failed as well to anticipate the utter and complete darkness—the blackness of outer space, of nothingness—of the desert night. Though Jesús "Eddie" built a blazing fire that lit up the rocks, brush, and trees for many yards around the camp, the overall effect was more unnerving than reassuring, especially at the edge of the circle where shoals of indeterminate light merged with the shadows advancing from the absolute darkness beyond. Worst of all were the noises—the unknown, unimaginable sounds proceeding from that darkness: the hurtling downward vibration pulling up abruptly in a trollish grunt that Jesús "Eddie" said was a bullbat, a noise like rattling bones that was really a fall of stones down the steep long canyon behind the camp, the ghostly whistle of the wind in the boughs of the stunted, hideously deformed pinyon pines standing black against a backdrop of stars as thick as frozen sand grains. With so much to nourish and stimulate his imagination, Héctor could if he wished—but did not, after the first attempt—imagine the stark mountainside ringing with the murderous shrieks of a couple of dozen Apache raiders breasting the steeps with heavy trunks on their backs in search of a secure place to bury the bloodied Spanish treasure.

The following day, he learned that a wilderness expedition entails ordeals far more unpleasant than unfamiliar sounds in the night. Crawling on all fours from the tent that morning, Héctor nearly set one hand on a stuporous three-foot rattlesnake stretched out in the morning sun, inches from the skirt of the nylon rainfly. (When he reproached his friend for his false promise that rattlers were not to be found on Ladrón Peak, Jesús "Eddie" replied that witchcrafters on the nearby Alamo Navajo Reservation had doubtless sent them to guard the treasure.) At breakfast, he had flies in his coffee and sand in his scrambled eggs to contend with, besides the ancient folding chair with a rotten canvas seat so deep it took him a full minute to pull himself out of it. And there were the daypacks to prepare, the water bottles to fill from the five-gallon jerry cans, the camp to secure for the day, and the fire to be doused. Camping meant a lot of work, Héctor was learning. At last the trek up the guttered, boulder-strewn canyon began, and he passed in less than thirty paces from a mild sort of Purgatory into the innermost circle of Hell.

Jesús "Eddie," wheezing like a bellows, led the way, carrying the treasure map tucked into the net pocket of his pack and a prospector's pickax secured to his belt. The day was already warm and both men, being seriously out of shape, sweated profusely. Jeans, Héctor discovered, were not designed for hiking, and neither were the Adidases he had on. The straps of his pack, containing among many other items the collapsible Marine Corps entrenching tool Jesús "Eddie" had added as an afterthought and weighing perhaps forty-five pounds, sawed at his shoulders, causing him to bend almost double in order to take the weight on the flat of his back. His legs ached, a burning coal seemed lodged in each of his hip joints, his lungs sucked air with a whistling sound through his parched open mouth, and his heart pounded like a drum at a Hopi fertility dance. Jesús "Eddie" was compelled by an appreciable beer gut to halt every twenty-five paces or so to catch his breath, a respite for which Héctor felt more than grateful. As the map failed to indicate a trail, the expedition was bushwhacking up the canyon that grew progressively steeper as they struggled among boulders and over gravel deposits that rolled like marbles underfoot, pitching the two men into the heavy undergrowth brought up by the late snow and the rains, the bladed yucca with their folded blossoms, and the datil that tore at their legs and clutching hands. At the lower elevations rattlers buzzed ominously from rock ledges and clumps of vegetation, and Héctor rendered thanks to the Almighty he'd insisted they bring the antivenin kit along in his pack. They fought the mountain until ten o'clock when they'd climbed, by Jesús "Eddie's" estimation, just halfway to the place marked by the *curandera* on the topo map. "Time we get up there, it'll be time to turn round and go down a-*gain*," he gasped in a nearly inaudible whisper. "Let's eat lunch, *compadre*. I'm goin to be anor-*es*-ist before this is over."

They reached the head of the canyon about noon, nauseous with heat and fatigue, and collapsed together on their backs across a shelf of rock. Feeling slightly recovered after a quarter of an hour, they sat up on the rock and looked around. The view of the Rio Grande Valley below and, far to the southeast, the hazed White Mountains rising above Alamogordo was stupendous, but of the lightning-split boulder and the sulphur smell there was neither sign nor trace.

"This is *malo, compadre—muy malo*," Jesús "Eddie" observed darkly. "Perhaps the *curandera* mis-*led* you."

"But you said yourself she could not say wrong."

"That is so, *amigo*," Jesus "Eddie" pondered. "The rock must be somewhere about here," he concluded. "We must look hard. It may take much time to *find* it."

"But we can't climb up and down here every day!" Héctor objected.

"That is true. We must carry the camp up on our backs and put it here, to save time."

Héctor stared at him, appalled. From where they stood the Dodge pickup was visible on the plateau far below, a speck of metal glinting in the sunlight like a scrap of tin can.

"Not the whole camp, of course. Just what we need to survive. A spike camp, the *An*-glos call it."

Héctor did not trouble to argue it with him. Why, he thought bitterly, if he wished to make a fortune, hadn't he gone to work on Wall Street and done it the easy way?

They spent the next two days carrying what they needed from car camp up to the head of the canyon in six trips, an ordeal that left both men ruggedly sunburned and a good five pounds leaner. Jesús "Eddie" raised the tent ten feet to the left of the waterspout, while Héctor, at Jesús's instruction, constructed a small firepit twenty feet downwind of it. When the camp was at last complete, the men stood with crossed arms to gaze upon their work and saw that it was good.

"If we do not find the treasure this trip," Jesús "Eddie" promised, "we will leave this spike camp here until we do. In that way, *compadre*, we will save ourselves much time and *ef*-fort."

Night fell, heavy with the drugged perfume of the yucca opening their tender white flowers to the velvet dark of the springtime desert. Cheered by the ragged orange flames and the fragrant drift of the pinyon and juniper smoke, comforted by the bottle of Jim Beam placed within convenient reach of the treasure hunters and by the spreading lights of Albuquerque poured out like burning jewels on the desert sixty miles distant, Héctor felt himself relaxing for the first time in forty-eight hours. Camping was not so bad after all once you got used to it, he admitted. And who couldn't, when you were so close to a buried fortune you could almost smell it? He and Jesús "Eddie," toasting their absent comrades at the Taberna Aztlán, drank a spot more than was good for them, and turned in before ten o'clock, determined to make an early start in the morning and confident of coming upon the split boulder before noon.

On account of hangover they got going an hour or two later than they'd intended. Also the boulder described by Hermana Carmen proved unexpectedly elusive, and the only perceptible odors were those of sun-heated rock and the oily juniper needles. The two men searched all day, with a break in camp for lunch and a hair of the biting dog, and returned at suppertime, disappointed and disgruntled.

"F--k the *curandera,*" Jesús "Eddie" complained. "If Beatriz don't report her to Father *What's*-his-face, I will, *compadrito.*"

"Maybe she just got the details wrong," Héctor suggested. "Or perhaps the split rock rolled downhill during the winter. Why don't we just start digging here, at the top of the canyon, and see if we come up with anything?"

But Jesús "Eddie" refused to accept this explanation. "There ain't no such thing as half-magic," he declared. "It's either *real* magic—or it ain't magic at all, it's phoney *ad*-vertising. If that priest don't kick the bitch's ass, maybe the Chamber of *Com*-merce will. *Amigo,* pass me that bottle—I feel like killing *somethin* to-*night.*"

They traversed the mountain slope in the vicinity of the pour-off again the next day with no greater success, retired to camp shortly before sundown, and sat in deepest gloom by the fire over a fresh bottle of Jim Beam to watch the full moon rise, swollen and orange like a huge Spanish dubloon, above the Manzano Mountains. Darkness fell, the friends had eaten nothing since lunch, yet so low in spirit were they that it occurred to neither of them to fix supper. "Maybe we need a metal detector—" Jesús "Eddie" began. He was interrupted by a sudden fall of gravel from the steep behind them.

"*¿Qué es eso?*" Héctor demanded in alarm.

"Mountain sheep, maybe," Jesús replied dubiously.

"Goats don't throw pine cones," Héctor told him. He picked up the one that, after striking him between the shoulder blades, had bounced and fallen against a piece of rock, and offered it to his friend for his inspection with a shaking hand.

Instead of accepting the pine cone, Jesús "Eddie" shrank from it, his normally rubicund face a sallow color in the ruddy light of the fire.

"*¡Fantasmas!*" he hissed. "It is the spirits of the Apache raiders guarding the treasure! O Jesus Mary and Joseph! The *curandera* said nothing of this. We have awakened them from their sleep after four hundred years, and now they look for revenge!"

Another pine cone landed on the rock beside the fire, and a third hit Jesús "Eddie" square on the back of the neck beneath the brim of his Stetson hat. Héctor did not reply to him. Having neglected to pass along to his friend Hermana Carmen's warning that the treasure site was a place of bad magic haunted by evil spirits, he felt strongly that now was not the moment to rectify the oversight. Under the climbing moon, Ladrón Peak was a study in ragged contrasts, bone-white rock opposing deathlike shadow. Overhead the stars, blanched by moonshine, appeared transfixed by suspense and horror. A sudden spate of pine cones incoming from the heights above struck all round like springy hail, and then they heard the scream. It was a terrible scream, like the fused cry of all the souls in Hell, rising upward toward the moon and falling back again. The sound lasted thirty seconds or more, then ceased abruptly. "Hail Mary full of grace," Jesús "Eddie" began. His voice died as three black figures holding what looked to be spears appeared simultaneously in silhouette against the sky on a shoulder of the mountain above the camp. He drew the .45 revolver and emptied the cylinder in the direction of the apparitions, the six successive crashes magnified unbearably by the surrounding amphitheater of rock. The figures vanished instantly and several moments of silence ensued, followed by an outburst of mocking goblin laughter from behind the ridge more terrible even than the scream had been. After that a descending chill, working its way downslope from the craggy heights above, seized them.

The treasure seekers lay awake throughout the night with their revolvers resting on their chests. They arose at first light, struck camp, and packed the first load for portage down to the truck, choosing only the most valuable items. The rest, they felt, could wait until the Apache spirits had got a handle on their tempers and quieted down a bit. Or until Hell froze over, whichever happened first.

On the drive out, a couple of miles down the jeep trail, Jesús "Eddie" was forced to pull off onto the grass hard against a juniper grove to make way for a Chevy Suburban coming straight at them, lurching and shunting in the dirt track. The Suburban was an older model from the 80's or earlier, high-riding above the chassis. It never slowed but passed the Dodge at high speed and in a thick cloud of the caking dust. Inside were four men and, back in the cargo space, an assemblage of what appeared to be excavating tools. The driver as he approached seemed to avert his face and swung the sun visor across the side window, partially concealing himself from view. Even so, Héctor recognized him, or thought he did. Unless he was much mistaken, he'd seen that face before—at night several months ago, pushing past him in the doorway of Hermana Carmen Cortez's ramshackle adobe in Belen.

EPILOGUE

Morning in America

A**FTER SO MANY YEARS** living in exile up north, Héctor had forgotten how pleasant fall in the Chihuahuan Desert can be, the summer heat banished for good and the first snows not yet upon the desert mountains that enclose the city on three sides. From his office on the top floor of the Museo de la Revolución in the Casa Pancho Villa, he had a fine view of Ciudad de Chihuahua dominated by the three conical hills, Cerro del Coronel, Cerro Grande, and Cerro Santa Rosa, and the twin bell towers of the Catedral de San Francisco rising from the city center. This morning the mountains appeared remote through a haze of poisonous cloud rising from the smoldering garbage dumps in the barrios that ringed the city at its perimeter and mingling with the bittersweet smoke of pinyon and juniper wood fires burning on hearths and within cookstoves across the metropolis.

Leaning above thick forearms crossed on the windowsill, Héctor surveyed his new domain with proprietary satisfaction. After three months, Chihuahua still seemed to him preferable to Albuquerque for its historical presence and the notable absence of diversity here. (In the hundred days since his arrival in the city, he'd not spotted a single turban or burqa in the streets, or anywhere.) Unlike the United States, which seemed to transform itself anew on a daily basis, Mexico didn't change much. Despite its substantial growth in recent times, Ciudad de Chihuahua remained in many respects the city Pancho Villa had known when he was governor of Chihuahua State and lived here, in this same house. From his vantage at the window Héctor, looking down into the grassy courtyard, could see the Dodge touring car, riddled behind by .45-caliber bullets, in which The Centaur had met his end in Hidalgo del Parral more than eighty years before. Living in Chihuahua and maintaining the computer system at the Museo, he felt closer to his hero than he had even in Namiquipa. As the department of the army in the Secretariat of National Defense in Ciudad de México operated both Casa Villa and the Museo, Héctor's colleagues in his new job were Federales almost to a man. Frequently—more frequently, indeed, than he was entirely comfortable with—the impassive looks they leveled at him from their flat, stonefish eyes gave him the impression of being face to face with the Villistas themselves, for so long the scourge, as well as the hope, of the Chihuahuan people.

In spite of his growing disillusionment with America and American culture, Héctor might well not have returned with his family to Mexico had the fiasco of Ladrón Peak and the buried treasure not occurred. At Jesús "Eddie's" insistence, Beatriz Juárez had forced the truth from Hermana Carmen by threatening to report the *curandera* and her witcheries to Father Ortega, the parish priest at Our Lady of Belen. Under interrogation from Beatriz, Hermana Carmen had confessed to having extracted a fee of $1,000 from the Treasure Hunter in return for directing him to the site she'd indicated to Héctor, minutes before. (Every footloose ne'er-do-well and dreamer, it appeared, had read that Camino Real column in the *Valencia News-Bulletin*.) Shocked by her unethical business practices, Héctor and Jesús "Eddie" together had petitioned the Chamber of Commerce for redress, without success. Immediately afterward, acting on impulse, Héctor had put his house on the market and begun a job search in Ciudad de Chihuahua. The house had sold within two weeks to a Chinese couple from Beijing at more than double the price Héctor had paid for it, allowing him to give cash for a handsome old home in Chihuahua in a fairly upscale neighborhood not far from Casa Villa. AveMaría, though she missed the American-style malls, seemed to be settling in nicely after finding an Assemblies of God church to her liking. Contracepción was doing as well as one might expect in a neighborhood school, despite being a year and a half behind her class, and had her first real *novio*, a nineteen-year-old aspiring *corrido* singer who wrote songs about narcos shooting police officers in cold blood. And Dubya attended preschool for three hours each morning, while his mother worked on the church's Crusade For Souls project.

Life here, Héctor knew, was good for the Villas. And yet something, he sensed, was missing. The Dream that had sustained his life for more than two decades was ended, and with its passing, existence, though pleasant enough, seemed to him flat and uninspiring—essentially meaningless. Unlike in El Norte, it was not morning again in Mexico every day.

El Día de Los Muertos, coming on October thirty-first and the first and second of November, gave him temporary cheer as a welcome instance of the rich historicity of Mexican folk culture. But Christmas was more of a downer than usual, owing to the absence of shopping malls, reduced family circumstances (the Secretariat of Defense was hardly a generous employer), and his aged mother's insistence that he and the family spend the holidays in Namiquipa, where she reproached her son endlessly for the remittances forfeited when the Villas moved from the U.S. back to Mexico.

Much of his restlessness, Héctor concluded, reflected the fact that there was so little to do in Chihuahua. When he ventured to mention the fact to his boss, *el Coronel* Baca had assured him that the bullring would open for the season in April. But Héctor, who had never been an *aficionado* of the *corrida* and in any event had developed an enthusiasm for NASCAR, was not comforted by the prospect of watching three men stab six bulls to death under a hail of *¡Olés!* or of pillows. Nevertheless, the *coronel*'s suggestion nudged his imagination. It was no good looking for Albuquerque in Ciudad de Chihuahua, he realized; *por consiguiente*, he must seek for Chihuahua in Chihuahua. With this aim in mind he bought a local guidebook, in English, at a downtown shop frequented by American tourists and spent several evenings perusing it over a bottle or two of Corona. Among the few entries to attract his attention, and his interest, was Rocas de Aladino, a rock shop located in an historic mining town 30 kilometers northeast of the city. Héctor had been fond of rocks since, as a boy in Namiquipa, he'd made something of a collection of the missiles that the older Montez brothers down the street had used to pelt him with.

"*Mi querida*," he told his wife, "next Saturday we will all drive out from town together and visit the rock shop I was telling you of the other day."

AveMaría gave him the look she'd used to give Dubya when, at around the age of two, he'd wanted to eat dirt.

"Rocks? You want to look at rocks? Why not lumps of coal?"

"But these ones are from an historic mine! There's an old town there, and everything."

"Coal comes from mines, too," she replied.

Contracepción, who'd looked forward to spending the afternoon with the *novio* at the neighborhood theater where the latest J-Lo movie was playing, protested, but Héctor insisted that this was a family outing from which no one could be excused. The drive to Aquiles Serdán, which should have taken half an hour, instead lasted forty-five minutes when Héctor found himself stuck at the tail end of a funeral procession going twenty-five kilometers per hour on the narrow two-lane highway without shoulders. When at last he saw a chance to pass, he counted forty-two vehicles on his right before being forced off the road onto the hardpan by an oncoming farm truck doing at least eighty and apparently without brakes. The country was barren desert, flat as a Wal-Mart parking lot and littered with rotting cacti and snagged plastic bags. AveMaría declared the sight made her so miserable she wanted to cry, just looking at it.

The old mining town of Aquiles Serdán sat a short way up a sharply narrowing *cañón*, facing across the precipitous slopes to the barren opposing hills. It was overlooked from the upper end by a decaying church of great age, built upon a bench of rock twenty or thirty feet above a row of small, dingy shops, most of them catering to the tourist trade.

"*¡No quiero ver rocas!*" Dubya whined. "*¡Más bien quiero encontrar dinosaurios!*" The boy, who'd recently developed a passion for collecting toy dinosaurs, had learned enough geology to associate the two subjects.

Héctor parked the Subaru at the foot of a flight of worn stone steps leading up to the level of the shops, and everyone climbed out. The town looked deserted, with the exception of two gringo tourist couples letting themselves into the church and a flock of small, predatory boys loitering at the head of the steps.

"*¡Señor, señor—venga conmigo!*" the boys shouted as soon as they saw Héctor. "*¿Desea un guía? ¡Venga, venga conmigo!*"

Héctor brushed them off impatiently, but one boy, a nice-looking, soft-spoken, and polite child, refused to take no for an answer. His father, he explained, was the proprietor of a rock shop. Would the *señor* care to come along with him and see it? Together the Villas followed, AveMaría dragging Dubya, loudly protesting, by the hand the entire way to the shop, where Héctor placed a peso in the kid's hand.

Inside, the proprietor introduced himself in a friendly way and proceeded to show Héctor his inventory. The rocks, indeed, were beautiful: rough, polished, and carved; minerals and gems; petrified wood, fossils, and geodes; carnelian, quartz and rose quartz, malachite, and blue calcite. Héctor was entranced and so were the girls, who kept squealing at each other from various parts of the shop to come look at this! On impulse, he bought, for twelve pesos, a malachite cougar (or was it an African lioness?) for AveMaría, and a geode for himself to serve as a paperweight. The girls also were buying, placing one item after another in the plastic sacks thoughtfully provided by the proprietor. Only Dubya seemed unimpressed. Instead of wanting to buy the whole store, as was usual with him, he was nowhere to be seen—or heard.

Where, Héctor wondered suddenly, was Dubya?

In panic the family ran outside, nearly forgetting to deposit their sacks with the proprietor. Héctor glanced swiftly around the small plaza and saw nobody. Even the gang of importunate urchins was gone. He raced to the flight of steps and looked down at the Subaru. Dubya was nowhere outside the car and Héctor had the keys in his pocket, having taken care to lock the doors. He looked back to the line of shops, half-expecting in his confusion to see one of the Dollar Stores where dinosaurs were always to be found. But the Villas weren't in Albuquerque anymore.

Contracepción was in tears and AveMaría nearly hysterical when they all heard sudden shouts punctuated by piercing screams from some distance off. Héctor, after listening with his head on one side and his hands cupped behind his ears, determined that the sounds came from behind the church. The next instant he was flying on swift new Adidases, leaving the womenfolk panting far behind. He vaulted a low iron fence and ran on, past the doors of the church from which a pair of curious gringo faces peered, around the corner of the building and straight into the street urchins pushing, pulling, and hammering with their fists at Dubya, crouched down in their midst with his arms over his bent head. They scattered, squawking, like ravens as he burst upon them and fled in all directions, some into the brush on the steep hill behind the church, others up the narrowing ravine where the town trickled out in a profusion of ocotillo and mesquite. Dubya lay sprawled on the bare ground, stripped almost naked of his clothes, including his new pair of expensive sneakers. Héctor snatched up his son and clasped him to his bosom—which was how the women came at last upon the two of them, as if the wooden statue of St. Joseph With the Christ Child had come alive inside the musty church and stepped outside for a breath of fresh air.

FOR WEEKS FOLLOWING the horrific attack on Dubya—Héctor was convinced it had been a kidnap attempt as well as assault and robbery—the Villas kept to themselves at home. Had the drug violence in México actually reached the point that it now involved seven- and eight-year-old kids? He put the question to *el Coronel* Baca, who seemed to pretend not to have heard him. Nevertheless Héctor, fearing the worst, kept the children at home as much as possible while urging AveMaría to take extra precautions whenever she went to church or the *supermercado*.

Therefore, despite the relatively warm weather, by late winter the Villa family was experiencing cabin fever worse than they ever had in the cold of central New Mexico. In New Mexico, too, there was spring break, which Contracepción's new school did not observe. In New Mexico, in March, the family had made a tradition of taking a trip together.

"¡*O papaíto!*" the girl complained one night at supper, "it's not fair! I'm so bored, and I never get to go any-place! Pu-lease, *papaíto*, can't we go *some*-place?"

It was thus, under pressure, that Héctor had the most inspired idea of his life.

"How would you like," he asked his daughter in measured tones, "to drive to Las Vegas for a week?"

"¡*O papaíto!*"

"Héctor, do you really mean it?" AveMaría breathed.

"¡*Quiero ver los leones!*" Dubya roared.

"¡*Muchos, MUCHOS leones!* What does the lion say, Papá? The lion says *RRRRRRRUUUUUUUHHHHHHHH!*"

And why not? Héctor asked himself. He and AveMaría had received their U.S. residency papers a month after returning to México, so the border crossing would be a piece of cake, for once. Even as the idea occurred to him, the Dream had stepped forward in his mind once more, a Lady clothed in green and bearing aloft a flaming torch, and he understood that, where they were going, it really was morning again, every day of the year.

About the Author

CHILTON WILLIAMSON, JR., was formerly history editor for St. Martin's Press and literary editor for National Review. For the past 23 years, he has been senior editor for books for *Chronicles: A Magazine of American Culture*. Born in New York City, he was raised in Manhattan and on the family farm in South Windham, Vermont. Since 1979, he has lived in Wyoming, except for two years spent in Las Cruces, New Mexico. Besides *The Education of Héctor Villa*, his third Chronicles Press book, Williamson is the author of three published novels and six works of nonfiction. With his wife, Maureen McCaffrey Williamson, he lives in Laramie, Wyoming.

www.ingramcontent.com/pod-product-compliance
Lightning Source LLC
Chambersburg PA
CBHW030521020726
47494CB00004B/1189